I0580825

The Keeper

JOAN VINCENT

North Street Publishing

The Keeper

Joan Vincent

"We are always the same age inside."

Attributed to Gertrude Stein

"The characters in this novel are fictitious and bear no resemblance to persons living or dead. Any names or characters, businesses or places, events or incidents are fictitious. Any resemblance to actual persons, living or dead, or actual events is purely coincidental." J.V.

Also by Joan Vincent

Fiction

Because Mother Liked to Dance

For children

Molly Marbles

The Legend of the Lost Lilies

Table of Contents

To Frank Vincent

"I love you the more in that I believe you had liked me for my own sake and for nothing else." – John Keats

Acknowledgments

My heartfelt thanks to author Carol Shields for keeping me inspired during that long ago workshop at the Humber School for Writers where The Keeper was born. Her enthusiasm and encouragement, intelligent, astute, and kind mentoring at the beginning of the project were crucial. How extraordinarily lucky I am to have worked with such a great writer.

Sincere thanks to Jan Berry and Lauren Kelly-Course for their steadfast belief in this novel, encouraging me to take it out of the drawer where it had been tucked away, waiting to be rediscovered. Wonderful readers both, they cheered me on to the very end with their perceptive responses and discerning suggestions.

Huge thanks to Emma Berry for her love, her generosity of time and wise counsel in guiding me through the byzantine universe of social media.

Thanks to Abigail Berry and Morgan Kelly for their love and always cheerful support.

Lastly, special thanks to my husband Frank, my first and constant reader and editor, for his unfailing support and devotion to me and the completion of this novel. I could not have done it without you.

Joan Vincent

Keeper (ke per), n. 1. A person or thing that keeps; 2. A person who tends or guards; 3. A person who owns or manages a place of business; 4. A person responsible for the behavior of another; 5. A person in charge of an incompetent or of animals; 6. Something that serves to hold in place, retain.

1

Rangy Barstow

What has he done? He lifts her head gently and cradles her upturned face in his powerful unwashed hands. *Oh, what has he done? Girlie, I'm sorry, I'm sorry—I never meant to do you harm.*

He'd been waiting some hours for the shiny white van that had just pulled into the underground parking garage, turning into the slot reserved for the architectural firm of Cole & Siegel. He was relieved when he saw she'd come alone this time.

He'd sidled up to the van and, through the side window, watched her remove her sunglasses and fuss with the contents of her briefcase as if she might have forgotten something. He'd touched the van's door handle gingerly at first, as if it were hot or rigged somehow, then pressed down, expecting resistance, for surely it was locked.

But it slid back so easily he'd laughed lightly and jumped in as if the van might suddenly start up and leave without him.

The woman in front did not turn her head, but in the rear-view mirror, her eyes met his, swelled with surprise, and before he could speak or pluck from his mind the words he'd labored over, she cried out, sounding like the wails of distress that so plague him on his night-walks through the city.

He'd lifted her out of the driver's seat, pulling her toward the back of the van. Still, she would not cooperate—kicking and thrashing and biting down hard on his hand—and as if she were a flame he'd carelessly ignited and must suppress, he struck her again and again until her body, extended across the seat back, lay silent and limp. He was left with her upturned face in the palms of his hands.

He has never looked so closely into such a creature's face. Her soft hair falls through his fingers as if growing out of a nest made by his hands, hair so fine he cannot feel its weight against his scaled and soiled skin. His eyes glisten, and he murmurs in wonderment. *Oh my, oh my!*

As if she can hear his voice, her body shudders, and shifts, one leg twisting awkwardly so that the heel of her shoe catches in the steering wheel, and the horn begins its insistent rhythmic blaring.

He panics, lets go of her, and begins backing out of the van when a glimpse of her face halts his flight—the flushed patches of skin where he'd struck her already darkening. There are spots of blood on her rumpled clothing and on his from where she'd fought back. *Oh, he's gone too far!*

He rifles unsuccessfully through his pockets for a rag and sees in the back of the van a swatch of cloth that looks like material cut from curtains his mother had once sewn. Hastily, he picks it up and spins the gauzy fabric around his wound, muttering *sorry, sorry*. He leaves the van and crawls across the cement floor of the underground garage, squirming beneath parked cars, one after the other. *Hurry, Rangy, hurry!*

He reaches the upper ramp and hikes over a steep wall, slipping into a pocket of concealed space, an architectural flaw. He'd watched it all that day a few years ago. Moses Rocket, where he'd worked all his life, had already shut down the morning he was wandering downtown. With nothing better to do, he'd stopped to observe a group of workers in a heated discussion, frowning and gesturing over blueprints, building a wall of concrete to enclose the blunder. For some time now, it's been a perfect place for him to hide out close to downtown.

Alert to noises of any kind, the van's blasting horn terrifies him. He lies on the damp cement floor, still and rigid as if someone has warned him he shouldn't make a sound or move his body. His breathing slows, and he remains transfixed with his hands pressed against his ears.

He feels so tired.

For some comfort, he lowers his head onto the wool fabric of the overcoat he wears, even on these hottest days of summer. *What have you done, Rangy?*

None of it turned out as he'd planned. He only wanted to speak to the woman, to tell her that the tearing apart of Moses Rocket had to stop. Remembering the breathtaking sensation of her silky-smooth skin, he tells himself *I only touched her gently. I didn't mean to hurt her at all!* He sobs in denial until, finally, his body shudders, sloughing off the violence of what he had not meant to do.

It seems like such a long while before the commotion of shouting voices and moving vehicles finally ceases, and he can squeeze his eyes shut, forcing himself into a hazy sleep of half-watchfulness, the kind he's used to.

In the dark and silent garage, his mind bends to the past to whirring gears and the machine shop's clattering motion inside Moses Rocket. As if it is something he can conjure up, he smells the odor of fresh oil he'd squirted intermittently into metal gears, into all places where metal rubbed continually against metal, necessitating his oily ablutions. Once again, he hears the voices of the men he'd worked with calling him. "Rangy, Rangy! Over here, Rangy! We're getting hot!"

They'd needed him! How easily he'd lifted those five-gallon cans!

2

Katherine

She wakes up clutching a sheet of coarse cotton that has softened with years of washing. It takes a moment before she knows that she's in her bedroom in the house where she grew up—her brother Luke's home that now belongs to her sister-in-law Lucy. She's only vaguely aware of what has brought her here.

The movement of leaves and twigs—a once-familiar sound of small creatures roving through Luke's flower beds—frightens her. She fixes her mind on the last thing she can remember—a tall man wheeling her out into spongy darkness. He'd stopped and leaned over the wheelchair, asking in a caring voice, "Miss, you are not going to be sick, are you?" when it was already too late. She'd heard Lucy say, "Clean her up as best you can, and I'll do the rest at home."

The room is dimly lit with a child's nightlight of moon and stars. She was eight years old when her father brought the light back from a business trip. Right before he'd left, she'd pleaded with him not to go, confessing that she was afraid of the dark. It was the time near the end of her mother's long illness, the end of her mother's life. Her father had soothed her, telling her that the sun was shining somewhere, always, in the vast universe.

"Everyone has to have their share, Kat, and the nightlight will remind you." It was a rare thoughtfulness. He was a busy and successful executive, usually away from home.

Something is luminous in the half-dark—what is it? Her one eyelid is swollen, sore to her touch, and begins jittering up and down. It's difficult, but she finally realizes that she sees nothing more ominous than a clear plastic bag. She strains to find what it might hold—it looks like one of her shoes—patent leather with a high slender heel. Where is the other? Her linen suit and the silk blouse she'd worn are hanging on the back of the door. What has happened? It's becoming a bit clearer, a curtain of fog gradually lifting, and she shakes her head and shuts her eyes, her heart pounding.

She believes she never really saw his face, but his odor—which smelt like garbage sitting around too long or cantaloupe rinds left in the kitchen sink—has stayed with her. That foul odor must be coming off her clothes. Her stomach cramps, and she might be sick again. She forces back the taste of sour liquid in her mouth.

The Keeper

She attempts to pull herself up, but her back feels weighted, pinning her to the mattress. Lying as still as stone, a feeling of horror comes over her—there is something she's neglected, something she was supposed to do, that brings her a sense of panic as well as failure. Moments later, she knows that it is Moses Rocket that concerns her. Images grow in her mind of all those she's worked with on the project, and the reason for her panic comes back to her not all at once but slowly, like watching a pot of water taking forever to boil. She is the senior designer on the Moses Rocket renovation but had not given the presentation she was responsible for.

Scheduled for one o'clock in the main conference room of The Charter Oak Insurance Company, it was the first of the four major presentations planned for the mill renovation. The tedious but necessary work was performed by Charter Oak's building committee and members of her firm at Cole & Siegel. It was a culmination of months of research, studies of projected needs, and meeting budget stipulations.

Breathing hard, she wipes perspiration from her face with the sheet. Her throat feels raw, and it hurts to swallow. Her tongue is dry, and the inside of her mouth is parched. She craves a glass of ice cubes, Dewar's, and a few drops of water, a drink she indulges in when she can't sleep because of a project crisis or worry. Her sense of time and the horrific circumstances that brought her here are skewed and distorted.

Determined to sit up, she tries again and finally gets herself upright, the dizziness fading slightly. She pivots on her backside, dropping her legs over the side of the mattress, and her back goes into a rubbery spasm of pain. She almost blacks out. Instinctively, she puts all of her weight on her arms and draws her feet up to the bedrail, sitting awkwardly in the dark room, afraid to move, afraid to remember all that has happened.

Nights on this side of the house have always seemed exceedingly dark. She can only imagine the field that Luke had cleared and leveled below this window when she was just a child, creating flowerbeds and planting trees and bushes that both he and their mother had loved—Japanese plum, flowering crab apple, pear, and mounds of sweet-smelling hyacinth. Tonight, in concert, the leaves rustle softly, shaking off the day's heat, a hum of contentment that had always comforted her.

Luke, Luke, she murmurs.

"What do you need, Kat?"

Lucy's voice startles her. She attempts to answer, but words won't come. She turns her head to the hanging clothes.

"Oh, I'm so sorry, Kat. I didn't mean to leave them."

Lucy carries them out and returns with a glass of water, holding out the two pills in her hand. "These are the same as the ones they gave you in the emergency room. The nurse told me you should take two more as soon as you woke up."

Katherine doesn't argue, but it's like trying to swallow stones.

"Do you need more water?"

Katherine shakes her head no.

"Want to lie down?"

"Yes." Her voice is raspy, but Lucy understands. "Let me help," she says and lifts Katherine's legs slowly onto the mattress, alarmed when Katherine gasps and her face crumbles.

"It's bad, isn't it—should I call Doc Cousins?" Submerged in a nightmare, Katherine won't answer.

Lucy stands patiently, confused and helpless beside the bed, forcing herself to look closely at her sister-in-law. Katherine's face is gray in the dim light, blotched with bruises. Her hair is tangled, and one eye is horribly swollen. She appears so hurt, disfigured, and vulnerable that Lucy is afraid even to touch her hand. She blots her eyes with a tissue. "Kat, I am so sorry," she whispers and turns away, walking to the window. Looking out to the seemingly peaceful darkness, it is all a blur. *Who could have done something so terrible?*

This attack on Katherine would have devastated Luke, yet she wants her husband here with her, with them—he knew how to comfort her and take charge of difficult, sensitive situations.

Bracing herself, Lucy returns to Katherine's bedside. Her eyes are closed, and she is now breathing heavily and seems to have fallen asleep.

Thinking the pills have taken effect, Lucy goes downstairs to the kitchen. She paces back and forth for a few minutes, then pulls a chair out from beneath the table and sits down. Should I call Doc

Cousins? A longtime family physician, he would come, even at this hour. Uncertain over what to do, she covers her face, weeping silently.

Katherine, aware that she is alone again in the room, resists the pull of drifting into the state of nothingness where the pills will take her. She looks for her phone, and it is on the nightstand, sitting beside a rotary dial phone, one of the artifacts Luke had insisted on keeping in this room as if it were something worthy and meaningful. It's not in working order, yet it holds a memory of her father giving it to her when she started high school so that she could have those long conversations with her friends in the privacy of her room. It was a thoughtful, kind gesture, and at the time, it had meant a great deal. Suddenly, tears run down her cheeks. She sobs and covers her mouth, afraid Lucy might hear.

She reaches for her phone, her hand trembling so badly it takes some effort before she can pick it up. The pills start to work, but she only has to wait through a few rings before Mac answers.

3

Mac

He is about to leave his home office, the room his children had christened "The Command Center," when he hears a terrible, indescribable racket. It is a ringtone they'd installed when they'd insisted on "helping" him set up his latest phone. He hasn't the heart to change it just yet. He likes the way when they hear it, they grin at each other with an undisguised air of knowing complicity, smugly delighted with their handiwork.

"Mac…"

It takes him a second or two to recognize her voice. "Kat?"

"Mac, I'm—I'm hurt. . ."

"What? I can't hear you."

"I need you . . ."

"Where are you?"

No answer—the line is dead. He is stunned. He finds Lucy's number and calls, apologizing that it is after midnight on the east coast.

"I don't think I'll get much sleep tonight," she says and tells him all she can recall.

"My god!"

"I still can't believe it, Mac. She was on her way to a design presentation at Charter Oak Insurance."

"W-what did he do to her?"

"No, Mac, she wasn't raped. She fought hard and is terribly hurt. Her face! Oh, I can barely look at her."

"Have they any idea at all who is responsible?"

"I don't know. Two detectives came to the ER, but she was too out of it by then to make any sense."

"I would have thought they'd keep her in the hospital overnight."

"I thought the same, but she insisted on leaving. She gave everyone a hard time—the doctor, the nurses, the aides. I've never seen her like that. As soon as her x-rays returned, they gave her a sedative and some pain meds. She demanded to be released, and the doctor told me she could leave if someone was with her. It might be weeks before she can be on her own. The meds knocked her out some, but even so, she got very angry when she realized I was bringing her here."

"You did the right thing."

"My friend Margaret helped me get her up the stairs. We got her undressed and into bed. She's badly, badly hurt! There's no way she can be alone—not for some time."

"Lucy, please tell her I'll be there as soon as I can—I'm not sure she heard me."

Clearly shaken by what Lucy has told him, Mac looks in on his children before going downstairs. He knocks softly, but his son Luke, named after Katherine's brother, doesn't answer. Mac opens the door. Like always, Luke is hunched over his drawing board. He turns and pulls one earbud out, looking at his father as if his space has been invaded. "What's up, Dad?"

He answers in a steady voice. "Just checking in, but I see you're busy—have a good night. We'll talk in the morning."

"Dad, you're upset. What's wrong?"

"We're all fine, Luke."

The door to his daughter's room is partly open.

Caroline is fast asleep, lying trustingly on her side. He gently smooths a lock of her hair away from her face that is so like his mother Veronia's, and he whispers, "Good night." For a moment, her face relaxes into a smile, and he wonders if she is dreaming, and if so, he's deeply grateful that it seems as if it is a pleasant one. She's clearly in another world.

Downstairs in the kitchen, he pours an inch of bourbon into a glass, goes out the patio door into a warm, close night, and sits in one of the deck chairs.

Realistically, he thinks it's almost impossible for him to leave just now. He started his own consulting business several months back, working from home. Evenings, while the children do homework or spend time in their rooms, he's nearby in his office, available if they need him. They are mostly caught up with friends and what is happening in their own young lives, yet on occasion, they come in wanting to tell him something or talk over some dilemma, and he puts all work aside. Years ago, after separating from his wife, he made the children his priority and has never wavered.

His business is thriving. He's got client meetings scheduled that he can't afford to cancel, and he'll have to ask Tom and Marci Baker if they're free to stay with the kids for a few days. And, yet, as he makes a mental list of all that's required before he can travel east for a short visit, he knows that almost nothing will stop him from going.

They had found each other on a school playground. It was lunchtime, and he was new at the school, having just moved to Connecticut with his mother. Like him, Katherine stood apart from the other children, absorbed in watching a group of older girls jumping rope as if she were wondering why or maybe how they successfully managed to hop above the rope to rhymes they were chanting. *"A is for apple, B is for banana C is for—"* How odd that he should still remember those words after all this time.

He thought she looked nice. Her hair was long and wavy, a pretty, sandy color. She was dressed in clothes that seemed to him then more like what you'd wear on special occasions, a dark blue skirt, a white blouse, and knee socks. He looked down at the orange shirt that his mother had brought back from New York City, a shirt he loved that had a streak of gray lightning down the front, a shirt he didn't think this girl might ever wear. But maybe she wouldn't care how he dressed. He walked over and stood next to her. He was almost a foot taller, and somehow that gave him confidence. "Hi," was all he said.

She turned to him, and after a somber moment of appraisal, she smiled.

He felt encouraged. "I'm Gerry McNulty, but my friends call me "Mac."

"I'm Katherine."

Her eyes were beautiful, the color of bright blue flowers. He'd felt his face redden. *Was it right then that he fell in love with her?* At the time, he'd felt brave enough to go on. "My mother and I just moved here."

"Where from?"

"New York City."

"My mother just died."

He was uncertain about what to say next. Then he said what he was feeling. "That's sad—I'm really sorry."

"Thank you," she said.

What do you talk about once you know something like that? Maybe talking about something else might be the best thing to do.

"Where do you live, Katherine?"

"What everyone around here calls 'the old farmhouse.'"

He knew where she meant. He'd already been told about the large white house at the top of a rise not far from the pretty white cape his mother had instantly fallen in love with so that the real estate agent had had to cancel all of the other showings.

Some trust, an unspoken connection, had been established during that first encounter, and they both seemed to know they would become friends. They began walking home together after school, both of them living close enough so that they didn't have to ride the bus.

The first time he brought Katherine home to meet his mother, Veronia stood at the door in a silky green kimono, holding a lighted cigarette, the scent of her perfume drifting through the screen. She glared frankly at both of them and didn't say much when he introduced Katherine.

His mother always wore a lot of makeup—eyeliner, face powder, and lipstick—and her shiny black hair fell loosely to her shoulders. Katherine thought she was the most beautiful woman she'd ever seen. "Your mother is pretty," she told him.

"Not pretty," he said with assurance. "Veronia's beautiful."

Seeming put out, she said, "You don't look like her."

"No, I don't look like her—"

She cut him off, sounding almost spiteful. "You must look like your father."

He didn't want to think he looked like the man who had abandoned them and also felt he needed or wanted to assert himself, knowing just what to say that might distract her. "My mother is a well-known actress."

He was surprised at how angrily she'd responded. "Come on, Mac! Movie stars don't live around here—not in places like this!"

"Veronia is an actress—she performs on the stage and can live anywhere."

He neglected to tell her that Veronia also had an apartment in Manhattan and had the luxury of Ollie, a housekeeper and cook who arrived at the Connecticut house whenever she was needed.

He remembers feeling a little self-satisfied walking away from her that day, and on this sad night, he smiles a bit grimly, thinking again *it was so long ago!*

Neither of them dated much in high school, and when she did, he felt so deeply jealous, so wounded, it almost made him sick. Unable to hide or disguise his feelings, he usually avoided her for a few days afterward. They went away to different colleges and saw each other during semester breaks. She called it "catching up," although they were always in touch. It took him a while before he figured out that she somehow needed him in her life.

She grew into a lovely young woman—smart, attractive, and ambitious. He felt afraid half the time, thinking someday she'd leave, although, in the end, he was the one who left, going 3000 miles west.

After college, she suggested they rent an apartment together in Hartford, and in a state of blissful disbelief, he readily agreed.

"Just for a while," she said. At the time, he hoped that would not be the case. *How naïve he'd been!* She was focused on her career and frustrated because she couldn't get a full-time position in corporate design. Companies were hiring only on a contract basis and with no benefits.

Neither of them had much money, but by pooling their resources, they found an affordable two-bedroom flat in Hartford's north end. Giddy with excitement, they painted the walls shades of purple from pale to a deep night color, almost black, put mattresses on the floor, and draped fabric samples she'd collected from various design jobs over secondhand tables. Her brother Luke gave them a few old bookcases, and Lucy put together a box of dishes and cutlery. They lived together chastely as good friends; although they'd been close for so long, no one believed it and thought they were destined to marry.

He was foolishly happy. He enjoyed cooking their meals and doing small household chores. He worked part-time and hunted for a job, seeking a good fit. He'd been intrigued by computers early on, focusing much of his education on them. They went home on weekends—he split the visit between time with Veronia and dinner at the farmhouse with Katherine, Luke, and Lucy.

It was a safe existence, a space of time between dependency and freedom. It soon got old for her, but he loved it and loved her deeply. When she sensed (what she had to have suspected all along and could no longer ignore) that he wanted something more from their relationship, she wasted no time "setting him straight" (her words). "Mac, you deserve more than I can give—"

"I guess I'd hoped all this time—" was his feeble answer. It hurts him even now to remember—he was heartbroken. He can also admit that he felt humiliated, with only himself to blame. She'd never promised or insinuated that there would be anything more between them than the close friendship they'd always had.

He was in a terrible state and supposed he was grieving. The pain he felt was unbearable, and to spare them both, a few days later, he packed up his clothes and left for California. Both families were shocked.

Veronia never really forgave Katherine. At the time, she declared that Katherine had "used" him. Their discussion regarding his relationship with Katherine erupted into an argument where hurtful things were said on both sides. From California, he'd written to his mother, asking forgiveness.

Over the years, he and Katherine have always kept in close touch but haven't seen each other much. Numerous times he's asked her to visit, to meet his children, but she's always turned him down, with one excuse or another. He's never pressed her. *What if he'd been more confident and self-assured? Would things between them have turned out differently?*

God knows she is the only woman he has ever really loved. He thinks again it will be difficult, even burdensome, to go east, and yet—what is that trite saying—*he'll move heaven and earth* to go to her.

In truth, he is somewhat bewildered by her call, especially by how he is feeling out here on this warm night, alone, overcome by what has happened. It is the same sensation he'd often felt from their very beginning, though in all the years of their friendship, this is the only time she has said the words, *"I need you."*

He swallows the last of the bourbon, staying out for a few minutes more, breathing in the exotic, unforgettable perfume of gardenias that in the future will always bring to mind Katherine and this night's decision to go to her.

4

Sy

He arrives early at Cole & Siegel for a meeting with Katherine's boss, Pete Larson. Their discussion will focus on staff, on who might be available, if necessary, to replace her as the senior designer on the Moses Rocket project. He thinks of the vacant drafting station next to Oscar's. For weeks, that is where he's imagined Apple at work. He frequently calculates the hours he'd spend alone with her if she were hired on to his project, legitimate late-night hours that would be charged to the client.

He checks the time, and with a few minutes to spare, he pauses in front of the 19th-century map that is pinned to the outside wall of his workstation. The map is a copy of a handsome and finely detailed drawing he'd discovered at the Hartford Historical Society soon after he was appointed as the lead architect on the project, a major renovation, creating badly needed office space close to downtown.

The map shows the original location of the main factory building, outbuildings, the expansive park-like grounds, and rows of red brick houses (known as "cottages") built for the workers and their families. In his mind, the map beautifully depicts a sense of community, purpose, and inclusion that he admires, and he looks at it with a kind of reverence.

Not shown on the map is the location of an ugly concrete building, a storage facility, put up without much foresight or deliberation by The Charter Oak Insurance Company after they purchased the Moses Rocket site in the 1960s for future use, dramatically altering the look and feel of the complex's original plan. Sy and the rest of the team frequently heap scorn on the building, referring to it as the "concrete cube."

At one of his first meetings at Charter Oak, Sy had lightheartedly suggested to the committee overseeing the project that the building might be demolished. He was pleased to learn that his suggestion had been passed on to upper management, where his proposal was considered. Subsequently, it was decided that the demolition costs would be too high.

Privately, in his office at home, he is designing a new entrance for the concrete building that will tie in with some of the old factory's noteworthy (he believes) architectural details. He'll present his idea when he's confident that no one can interfere, offer suggestions, or change it in any manner, particularly Will Swanson, Charter Oak's project coordinator, the surly man Sy must communicate with on a daily basis.

He often wonders why the company appointed Swanson to manage the project. Swanson knows little about design or architecture and often seems disorganized and defensive. If it weren't for his assistant Tillie Watson, the project could well be a disaster on the company's end.

Swanson also seems to have a particular dislike for this assignment and design professionals in general. During meetings, he takes every opportunity to make needlessly rude, arrogant, and disparaging comments that Sy does his best to ignore. A confrontation with Swanson will set things back, and Sy's ultimate goal is to keep the project moving toward completion. "That's your mission," Jed Cole had told him when he assigned him to the project. "Charter Oak wants the project well managed and kept within budget."

Sy got off to a good start. He'd asked Jan Neery, one of the firm's graphic designers, for help. She was professional, positive, and focused, discussing strategies for the initial overview meeting with Swanson and the full committee at Charter Oak, department heads, and middle-line managers.

Jan agreed with him that they should stress the enormous appeal of the housing units, an enticement for Charter Oak employees who would have the first opportunity to purchase them, and for singles and young couples, even retirees attracted to city life. "Then lead the discussion into the renovation of the Moses Rocket building and the redesign of the concrete cube," Jan suggested. The strategy worked.

In her perspectives for landscaping the site, Jan emphasized the natural world, imbuing the cottages with the Victorian theme of going out to nature. Her watercolor sketches looked as if they were torn from a book on 19th-century English country gardens. Stone paths led to the original heavy wooden doors she'd crowned with wisteria vines. Clematis and old-fashioned roses clung to the façades, and ivy tumbled out of window boxes. Side gardens held a profusion of foxglove, sweet William, and bluebells.

Sy was cautious when discussing the landscaping, using words like "projected" and phrases like "these sketches will enable folks to see how the cottages might look with some attractive plantings." He made no commitment that Charter Oak would actually provide the specific flowers or shrubs shown in Jan's drawings for the cottages or for the rest of the site.

The committee was pleased. Swanson had turned to him and said, "Now you people have finally given us something we can all relate to."

Sy overlooked yet another one of Swanson's "you people" remarks and was thrilled when the sketches were displayed in Charter Oak's main lobby downtown. The prospect of working and perhaps moving to what some called "a campus-like environment close to downtown" excited employees.

At Cole & Siegel, Sy is not only working toward a partnership, but he believes that if the project is successful, there will be press coverage and notoriety. He'll be instrumental in accomplishing what some newspaper articles have already decreed is a visionary idea—the saving and restoration of Moses Rocket.

He'd been restless all night after Jed's call, explaining in more detail why Katherine hadn't shown up for the presentation. "Can you manage without her?" he'd said, sounding worried.

"I'll do my best, Jed, but we might have to hire additional staff."

"You have to get an okay from Charter Oak. That won't be easy, and we're not sure yet how badly Katherine is hurt. She may be back sooner than we expect."

Sy thinks how much easier it would be to move the project ahead without Katherine but knows better than to say so to Jed.

From the beginning, Katherine was too passionate about Moses Rocket, arguing with him over decisions for which she had no responsibility, making his job more difficult. Her rants on the "integrity of design" exhausted and, at times, enraged him, although he silently agreed with many of her insights and often costly suggestions.

But he walks a fine line on this project, balancing architectural integrity and an almost sacred covenant to preserve the past—the design's original intent—with practical solutions that can be implemented quickly and within budget, designs that Swanson and the committee will sign off on.

Katherine has been at the firm for years. She doesn't seem particularly close with anyone but her friend Holly and her sister-in-law Lucy. However, the professionals she interacts with respect her. Her design work, and her ideas, are invariably well received. Jed has mentioned to him that she's a rare asset, meaning she works both creatively and competently with corporate clients, having had the experience of working within a corporate structure before coming to Cole & Siegel.

The tensions between them started a few weeks into the renovation. She requested a meeting alone with him in the first-floor conference room. She was waiting when he arrived and immediately began by criticizing his handling of the project.

At first, he listened calmly to her complaints, needing to know where he had to defend himself to the firm's partners if their disagreement went that far. He barely paid attention to her speech about the integrity of design and hints that he had to trust his team. In other words, he let her "get it all out." She then crossed a line, accusing him of letting Swanson control the project, and he'd had enough. The meeting ended in a shouting match.

News of conflict circulates quickly through the firm. He was in the men's room when Scott, one of the interns, asked why he and Katherine had quarreled. It was none of Scot's concern, and the question irritated him. Thoughtlessly he'd shrugged and said, "She's on the rag."

The Keeper

The crude remark, reminiscent of one that his teenage workplace mentor Joel Schopenhauer might have made, had slipped out. If Scott, or anyone, ever brings it up, Sy will deny he ever said it.

On his way down to the design department, he pauses at the reception desk to ask Violet about Katherine.

"Have you heard anything more?" he says with concern. Violet looks up at him quizzically and shakes her head. Earrings of three squatting monkeys—the see no, hear no, speak no evil icons—sway back and forth. "I know as much as you," she says.

He senses a note of insinuation, of blame. "I'll be in the downstairs conference room."

"I've got that already," she says, pointing to the daily calendar.

Violet's manner, the way she guards her post as if it were a strategic checkpoint inside a country on the brink of war, often annoys him, but especially so this morning. He worries that she—or maybe others at the firm—believes he's responsible for what happened to Katherine. Parking is at a premium downtown. At the start of the project, he emailed Swanson (a copy is in the project file) asking for parking adjacent to the home office where the meetings and presentations are held, explaining that the team often brings materials they are unable to carry from the garage.

Swanson turned him down in a quick email back. "Why should our people lose spaces to Cole & Siegel or any outfit that's working for us? You have two options. Your staff can park temporarily in the visitor spots, notify the building department that help is needed, and one of the men will go out and bring in the samples. Your second option is to call the building department ahead of time and arrange to drop materials off at the loading dock and then park in the municipal lot close by."

Sy felt it would be futile to press him further. Swanson may even have requested spaces from Security at Moses Rocket and been denied, although he'd never admit it.

He moves as quickly as he's able through the design department, but Deborah Keneally, the junior designer on the project, sees him coming and steps away from her drafting board, stopping him in the aisle. A good and dependable worker, her sweet face is paler than usual. "Katherine—is she going to be all right?" she says, looking tearful.

"She's at Lucy's, Deborah. That's all I can tell you, all I know," he adds gently. She is so distressed that he starts to put his hand on her shoulder and pulls back just in time. Touching the body of a colleague of either sex, for good reasons, is no longer permissible.

Reaching the conference room, he pulls hard on the door that is frequently jammed and walks into chaos. The room is a catch-all— a depot for the project remains. The table is littered with presentation boards and samples of building materials, and most meetings here are hurried and take place with people standing up. The steel skeleton of a chrome and leather chair lay there still displayed, used during a presentation to convince a reluctant client about the wisdom of its uses here. Also, yards of baseboard, stacks of carpet samples, boxes of floor and carpet tiles, ceiling strips, some black polyvinyl piping, and even a clerestory window a dealer left behind.

All of the staff put materials they no longer have any use for in here, thinking that interns would spend a day decluttering the room. In reality, interns are used more profitably, building models and making up presentation boards, legitimate hours that can be charged to clients.

Ventilation and air conditioning have been disconnected as a cost-saving measure, and the thermostat is set at 50 degrees so the pipes won't freeze. For some reason, the building's drifting odors— mildew, food, chemicals— migrate into the room. The room's one advantage is privacy. Employees from all three floors use it. Pete is already there when Sy walks in.

Sy is dressed in khaki trousers and a blue oxford shirt, seeming relaxed, cool, and under control. Pete looks almost as disheveled as the room in a rumpled dark gray suit, white shirt, and striped tie, loose at the neck. His thick hair falls carelessly on his forehead, and he pushes it back impatiently.

"Damn, Sy, I can't believe it. What the hell kind of security have they got over there? My whole department is spooked. They've all used that garage at one time or another. I told Jed my staff can no longer park there without a security guard."

"No, no one should go in alone."

"Never again on my watch," Pete says.

"How is she?"

"Not so good. I just spoke to Lucy. Katherine will stay with her for the next few weeks."

"She should take all the time she needs." Sy hesitates, gauging if this is the right moment to discuss hiring additional staff, hiring Apple. Is the incident too new, too raw, to suggest a replacement? It might show a lack of sensitivity.

"What's on your mind, Sy?"

"I'm concerned about staff for Moses Rocket. Who will fill in for Katherine?"

"Deborah fills in—that's what juniors do when a senior is absent."

"Have you any idea how long Katherine will be out? If this were a few days, a week, we could manage." Again Sy hesitates and adds, "Is it certain she'll want to come back?"

"Why wouldn't she?"

Sy has gone this far and presses on. "The threat of rape and actual rape. Isn't it the same for a woman?"

"What in hell are you talking about, Sy?"

Sy is going too fast and needs to stop, but before he can, he blurts out, "What kind of emotional shape is she going to be in? I spoke to Swanson this morning. He's concerned."

"As long as the work gets done, it's our problem, not his."

"That's what I'm asking. Who can do the work? If Deborah moves up, who does hers? Your whole department is working overtime as it is."

"I'll make adjustments and let you know."

"It's got to be soon. My client is sympathetic, but they've got a schedule they have to keep, people on their backs—"

"You're joking—they spend half of the day in meetings and never get one thing decided. You said that yourself. Not one of them has the balls to make a decision, to take responsibility—"

He should have waited. Soon it would be obvious they'd need more help. "Pete, you're upset—we all are—"

"You bet I'm upset. Ever since Jed called, I've been asking myself why Katherine was alone. This was a major presentation. She should have had someone with her."

"I spoke to her twice the day before the presentation. She said she was ready. As far as driving down alone, isn't it her responsibility to coordinate with her staff?"

Pete takes a deep breath before answering. "What's going on with you, Sy? What's your angle?"

"My angle? Listen, Pete. Swanson's not happy. She went overboard—"

"She knows what she's doing, and you know that as well as I. As for the carpeting, no one's installing wall-to-wall— it looks trashed after the first few weeks."

"She spent far too much on the analysis. The trips to New York, to Boston—"

"You approved those trips."

"I gave her the time to do an in-depth carpet analysis, a comparison."

"You knew up front they wouldn't go for modular carpet. You covered yourself, having her do the analysis."

"That's not fair. I knew Katherine would be thorough. I hoped the analysis would persuade Swanson it was an outdated, expensive idea."

"You should have told him straight out that wall-to-wall was a dumb idea."

"The VPs moving over want the same carpet they have in the home office."

Pete gestures with irritation and the papers he's been holding spin to the floor. He bends to pick them up, and Sy pulls at the stuck door.

"We're not finished here," Pete says. "Katherine deserves a chance to get back on her feet."

"Of course she does."

The door finally gives. "Sorry, Pete. I've got a meeting at Charter Oak—let's catch up later."

On his way upstairs, he knows it would have been a bad idea to bring up hiring Apple and is relieved he hadn't.

5

Violet

For most of her working life, Violet LaTresse had clerked at the West Hartford post office. She was a valued employee. She always arrived early and was often the last to leave. She was dependable and hardworking. Those qualities came naturally to her—she'd made her own way in life from her earliest years.

Then after twenty-seven years, she was fired. Mr. Wynburn, her boss, had put it as nicely as anyone could on the morning he told her, using words like "resign" and "retired." "I saved your pension, Violet. It was the best I could do for you."

She's never blamed him.

He'd been a good boss and was always fair. After all, she'd been caught—what's that expression—"red-handed?"

Would she have opened that particular envelope if she had that moment back? The writing was not as frantic and worried-looking as on some others, although she'll always remember how dark and swooping the letters were.

She could see that someone had pressed a pen quite hard on the paper's surface, a signal to her of distress. She hesitated before sliding her thumb into the flap on the back of the envelope.

For many years now, sensing a cry for help, Violet has opened other people's mail. She saw herself like the man on that TV show she used to watch long ago, where he gave some poor soul a million dollars. She'd loved it. That's where her idea came from. She felt she might do some good with the savings she had, and it had made her job more interesting after so many mostly uneventful years, a reason to get out of bed each morning.

On the day that turned out to be her last, she had no idea a Postal Inspector was in Mr. Wynburn's office. Usually, he warned his workers the day before, reminding them what had to be done and how to behave. She always did her job properly during postal inspections.

She was stunned, looking up from the letter she was reading to find the red-faced Postal Inspector standing by, trembling with disbelief and rage.

Violet is a woman who prides herself on seeing life "as a glass half full." She muses over the difference she's made in the lives of some she's helped, like Hannah. Violet paid her tuition for her first year of college, and now Hannah works as a highly successful marketing consultant. And Aaron. He had protruding teeth and needed braces. His schoolmates regularly made fun of him, and he was a target of bullying. He grew into a handsome young man and is now in law school, wanting to work for the handicapped. And Timothy. He ran away and got in with a rough crowd and had no way to get back home. She notified his family, who were desperately trying to find him. She bought him some new clothes and paid his train fare back to Minnesota. Once strangers, many of those she's helped have become like family. They all keep in touch regularly.

Violet has no other relatives. Her beginnings were something like you'd read in one of those old-fashioned stories that sometimes appear around the holidays about an abandoned child. It is true she was left at an orphanage on the lower east side of Manhattan on one brisk March night, but no one had mistreated her, nor had anyone smothered her with kindnesses. She grew up in a clean, spare environment, was well educated by the Sisters of Charity, and was taught how to take care of herself. Her life was guided by aphorisms like "Do unto others," and "Turn the other cheek," which was at times hard for her. She could be sharp-tongued when provoked.

She left the orphanage at sixteen, first working in a Hell's Kitchen restaurant for a German couple who'd recently immigrated to America—Louise and Adolph. Naturally frugal, she saved as much as she could. Then she was hired at a post office in New York

City during the Vietnam War when additional help was needed, eventually transferring out to West Hartford, Connecticut, a form of retreat into a quieter place. She bought a small house and was nicely settled until she lost her job.

She is not ashamed she opened personal mail—caring little for gossip—and for the most part, she'd always minded her own business—she'd been taught that, too, early on at the orphanage. She was only interested in the needs of those who'd come to that place in life where a bit of help could make a difference. After a few lines and a quick read down the page, she always put the letter back into its envelope after making a note of how she might reach the sender.

The result of what she thinks of as "innocent eavesdropping" was that one day she had a job at the post office, and the next day she found herself out of work. Oh, she learned a hard lesson! If only Mr. Wynburn had warned them!

Her philanthropic impulses are gratified at the Homeless Shelter's soup kitchen, where she volunteers three nights a week. That's where she met Nan Cole, Jed's wife. During a coffee break together, Nan told Violet that her husband's firm was looking for a receptionist.

Violet figured people find out things sooner or later and told Nan the truth about herself up front. Nan sympathized and made an appointment for Violet to meet Jed.

She was very nervous during her interview with Mr. Cole, a broad, heavyset man with a large head, a smattering of wispy hair, and a surprisingly good-looking face. He was dressed neatly in no particular style and looked solid, trustworthy, and a bit rough, not at all like his wife, Nan. He hired Violet with a promise (he'd asked her to make) that she'd open nothing—mail or files—unless specifically asked. And she never has.

Character traits and lifelong habits are hard to change, though. Violet watches everyone at the firm and makes a mental note of who comes in and out of the lobby and with whom. She knows a great deal about her fellow employees' lives and work habits, or at least thinks she does, without snooping conspicuously into their privacy. She sees that Cole & Siegel is a microcosm of the outside world and harbors the same intrigues, manipulations, infidelities, disappointments, and heartaches. So far, there is plenty here to keep her inquisitive mind and idealistic impulses occupied.

6

Lucy

She comes slowly up the long drive, looking up at the tall, white farmhouse with its oversized chimney framed in an azure blue sky. On all sides are Luke's marvelous flower beds, a dazzling, breathtaking hodgepodge of color. A wonderland for bees, birds, and butterflies, she thinks. But not for you, Lucy.

The climb leaves her breathless. Reaching the stonewall, she comes upon a bed of yarrow with limp and wilted stems. She'll need to water later on—a task Luke had looked forward to that she dislikes. And now there is Ellen's car parked beside the house. "Damn," she mutters, not in the mood. Ellen takes work, and Lucy hasn't the energy.

She waves hello, and Ellen's tall, thin frame unfolds from its sunny position on the porch steps. "It's about time you showed up, Lucy."

"I was out for a walk."

"I can see that. How is my niece? Out of bed?"

Lucy shakes her head no. "It will be a while," she says, leading Ellen to the side porch entrance. She doesn't want to speak, to explain how badly Katherine has been hurt. It will be a while before she can get out of bed on her own.

"I saw Doc Cousins leaving," Ellen says. "He had his nurse with him."

"She had a rough night. I thought a visit with Doc might help," and she tells Ellen what she already knows. "After all, she's known him all of her life."

But Ellen is aware that Lucy is more than upset. Since Luke died, she's been lost in grief, and now this new horror, and she doesn't interrupt, allowing Lucy to finish.

"Doc has seen her x-rays, and she trusts him to tell her when she can return to her own apartment and work. That's what she wants."

"She never liked being told anything more than what she wanted to hear."

In Katherine's present circumstance, the remark sounds harsh to Lucy, but she has to let it go. It is altogether too easy to get into a testy row with Ellen.

"I haven't had any breakfast," Lucy says. "How about you?"

"I had it at six like every morning," Ellen says, as if it is a crime that Lucy can't take her meals at appropriate times. "I brought you supper—I had to leave it out here on the porch. I couldn't get in; everything's locked up."

Lucy picks up the casserole and thanks her.

"You need to get that in the fridge before it spoils."

Lucy sighs. Inside the house, faded green shades that she hasn't much liked have kept the kitchen cool and dim. She flips one up, hoping it will fall to pieces so she can replace them all, but it just rattles efficiently to the top, like always. "The sun's moving to the other side of the house," Lucy says.

"When did you get a microwave?"

"A few months back."

"I guess I'll be the last person on the planet without one."

Lucy fills the kettle, carries it to the pantry, and Ellen follows. Lucy won't turn on the burner until she checks on Katherine. She notices the stove needs cleaning and hopes Ellen won't.

"What an inconvenient place for the stove," Ellen says. "I always wanted to ask, your idea?"

"Luke's."

"What happened to the electric stove I used?"

"Wore out."

After Luke's father, Harry, moved to Florida, Lucy and Luke moved from their newly remodeled home on the outskirts of Hartford to the farmhouse that had been built more than two hundred years ago by the Wicks, Luke's maternal ancestors.

One of Luke's first projects was restoring the wood-fired stove in the kitchen. From the beginning, Lucy heaped all of her frustrations of giving up a home she loved onto the ancient, squatty appliance. "The heat from that stove in the summertime, Luke! How did women endure it?"

"Stoically, I imagine," Luke said. "What choice did they have?"

She actually enjoyed the stove, especially in winter when it heated the downstairs rooms and lifted the odors of what simmered in pots or baked in the oven throughout the house. And it was surprisingly efficient. But she refused to light it in the warmer months. Neither she nor Luke liked to grill, and Luke's solution had been a hot plate.

When it became obvious that they couldn't cook a whole meal every night on a hotplate, he reluctantly agreed to purchase a narrow 4-burner gas stove, telling her it could go in the pantry.

"The pantry, Luke? The pantry!"

Stubborn and territorial about any changes in the house, he said, "Yes, Lucy," in a tone of finality that proclaimed in her mind that he had a history here and she did not.

The stove was installed in the pantry, the room with access to the original well, besides an old rinsing sink—an awkward and inconvenient location, back and forth from the kitchen to the pantry.

Once upon a time, Lucy enjoyed cooking but gave that up after Luke died. Now she relishes the catered food from Abi's Gourmet— the cold salads, the hot dishes like apricot turkey meatloaf, the crusty home-baked bread, and the choice of desserts— a slice of Key Lime pie or lemon pound cake—food she hasn't thought about or had to plan for that provides some small pleasure.

"I'm all sweaty," Lucy tells Ellen. "I'm going up to change out of these clothes."

"Should I come with you? I'd like to see her."

"Better to wait. She might be asleep—the pills knock her out."

Upstairs, Lucy quickly removes her sweats, showers, foregoes moisturizing, and changes into cotton slacks and a t-shirt. She taps lightly on Katherine's door. "It's only me," she says softly.

"Come in," Katherine says and thanks Lucy for locking up the house. "Ellen tried to get in, and I was so afraid you'd left one of the doors open. I don't want her seeing me like this."

While assisting Katherine, Lucy avoids looking at her, and she turns away quickly, her heart thump thumping so that she puts her hand to her chest. "How did it go with Doc Cousins?"

"He says I'll be fine."

"Good, Kat. That's good."

"It will take more time than I imagined."

"You're welcome to stay as long as you want."

"Yes, thanks."

"You're not a burden, Kat. I like working from home."

"And I'm anxious to return to our place of work." They both smile stiffly.

It is all they can do under the circumstances.

"I better go down," Lucy says. "Ellen might charge up here any minute."

Lucy brings a tray with two cups of tea and a plate of cookies out to the porch.

Ellen glances at her watch.

"Sorry, Ellen, I had to shower." She sets down the tray, and Ellen snatches one of the cups. "I don't use sugar."

"I didn't put any in."

"She's still asleep?"

Lucy nods, wishing Ellen were not here. The sight of Katherine shocks her whenever she goes into the room, and she needs a space of quiet to steady her nerves. She brings the cup to her mouth and keeps it there. Ellen may or may not know that Lucy has done so because she cannot answer her truthfully and tell her that Katherine is awake, but she doesn't want to see you just yet. No, Lucy couldn't do such a hurtful thing.

"I hope she's not planning to go back to work this soon."

"I don't know."

"She should take some time off. Quit altogether for a while. She can afford it. My brother left her a small fortune." Lucy sips her tea silently. A discussion with Ellen about what Katherine will do is pointless. Luke used to say, "Katherine is stubborn and independent, and Aunt Ellen is a 'know-it-all,'" adding that they never got along.

Thankfully for Lucy, Ellen also seems aware that she has little influence on Katherine and switches to a new topic. "The property looks nice. Who did you find for the yard work?"

"Silvano's Nursery."

"Must be expensive."

"I checked around first." Why the fib, Lucy? She'd hired Silvano on the phone, the largest nursery in West Hartford, the one call she made.

"I can't get anyone to work at my place. They come and give me an estimate and then don't return my calls."

"I could ask Silvano."

"Is he reliable? I only hire quality people."

"You decide. He's been a godsend for me."

Silvano's men have taken charge of the outdoor tasks, caring for the property and imposing order, as Luke had. The task she's been left with is to water some of the flowerbeds, but sometimes she forgets or doesn't want to remember and feels terrible that she's been neglectful.

"Sure you don't want a cookie, Ellen?"

The question seems to aggravate her. "You know very well, Lucy, that I don't have a sweet tooth."

Lucy bites emphatically into her third.

"Well, what are you going to do with this place? It's been a year."

"I don't know."

"You don't have to stay way out here. You're a young woman. Fifty-two is nothing nowadays!"

Lucy laughs softly, disconcerted her correct age has been spoken aloud. Shouldn't she be proud? Shouldn't she welcome age? Not yet! Not yet!

"It's peculiar how people think of age," Ellen says. "When I turned thirty, I wasn't married, although people expected me to want a husband and children. Their presumption sometimes made me angry. What's that term people use nowadays? *Pissed off.* An awful expression!"

Ellen smiles triumphantly as if she's keeping up with how a younger generation might express their anger. "But that's how I felt at the time. I fairly slid into forty. I was doing well at the bank by then. Believe it or not, I was learning to keep opinions to myself, at least at the office. But fifty rocked me. Fifty means half your life is over. And then, of course, for women, it's worse. The Change. A stupid word for it—but I suppose accurate. Happened to you yet?"

"No, it hasn't."

Liar! Liar!—what is the rest of it?—*pants on fire*? Eyes glazed, face puffed, skin unhealthily flushed. She knows how she looks and worries one will come while she's at work—it's a miracle it hasn't already happened. She's put off her yearly physical, searching for a female internist.

When she says, "My breasts are sore," she wants more questions, no platitudes, and a few solutions. All of her life, men—perfectly kind, capable, and professional men—have been telling her to "scoot down" an examining table. She has no wish to hear it again. *Who are you kidding, Lucy?* On your next exam, you'll scoot down the table, awkwardly wrinkling the paper sheet, feet in the stirrups.

"Soon it will," Ellen says as if she suspects Lucy's fib but forgives her or at least is willing to overlook it. Suddenly, she jumps up from the chair. "Time to go! Tell my niece I was here?"

"I'll tell her, and thanks for the casserole."

"What was the name of that man who does the yard work?"

"Silvano. Silvano's Nursery. I'll get the number for you."

"Are they in the book?"

She remembers Ellen hasn't yet succumbed to the age of computers.

"Should be—under landscape."

"Don't bother, then. If I need it, I'll call you."

Lucy walks with Ellen to her car, assuring her she'll keep her informed about Katherine when they hear the sound of tires crossing the gravel and see a pick-up edging cautiously up the driveway. "Wait," Lucy says. "That's one of Silvano's trucks."

A man climbs out, and Lucy says, "It's Silvano, the owner." She recalls telling him she'd be here, taking time off to stay with Katherine.

"So, this is the great Silvano!" Ellen crows.

He gives Ellen a big smile.

He is taller even than Ellen. His hair is cut short and fringed with silver, lightly waved. But already this early in his day, the waves have curled. His eyes, a deep dark color, reflect a brightness that seems mischievously curious.

His mouth is relaxed, and he carries an air of confidence that everything will turn out all right. He's wearing gray slacks and a checked shirt that fits him well.

"I like your boots," Ellen tells him. "They look sturdy."

"They are Italian, like me."

"With a name like yours, what else would you be?"

He laughs softly. "Lucy, I stopped by because your place needs water. We've had no rain for weeks now."

"I was going to do it later—"

"No, it's too much for you. My men are working in Pilgrims Corner. They'll come by and do it."

She's relieved she won't have to drag out the hoses and keep track of the various timers. "Don't forget to add the hours to my monthly bill."

"Don't worry about it."

"We were just talking about you," Ellen says.

Lucy blushes and quickly explains. "Ellen needs some work done on her property—"

"Well, it's not guaranteed I'll hire your outfit," Ellen says. "You come out and give me a price first."

"Of course," he says, and Lucy can see that he's enjoying Ellen's directness.

They agree on a day, and Lucy thinks it's kind of him, not to mention that he rarely goes out to a prospective customer with a property as small as hers.

Once he is gone, Ellen turns to Lucy, her eyes glittering. "What an attractive specimen!"

"He is a nice man."

"Yes, well, look, I have to leave. You know where I am if you need a hand."

"Thanks, but I wouldn't know Kat was here if I didn't have to help her out of bed."

"Remember, Lucy. I helped raise her and lived here for a while in her early years after her mother passed. I know full well how independent she is and how stubborn!"

Ellen turns suddenly and walks toward her car, straight-backed and urgent, as if she's got a hundred things to do. Secretive about her own age—somewhere in her mid-eighties—she is healthier and more energetic than most of the older women in Lucy's Widows Group.

"I'll be back," she calls to Lucy.

Of course, you will. This was your home for a long while, too, yet I—the only one of us born in a city—am living out here in what this family calls "God's country."

The Keeper

Lucy sets the empty mug on a round chestnut plank table, an heirloom, a piece of furniture crafted by one of Luke's maternal ancestors. For a long while, she rocks steadily in the black wicker chair.

At the end of the drive is a cemetery, a square parcel of land Luke had painstakingly landscaped, where a dozen or more Wicks are buried. The holly berries have not yet reddened.

She and the berries have been at war—that is how she feels whenever she looks at them. Lately, she's been looking for them— they remind her so of Luke and how they'd quarreled the day he transplanted them into the cemetery.

It had been a Saturday, a long week of work behind them. She'd wanted to drive to Hartford to a Modernist show at the Athenaeum. She was looking forward to the exhibit, dinner, a night out in the city, and lively companionship. It was ten o'clock in the morning, but Luke already looked tired—he'd been working in his gardens since six. "I don't understand you," she said.

"What, Lucy? What don't you understand?" he asked sadly as if wanting forgiveness for who he was.

"I don't understand why you spend all that time in the garden! Digging, digging, always digging!" she cried, not wanting to hear again why soil needed nourishment.

"Once I get these hollies planted, I'll shower and—"

"The hollies were fine right where they were!"

He climbed into the seat of the old truck he kept for farm work, the stunned-looking bushes encased in burlap, listing in the back.

"Who ever heard of planting holly bushes in a cemetery, anyway?" she shouted as he headed down the drive.

"For the birds that winter here," he called back as if she'd been born in such a place, she would have understood.

Last winter, grieving for him, snow clinging to the spiny-toothed leaves, the bright berries the birds swooped in for had seemed like a reprimand.

Luke had changed after his father sold the land off for the nearby housing development—Pilgrims Corner. Normally a kind and generous man, Luke became almost obsessively protective of the property. When people from the development explored the cemetery, he behaved selfishly. "It's not a local attraction, Lucy," he told her, wiring a Keep Out sign to the gate.

"They're only curious, Luke. Those graves go back to the 1700's—"

"It's none of their business!"

The people from the development sometimes ignored the sign. She thought Luke would give up the fight, but instead, he installed a lock on the gate. "You can't keep them out," she warned. He vowed he would, yet some climbed over the stone walls, needing to satisfy their curiosity about the people buried here so long ago.

It was how she met Margaret, her friend who lives in Pilgrims Corner. She'd been out for a walk and found Margaret in the cemetery on her knees.

For a few minutes, she watched her transferring grave markings onto large sheets of paper. "Oh, you've caught me," Margaret said, looking somewhat embarrassed, and yet she continued on as if she had a right to be there.

"It's okay," Lucy told her. "I understand the artistic impulse, but you probably shouldn't do it evenings and never on the weekend when my husband is at home, working around the property."

"You don't mind?"

"Not one bit." She invited Margaret in for tea. They've been close friends ever since.

Margaret is a single mom, energetic, cheerful, and talented. She draws beautifully and frames these tracings. Lucy supposes it is an art of some sort. Then from out of her memory drifts the odors of the canvas, of paint. The tubes of color left up in the loft, dried out, unused. Her art lost to her. Not something she wants to think about.

After Luke died, she removed the sign and the lock from the cemetery gate, caring little about who wandered through. Soon cemeteries will be extinct—no one will be buried. Again, she relives the shock, and her fury, over Luke's last wishes.

His death had been sudden and unexpected. The three of them—she, Ellen, and Katherine—had been in the kitchen, dazed, attempting to talk over funeral arrangements, not believing Luke had passed, not believing what they had to discuss, and only Ellen's practical-mindedness kept them focused. The phone rang, and Ellen, nearest to it, picked up. A partner at Luke's law firm asked to speak to Lucy, and she refused—she could not speak with anyone—and asked Ellen if she'd take a message. Hanging up, Ellen announced that Luke had wanted to be cremated.

"No, Ellen," Lucy said.

"It's his handwriting, Lucy. They've verified it."

Lucy wanted Katherine's support to bury Luke in the earth he'd so loved. But she may have been equally stunned and said nothing. For her part, Lucy felt betrayed, learning Luke had kept such a thing from her.

She was uncooperative regarding all of his last wishes. In fact, she behaved badly. Her memory, the one she holds, is of Luke as a young man, his strong body, lovely in its nakedness, always radiating warmth.

After years of marriage, they'd made a corny joke of it, calling him her personal "heater" when she snuggled against him. No, the ashes had nothing to do with Luke or with her, for that matter. "It's not Luke to me. I don't care what you do with them," she told Ellen after the service, inwardly boiling with sorrow and disappointment that her husband, her beloved lifelong companion, had been reduced to ashes.

For once, Ellen seemed at a loss. She clasped the metal cylinder against her as if the contents might spill over, and as soon as they arrived at the farmhouse, she placed the ashes inside a built-in cupboard in the dining room. Latching it shut, the door hasn't once been opened.

What are all these memories but threaded sequences of her life? *Her life,* which she believes has somehow gotten away from her. Individual responsibility, her father had preached, encouraging her to architecture and never mind that it was a man's profession. "Each person makes his or her own life, Lucy."

She was not yet in her teens, walking with him through the streets of Hartford. She'd been holding a pretty yellow rose that her father's close friend Johnny Crane, out working in his prized rose garden, had given her as they passed by. She recalls that on that same day, her father brought her to the Moses Rocket complex. He related the building's history as one of the first mercantile plants in Hartford, and he'd gone to school with people who'd lived in the picturesque brick houses. If he were alive, he'd be bursting with pride that she was part of a team engaged in their renovation, albeit a small part.

Yet she'd followed his advice from long ago and, for the first time at the firm, had asked to lead a project.

She can at least hold her head up when regrets—the could haves, would haves, should haves— overwhelm her.

When Charter Oak awarded the bid for Moses Rocket to Cole & Siegel, her colleagues were not at all enthusiastic. They'd heard rumors that people in upper management like Will Swanson were reluctant to leave the sweeping grandeur of the home office in the city's center for an undesirable location in a stripped-down mill building.

She'd been assigned to work on the bidding proposal submitted to Charter Oak and met with Will Swanson, warned beforehand that he would be difficult. She was both surprised and relieved that he was courteous and open with her. She listened carefully, noted his concerns, and returned from the meetings feeling assured they could work well together.

Jed Cole and Luke were friends. From time to time, they met for lunch and sometimes partnered on projects for the Chamber of Commerce. Jed and his wife Nan had been to the farmhouse for dinner and parties. So she approached Jed both as a colleague and a friend, coming into his office with a degree of confidence, knowing she was the only established architect at the firm really interested in the project architect position. She said confidently, "Jed, I'd like to lead the Moses Rocket project."

He'd swiveled his chair and grinned at her. "So you like those old buildings, Lucy?"

"It so happens that I do, and I believe I can work well with Will Swanson. From what I've seen, he knows almost nothing about renovation—not on this scale. He needs assurances. I've also noticed that he is insecure about the job he's been asked to do. I think he'd trust me," and she went on to describe how well they'd gotten along during meetings.

"All right, Lucy."

They parted with the notion that he'd talk it over with his partner, David Siegel, and let her know.

A few days later, the firm announced Sy as the project architect for Moses Rocket. He'd been with Cole & Siegel for three years and was only recently promoted. She was disappointed, outraged, and shaken that Jed hadn't told her beforehand. She thought his silence reflected on her work. She went to his office and, as calmly as she could, asked him to explain.

"Why Sy? I've been here longer, and I have more rehab experience." She felt as if she'd lost all dignity in their exchange, telling him—almost pleading with him—what he should have known.

"It was Charter Oak, Lucy. I meant to get back to you before it was announced, but it's been so busy here." He shrugged. "I'm sorry about that."

With an edge of weariness in his voice, he told her that he and David had agreed that she should lead the project and put her name forward. "But Charter Oak wanted a man to lead the project, and Sy was the only one available."

"You mean the others here didn't want it!"

His tone changed, and she almost heard in it something like "Grow up, Lucy!" although she was so upset by that time, she might have imagined it. "Charter Oak is an insurance company, and you know as well as I what that means. Every VP moving to the site is a man."

That night she cried in Luke's arms and again when she learned Katherine had been appointed the Senior Designer. It would have been an opportunity for them to work together.

A week later, the firm appointed her to be part of the team. Jed spoke to her in private. "Keep an eye on Sy," he said with that complicit, Cheshire cat grin of his as if he'd managed to come through for her after all.

Her function is to review all of the blueprints, the very work she performs for the other PAs. She is also expected to make suggestions on architectural details and to attend meetings when Sy thinks her presence is necessary—a rare event so far. In fact, she thinks he schedules her for a meeting at Charter Oak once a month, almost as a courtesy, so that he can defend himself if she complains to Jed about her lack of involvement.

Her decision not to quit when the firm overlooked her has been an ongoing concern. Why didn't she put her job on the line when she confronted Jed? Has she lost all confidence?

At Cole & Siegel, she uses a few of the skills that earned her a fifth and then a sixth-year scholarship at MIT. She thinks of the model office building she designed for which she'd won an award and, yet, what has she really accomplished since? She's hardly scratched the surface of her potential. Why has she put up with it for so long? "Everyone makes his or her own life, Lucy." There is her father's voice again.

The Keeper

It seems no matter how hard she works, how patiently she waits for promotions, or how much they are deserved, recognition is precarious. Or when it comes, it's not what she expects.

At the firm, her title is Project Architect, yet she's never been in charge of a major project, only smaller jobs like the addition for St. Agnes' Clinic.

Her thoughts are scattered, and one leads to another. What is it like job-hunting for a woman in her fifties? Can she compete? She thinks she would have to more than prove herself at any new firm.

In fact, she'd have to dazzle them if the one she'd worked at for years hadn't supported her, giving in to the client's insistence that a man be in charge, assigning the job she deserved to someone with less experience.

Her eyes drift toward the cemetery and its weathered granite, monolithic posts. She stares at them for a long while. They appear to have vacant eyes, flattened noses, and spired heads. She is not mistaken. They are looking back at her as if there is something they would like her to know.

Her glance shifts to the cemetery's iron gate—someone has left it open again.

7

Rangy Barstow

He wakes up in the underground garage, and as if it had all happened moments before, the woman he has unintentionally hurt appears to him. He shuts his eyes, shakes his head, and makes her go away. *He had not meant to hurt her, not at all!*

Overcome with shame, he thinks of his mother and his promise to *always be a good boy.* "Sorry, sorry," he whimpers, his eyes lowered as if Mom and Dad were there watching him.

He traces the source of a throbbing pain to his right hand and unwinds the strip of white mesh, now brown-stained with his blood. The wound has dried, and for a moment, he studies the torn, raw skin and what looks like the marks of her teeth. She had bitten down hard and wouldn't let go, blood dripping everywhere!

Not my fault!

He throws the stained cloth into a corner, heaped with the rest of his litter, and climbs out of his hiding place.

It takes a few moments for his limbs, stiff as sticks, to adjust and for his blood to circulate.

Then he moves furtively in the shadows toward the exit, stumbling once or twice. "Hungry and wore out," he mutters.

Outside, he walks in the city's gray dawn with his head lowered. Mostly the streets are quiet, and the few people that pass by him do so in a hurry.

When he is far from the garage on the familiar road toward the Capitol building, the sky begins to brighten. He looks up at the blue of it and the white puffy clouds sailing slowly through and smiles. His gaze shifts to newly constructed office buildings, and he thinks how ugly they are with none of the splendor of the older ones he's used to—no columns of stone, no bricks, no arches, peaks, no wide staircases or walled landscaped gardens. Oh, how he despises these tall, flat structures! His dislike is small, though, compared to the disdain he feels for how Moses Rocket has been changed, and he worries as always—*What happened to his neighbors who, like him, were told to leave their homes—where have they gone?*

He enters a small park and sits on the bench closest to the street. The towering branches from century-old trees above him sweat, showering him with overnight dew, and he lifts his face to moisture, air, and light that is precious after his long hours underground.

He thinks again of the woman he has hurt, wondering where she is right now. He must find her and tell her he is sorry. He approached her because he thought she was important. He thought she would help. He'd often seen her visiting the construction site. He even spoke to her once, a while back, and had liked what she'd said.

It was that night when he'd come into Moses Rocket right after it had been gutted. He looked around, feeling sick and scared by the destruction, and the almost empty space, the changes to his former workplace. He'd heard voices from upstairs and wondered who was in the building at "suppertime," Dad used to call it. Curious, he hiked up a jury-rigged ladder, and to his surprise, the woman was there with that man in charge, the one who always wore a yellow hat and had a line of dark, bushy hair above his eyes that spooked Rangy. He was the same man who checked the alarms before leaving the site at the end of the day.

Through the long windows, the setting sun had been low on the horizon, casting a soft light on the brick walls, wide floorboards, wooden piers, and oversized beams. Old factory spaces were not as dark and gloomy as some people thought—natural light was essential and had been planned for. He thinks about how Dad had often pointed out these facts, and it is painful to remember that once he'd had a life where people taught him what was important and cared about what happened to him.

Like old times, he could see from one end of the floor to the other. A cross draft freshened the open space, bringing hints of oil that, for over a century, had permeated the wood.

His heart had raced with joy thinking how the men had once called out to him. He'd had responsibilities! Now all the machinery he'd once kept slick and oiled has vanished.

Unseen, he'd listened to the conversation between the woman and the man with the yellow hat.

"It's beautiful, empty like this," she said, standing near a window. "It's almost a shame to clutter it up with people and workstations."

"So you want a museum?" the man said and laughed.

"You know what I mean."

"Yeah, I do. But then I remember that people, even kids, had worked twelve, sometimes fourteen hours a day, six days a week in this building."

She looked out toward the chimney of Rangy's former home, the place of his birth. "The cottages are lovely," she told the man.

Hearing her say that somehow filled Rangy with a sense of happiness. It was like coming upon some nice music when he could think that not everything had changed, that people still listened to songs where they could understand the words. But the man only laughed. "Not my idea of cottages," he said.

Rangy had not liked his tone.

"The people who used to live in them called them that," she said. "They're small and perfect. Each has two fireplaces, a decent-sized kitchen, a sitting room, and two rooms up. Only one bath, though. Sy should include a half-bath on the first floor, but I can't convince him. He tells me it's too expensive, not in the budget. I tell him it will make the units more valuable."

"The people who worked here were probably too hungry and tired to appreciate what they had."

"I don't know about that, but I'm glad they're being saved. It makes sense for people who work in the city to live here if they want to."

"I guess it depends on what kind of work you do. Some nights I want as much distance between work and home as possible. Quiet, some food, and my bed—that's all I need. I'd rather hear my neighbors plowing their driveways, mowing their lawns than police sirens."

"Come on, Mike. The city's a great place to live."

He shrugged, and they left it at that.

"But it's a sin to pour concrete over these wood floors."

"It is too bad, but they're soaked with oil."

"Can't something be done to save them?"

"Fire codes. We can't take a chance. Do you know they kept five-gallon cans of oil up here? Spilled all over—"

Rangy could no longer stop himself. He had to speak to the woman. "Hello!" he shouted. "Is it all right if I come out?"

Neither one answered, so he thought it would be okay and edged out from behind one of the wooden supports.

"Figure I'd better holler. I didn't want to scare nobody."

At first, the man and the woman looked at him as if they didn't believe what they were seeing. Then the man came toward him, mean and angry-looking, shouting as if Rangy had done something wrong. "Who are you?"

He spoke up like Dad had always told him. "Rangy Barstow!" he said, sounding as if it were one word.

"Who? Who did he say he was?" the man said to the woman.

"He's *Rangy Barstow,*" she said.

Rangy smiled at her.

"What're you doing in here?" the man said.

It sounded like a threat, and Rangy didn't answer, stepping back away from him toward the ladder. But he'd come this far and had no intention of leaving without speaking to the woman.

He'd always had a difficult time with his speech and often stuttered, especially with strangers, but that night words just flowed out of him. "Hey girlie, see over there?" he said, pointing to the far end of the floor. "Third window from the end is where I used to work."

She said nothing back to him; it was the man's fault because he kept hollering, and she couldn't hear what Rangy was telling her. So, he shouted, too. "Girlie, see that chimney you were looking at? I lived right there. All my life."

But the man wouldn't shut his trap!

"Listen, Buddy. You leave right now, or I'll have you arrested!"

Rangy headed for the stairwell, and the man shouted again. "Not that way! It's not safe!"

"You don't know nothing," Rangy muttered and ducked under the rope.

"Wait!" The woman called out, but he'd already climbed down out-of-sight—although he could hear what she said. "He might know something interesting about the building, Mike. Rangy Barstow," she said, scribbling his name on a corner of the blueprint she was holding. "Maybe I could look him up in the archives."

Archives. Rangy had never heard such a word, had no idea what it meant, and it almost frightened him more than the man threatening to call the police. *Was it possible that he was known in some place called "Archives?"*

"How the hell did he get in?" the man said. "This place is locked up tighter than a drum. I chased a few from the site this winter when I found them asleep under the excavating equipment, but no one's ever gotten inside."

From the park bench, Rangy mutters aloud, "That's what he thinks, and like I said before, that man knows nothing!"

Rangy shuts his eyes, envisioning how each night, despite the alarm system and the vigilance of this construction manager, he freely roams the building, inspecting and bemoaning each of the changes made. He is determined to stop the destruction of so much that has made his life purposeful. He must also search for the woman he hurt to tell her he's sorry. It's the right thing to do. It's what Mom and Dad would have expected.

Feeling loneliness, sadness, a confusion he doesn't understand, Rangy leaves the park.

The city has come alive. One after another, buses pull in, and people file out of them, heading into office buildings. The food and coffee vendors roll their carts past, and the odors stir his insides, but he can't stop. He's gotten himself into trouble, and he needs to get back to the two-story red brick building that sits among a row of similar ones that are all vacant now and forbiddingly boarded up.

What can he do to stop this work on Moses Rocket? Thinking so hard it is almost painful, he reaches into the spaces of his mind and memory, grasping for enlightenment, for some new idea or maybe a plan he might put into action.

Reaching the cottage, he looks left, then right, and then turns quickly into the alley, glancing at the weeds, the crabgrass, and the stalks of dried-up flowers in the small yard. Until this year, it had always been carefully groomed and watered. He'd like to pull up the weeds and plant tomatoes and cucumbers, as he had in the past, as his father had, even a row of marigolds at the margins, but he knew he'd be found out and made to leave again. He groans, releasing some of the pain of failure and helplessness that he experiences each time he returns here.

Raising one side of the door on the cellar hatch (that had been nailed shut before he'd torn it open), Rangy takes five steep steps down and closes it soundlessly. Then he opens and quickly shuts and bolts a heavy, wooden, over one-hundred-year-old door. He goes straight to the cupboard that, in Dad's time, had held small tools and where Rangy now stores a supply of food that rodents can't get at. He takes a box of crackers, a jar of peanut butter, and a plastic knife and settles on the floor, preparing his meal. For a few more hours, he feels safe.

8

Sy

"Julie," he says softly to his wife, careful not to wake their daughter, Heather, slumped over in the car seat, fast asleep. His wife doesn't answer, and he turns to look at her. Her eyes are closed, her breath coming evenly and deeply. She must have fallen asleep as soon as they all got into the car.

This fall, Heather will be starting kindergarten at The Academy, a progressive private school Julie and her sister Leah had attended. He'd wanted Heather to have a carefree summer, but Julie insisted on enrolling her in a six-week Pre-Kindergarten class. "The Academy will be very different from what she's used to at Montessori, and this program will help her make the adjustment."

When they returned home from a short vacation at the Cape with Ben and Silvia, Julie's parents, Heather started the Pre-K class. Some mornings she wants to sleep in, and they have to coax her out of bed. Some mornings she cries pitifully. He soothes her and feels helpless.

Tonight, at the conclusion of the course, he and Julie sat down with Mrs. Corliss, Heather's teacher, a soft-spoken, pleasant, middle-aged woman that Heather grew to like. During the discussion, Julie made notes of anything relative to Heather's development. Sy is aware that she'll want to talk all this over with him later on while the conversation with Mrs. Corliss is fresh in her mind.

They'd waited years to have a child, and Julie wanted to be a good, perfect Mom. Recently, he'd suggested she might back off a bit and relax her oversight on some of Heather's activities. "We only have one shot at this," she reminded him.

He is sorry that Heather is an only child. He remembers as a kid how odd and disconnected he felt at times because he had no brothers or sisters. Julie has a sister named Leah. She is single and a film producer in Los Angeles. She is fond of Heather, and they are on the phone frequently. Heather adores Leah and tells Julie that "Aunt Leah is fun." Despite Julie's objections that her sister will spoil Heather, she is also a giver of wonderful and surprising gifts.

They are a small family.

His parents have passed, and he's grateful for Julie's. Ben and Silvia are warm, kind-hearted, and generous to a fault.

They openly worship Heather and spend a good deal of time with her.

It's been a long day—another frustrating meeting with Will Swanson. The air-conditioned car and the quiet, smooth ride is calming. He takes a deep breath, letting it out slowly. There is something pleasurable about the three of them moving along in the silent car, and he bypasses the highway ramp for a slower-paced trip through neighborhoods that are mostly quiet at this hour.

Coming to an intersection, he sees a young woman standing beneath the glare of the street light, waiting to cross. He slows the car. She smiles and waves a thank you, and he waves back, thinking there is something about her that reminds him of Apple. Perhaps that this woman is alone on an already dark summer night and vulnerable. That thought leads to what has happened to Katherine and the question of how long she'll be out. He reminds himself to send her a note. He should call, a courtesy, to bring her up to date on the project but senses that might be awkward for both of them.

His thoughts shift swiftly back to Apple. *Apple Messina.* He allows himself the quiet joy of remembering the first time he ever laid eyes on her.

His father's medical practice was a four-room addition attached to one side of their spacious home on Poplar Street. After coming home from school, Sy first had the snack his mother always left for him in the kitchen, and then he'd go next door to the waiting room.

So that no one could sit beside him, he sat in the middle of a two-seater sofa in front of a bay window tucked into an alcove. He did his homework, looked through magazines, or studied the patients, curious about what might have brought them here. At times, when his parents were out together, he took the key to the filing cabinet holding patient records out of his father's desk and went through them. Often, it was almost like reading a book he would not have been allowed to read, and he was shocked. Some people had hard lives, just as his father always said, and sad and terrible things happened to them.

Most of the time, he found the atmosphere in the waiting room warm and friendly, as if all these patients were extended family. A few plants his mother tended hung from ceiling hooks and moved slightly as if lightly pushed whenever the door was opened. Magazines were piled neatly on a low table in the center of the room. There was a row of chairs where people sat when they arrived, across from a wall of long, high windows overlooking a garden filled with bushes, flowers, and ferns. It was his mother's idea. His father thought it would be too expensive, but his mother said patients would like it, something nice to look at, to take their minds off their worries.

At thirteen, almost fourteen, Sy was shaped like a barrel, "short and pudgy," a girl in one of his classes told him. He'd laughed as if refusing to take her seriously. Though it had stung, he quickly walked away from her. He couldn't help that he always felt hungry, and his mother was such a good cook.

His eyes were a deep brown color, his hair was always neatly combed, and he had a clear complexion, unlike some of the other kids at school. The teachers and counselors described him as a quiet and shy boy, an excellent student. He was born late in his parent's marriage, and the clothes his mother selected looked much like what his father wore—starched shirts, vest sweaters, dark pants, leather shoes. He was always polite and distant with his classmates, as if he were much older, and they left him alone. Yet, something in him changed after he saw Apple Messina. *He wanted her to notice him.*

He'd been unusually hungry and restless that day, counting the minutes on the wall clock until dinner—roast chicken, mashed potatoes, string beans, and corn. Jell-O with whipped topping. He wished his father would finish up and quit on time for a change. Then the door opened, and Apple came in, followed by her mother. She was a slight and spindly girl with pale skin and long silky hair, a sharp contrast to her mother, a short, stout woman with large oval eyes and thick eyebrows. A towel was wrapped around one arm, and Sy heard her explaining to Donna, the receptionist, that she'd had an accident and needed stitches.

"The bleeding won't stop," Mrs. Messina said. "It bled right through the towel!"

"We'll get Doctor Greene to look at you right away," Donna said, bringing her in to see Mrs. Degnan, the registered nurse who assisted him.

Apple sat down in the row of chairs, looking out to the garden. She glanced at him and then turned away as if he were just another patient. She was dressed in jeans rolled at the cuff, a red plaid blouse, white socks, and blue sneakers. She wore a chain around her neck that disappeared into the V of her blouse. He wondered if it was a religious medal. Messina. The name sounded foreign. She might be Catholic. Maybe she went to Saint Colombo's? A charm bracelet—links of silver—shimmered from her wrist. He studied her until Donna grinned at him in a silly way, aware that he'd been staring at Apple. His face turned red, and he didn't look at Apple again until Mrs. Messina finally came out, and she stood up to join her mother. "I'm all right, Apple," she said. "The doc fixed me up fine."

They approached Donna to make an appointment to have the stitches removed. "Four o'clock is good," Mrs. Messina said, noticing the daffodils. "Apple, aren't they beautiful?"

Apple glanced at the flowers, blushed, and smiled. Sy wished she had answered her mother so he could hear her voice.

Afterward, he thought about her almost constantly. For several months, his appetite waned, and he lost enough weight to fit into a pair of blue jeans that he bought himself at Gus's Army and Navy. Appraising himself in the dressing room mirror, he admitted that he appeared a little older and maybe looked somewhat like the other boys his age, although he felt no different inside. He began spending less time in the waiting room and much of the after-school hours riding his bike through the busy sections of Poplar Street, hoping he'd see Apple Messina somewhere.

He'd overheard his mother wonder to his father if there was something wrong, and his father had said their son was growing up. "That's all it is." Hearing his father's answer somehow comforted him.

Sy felt so let down when Mrs. Messina came alone to have her stitches removed that as soon as Donna left for home that day, he searched the office records for Apple's address. Number 16 Garden Street, right off Poplar. He'd been in that neighborhood with his mother to buy bread at the Italian bakery.

The day was warm and blustery when he started out on his bike. He pedaled furiously down Poplar, excited by thoughts that he might see Apple again and worried with questions. *What would he say to her? Why would she even remember him?*

Reaching Garden Street, a narrow one-way, he rode slowly down the block and paused at number 16.

He got off his bike, pretending to fiddle with the chain so he could get a good look at the house. It was small and built close to the homes on each side, white with glossy black shutters. An attached garage in the back rose up, almost dwarfing the house. The front windows were too small to get a look inside.

He got back on his bike and rode up and down Garden Street four times, hoping to see her, but never did and rode home with a heavy heart.

From the back seat of the car, Heather calls out, "Daddy, Daddy, I'm tired," sounding a bit frightened.

"Don't cry, Heather. It's okay—we're almost home."

He turns onto a road of houses set well back from the curb on two-acre lots—a mix of traditional and contemporary homes. He'd bought one of the lots, intending to design the home and build it when he and Julie could afford to, but her parents surprised them with a large contribution, encouraging them not to wait. He and Julie worked on the plans together—it was a happy time.

He presses the garage door opener, and Julie sits up and grins sheepishly. "Sorry, I didn't mean to fall asleep."

She looks earnest and quite lovely, and he places his hand gently on her arm. "It was a big day, Julie."

She goes ahead into the house, and he takes Heather out of the car seat and straight upstairs to her room. Only wanting to sleep, she squirms while he changes her into pajamas, but as soon as he puts her into bed, she takes hold of the stuffed toy she has slept with for as long as he can remember and cuddles it into her small chest and is out for the night.

How he loves her! Overwhelming feelings of pride and tenderness come as he looks down on her. She is so young, so small, to be the object of so much of Julie's intensity. During their discussion this evening, he'll impress on her that Heather needs a break from scheduled activities. He'll plan something special the two of them might do together, a father/daughter outing, somewhere frivolous so that she can run around freely, laugh, and play before the regimen of school and Julie's almost obsessive perfectionism reignites.

Downstairs, Julie is waiting with cups of tea so they can discuss Mrs. Corliss' report. "This is important," she says. Caringly, he replies that it is, wishing he'd told her that he'd have preferred a glass of wine.

That night he and Julie make love. She falls asleep in his arms, and he lies awake, not wanting to think of Apple, yet her vision drifts into the room, into the bed, into his very soul so that feelings of despair and guilt flow through him. As if she is aware of what is happening, what may happen, Julie shivers lightly. It is cool in the room, and he releases her, pulling a light blanket up from the bottom of the bed. He hesitates before placing it over her, smoothing his hand over her lightly flushed cheeks, breasts, and stomach—she has such lovely skin and a firm, young body. There is a purity about her, he thinks. No other word would do as well to describe his wife's emotions and her motives. In bed, in lovemaking, they are in sync. In so many other ways, too. He admits that perhaps she is somewhat predictable, yet he has often found that quality steadying—there is too much of it lacking in his professional life.

Even now, in these moments when his desire for Apple is a force over which he believes he has little control, he cannot imagine a life apart from Julie.

He leaves the bed quietly so as not to disturb her, stopping on the way out of the room to lower the air-conditioner, and then he slips into his office, softly shutting the door.

He thinks what a strange and maybe ridiculous figure he might make—a grown man, sitting almost naked at his desk in the middle of the night, desolate with desire he does not quite understand for a woman who is not his wife.

9

Katherine

Although she doesn't remember them, Detective Hays and Sergeant Vickers, the same officers who came to the emergency room after the attack, are in the bedroom, attempting to interview her, and it is hard going.

Detective Hays, young and haggard-looking, in need of a haircut, seems uncomfortable. Katherine supposes the bruises on her face and her still swollen eye are disconcerting for him. At the same time, Sergeant Vickers seems more composed, and Katherine wonders if she has accompanied him here because she is a woman, and it will be her job to talk more personally, maybe ask sensitive questions, about what happened.

Detective Hayes speaks to her but keeps looking out the window as if he is embarrassed about interviewing a woman in her bedroom, although Katherine is dressed in sweatpants and a t-shirt and is sitting up in a chair.

She is still too weak to manage the stairs, and when Lucy told her that the officers would be coming, she said she would only see them if she were out of bed and fully dressed. Yesterday, while she was immersed in the huge clawfoot tub of warm water and Epsom salts, a recommended and soothing treatment for her injured back, she could hear Lucy and her friend Margaret carrying up an armchair from the sitting room, placing it next to the window overlooking Luke's gardens. Katherine has never met Lucy's friend, and even though Lucy tells her how helpful Margaret has been, she has no wish to do so. Margaret lives in Pilgrims Corner, the nearby housing development that caused Luke so much stress and heartache and most likely was partly responsible for his death.

Katherine has had little experience with law enforcement and had expected them to show up in uniforms. Still, on this hot, humid day, Detective Hays is dressed in a tweed sports jacket and tie, while Sergeant Vickers looks cool and professional in dark slacks and a light blue shirt.

"Sometimes it takes a while to recall what's happened in a circumstance like yours," says Detective Hays, hands in his pockets again while glancing out the window.

Katherine looks squarely at both officers. "I've already told you what I remember."

"It's not much for us to go on," says Sergeant Vickers. Her voice is quietly firm, and she is direct. "Whatever comes back to you. Facts, anything you might be thinking, could be helpful."

Facts. Katherine is almost forty-one years old and 5 feet 7 inches tall. She keeps her weight under 135 pounds. Her hair is not all one color, and she is particular about details but has put the color brown on her driver's license, a word she believes is the most accurate. Her eyes, she thinks, are not her best feature. They are too small. Unmarried, she refers to herself as a career woman. She works at the architectural firm of Cole & Siegel. Her title is Senior Designer. In charge of large projects, she has direct contact with clients.

She'd admit (if she confided in anyone) that she's competent, that her peers envy her achievements—her experience in New York at the apex of design, her early decision to find work in the corporate world when design there was still a fledgling profession. And her luck, *her damned luck,* she might laugh and say about her work, for being at the right place at the right time.

While the officers encourage her to think back and remember, she is picking at threads in the chair's linen print fabric that is completely worn. Its once exuberant blossoms faded to almost indistinguishable rosy blotches. It was her mother's favorite. For months after she died, Katherine came home from school and went directly into the sitting room, hoping she'd find her mother in this chair, waiting for her. Her eyes fill up, and she quickly brushes them.

She has stayed away from this house since Luke passed—everything here reminds her of what she's lost.

"Katherine," says Detective Hays.

"Sorry," she murmurs.

He begins explaining that her assailant had attempted to pull her into the back of the van. "During the struggle, the heel of one of your shoes jammed in the steering wheel, activating the horn. Do you remember that happening?"

She shakes her head tiredly. *Don't they understand? I don't want to remember.*

"The horn must've scared him off—that's what we think," he says.

She imagines herself in the van when the security guard found her—a cartoon-like image of a woman spread across the backseat, her feet where her head should be, something to laugh at if it wasn't so terrible, so terrifying.

"If he'd had a weapon, he would've used it. I—we," he says, turning to Sergeant Vickers—"believe this assault was a bungled attempt at rape."

What Katherine is thinking is that this incident should not have happened, and she is responsible. She was so tense over the upcoming presentation that she'd neglected to lock the van's back door after dropping off sample materials at Charter Oak—a security precaution she normally adheres to when she is downtown.

"As you might suspect, Katherine, somewhere in America, a woman is raped every two minutes," says Sergeant Vickers, citing the statistic as if Katherine's situation is not in the least uncommon. But Katherine has never thought about how frequently rape might occur, and what Sergeant Vickers is saying frightens her. She wonders if she'll ever feel safe downtown or anywhere again.

Detective Hays goes on. "When we questioned you in the emergency room, you told us that a man named Wallace, who met you at Charter Oak's loading dock, might be responsible. We can assure you he is not a suspect. By all accounts, he delivered the materials and then had lunch with his co-workers. He never left the main building."

During her lucid moments, Katherine has visualized Wallace as her assailant and is not prepared to believe what Detective Hays is telling her. She thinks now of the first time she saw him just as she pulled up next to the loading dock. As Tillie had promised, a man would be waiting with a cart to bring materials into the building.

Katherine got out of the van, greeting him in a friendly manner. He'd looked inside the van and said unpleasantly, "Does all this have to go?"

"Yes, to the main conference room, on the second floor, please."

"I know where it is."

The badge pinned to his shirt had his name—Wallace—small-eyed and lean. With all she'd had on her mind, anticipating the presentation, she might have forgotten about him, but he'd been needlessly rude. She thought he must be new—she'd never run into him before, and she thought she would mention his behavior to Tillie. Katherine feels responsible for her team and wouldn't have wanted any one of them to interact with Wallace, especially the younger interns.

Wallace had lifted the first board, the one showing the ceramic tiles. It was so heavy when she and her co-worker Henry Briggs were loading the van that she'd asked him to save it for last so that it could be removed more easily if she had to do it herself.

Wallace dropped the board roughly into the cart, and she almost said, *"Be careful,"* but stopped herself. Men in the building department have great power over the inner workings of a complex, and she needed the materials to arrive in the conference room on time and intact. Nothing would unsettle Will Swanson like a needless delay, searching for lost materials, or worse, if they arrived damaged.

When Wallace went back to the van, she'd managed to remove the tile board from the cart, intending to place it on top of the other materials once he finished unloading.

He pulled a rag out of his uniform pocket and wiped his face.

"It is hot, and I appreciate your help," she said stiffly.

Silently, without looking at her, he slammed the last board from the van into the cart.

She didn't ask for his help, and he made no move to assist her when she slid the tile board to the top of the cart, watching nervously while he steered it up the ramp and into the building, jostling materials that represented months of work.

She drove the two blocks to the parking garage, worrying over the man's carelessness, entered, stopped to get the parking ticket, and drove into the spot that was reserved for Cole & Siegel that day. Turning off the ignition, she removed her sunglasses and reached for her briefcase when she heard the click of the latch behind her.

Her breath comes quickly. She feels a pounding inside her chest. Sergeant Vickers looks at Detective Hayes and shakes her head. Then she takes a card out of her jacket pocket and places it on the table next to Katherine. "We know how hard this is. If you think of someone or some detail that might be relevant, day or night, please contact us right away. Both of our numbers are on the card."

What Katherine recalls is the rank odor of the man's body in the close confines of the van. Just thinking of it causes upset and near panic. She hasn't the words to tell them.

When they are gone, she's tired from sitting up, and her back muscles are spasming. It will get worse if she doesn't lie down. She wants to make it to the bed on her own and stretch out but is afraid she might fall. She's tempted to ring the small bell Lucy has left on the table so that Katherine can summon her. It was a thoughtful gesture, and Lucy couldn't have known that it would bring up sad memories.

Her father had been mostly absent during her mother's long illness, but Luke was devotedly present. In the night, the chime of the little bell from her mother's room, a signal that help was needed, sometimes woke Katherine, and she would listen to Luke's muffled footsteps going past her door and down the hall to their mother's room. She only felt safe enough to relax and fall back asleep once the house quieted and darkened again.

The clock on the nightstand reminds her it is time to take the pills, lying beside a carafe of water that Lucy regularly freshens. Katherine does not like the sinking sensation or the darkness she descends into once the pills take effect, and she turns her head to the late morning light on Luke's field.

She smells the warm scented air and hears the high-spirited chirping of birds. Luke was twelve when she was born, and for as long as she can remember, he spent most of his time at home outdoors. He grew up to be over six feet tall, and working outside, he wore an unusually large, floppy hat that he'd said kept the sun off his face. From this window, she'd often watched him. He'd seemed something of a giant, standing on tree shadows, leaf and sun-speckled, calling her name, urging her to come outside. *"Look, Katherine, almost everything flowers before the leaves unfold. These yellow-green buds are as small as drops of rain."*

Looking down on the flowerbeds, they seem all wrong, clipped and pruned to perfection by the workers Lucy has hired. For Luke, weeding and shaping was an art form. When he was through with the task, the beds looked natural, as if the flowers had sprouted in profusions of their own design.

The Keeper

She feels almost desperate to get back to her Hartford apartment. The muscles in her back begin to spasm again, so she is afraid to move. She looks again at the bell that will summon Lucy but can't bring herself to pick it up.

For some moments, she follows a flinty, narrow expanse of light moving across the ceiling, the fading papered walls, the worn floorboards, and a high antique chest. A step stool Luke had made for her on her sixth birthday so she could reach a number of small drawers at the top is still sitting beneath it.

On the wall above the chest is a Victorian print—a snowy landscape with a family of deer, a majestic buck with oversized horns in the forefront in a protective stance, a doe and fawn in the background—a sentimental portrait of the natural world—a print she'd normally mock. As a child, though, the scene had comforted her, especially during the final weeks of her mother's life when the bell rang more often, and Katherine would stare at the picture, wishing with all her heart that she, too, were out in the snowy field.

She's been waking up nights here, thinking she hears someone talking outside, wondering if the voices are coming from the housing development or whether she imagines them. She has moments when the familiar sounds of nocturnal animals make her afraid her attacker is lurking about. Then her heart beats frantically, keeping her awake.

She picks up the card lying beside the one Sergeant Vickers left. On it is the name of a trauma counselor, Dr. Richard Rablen, a psychologist—a cognitive behavioral therapist—the ER doctor had recommended. The idea of talking to anyone regarding how she feels about what has happened is distasteful and frightening, something she'll have to deal with, and she'd rather just put it out of her mind and have her body heal so that she can get on with her life. She's been badly hurt, she reasons, but she was not raped. *Raped!* She can hardly whisper the word.

She touches the welt beneath her eye that had not required stitches but would take time to heal. She lifts the t-shirt she is wearing and examines her bruised, discolored skin with a mixture of disbelief and horror. She quickly pulls the shirt down over the bruises, wanting to deny they are there on her body or that someone wanted to violate her in a most terrible way.

She wonders if Sergeant Vickers noticed the card and thinks she probably had—she's been trained to observe.

Her eyes fill up with angry tears—she's lost her privacy, a thing she cherishes. Just when she thinks she can't bear the pain of sitting up any longer and she might have to use the bell, Lucy comes in. "Would you like help to get into bed?"

Katherine nods and, once she is back down, sighs with relief.

"How about some lunch?"

"Too tired. Maybe later."

She feels thoroughly exhausted from the police interview and is grateful that Lucy doesn't linger.

She hears voices outside again and recognizes that it is Lucy and Silvano, the landscape contractor Lucy hired to care for the property. Feeling that there are trusted people close by, she tries to relax.

Her phone goes off, and she wonders if she should answer. It might be Mac. She hadn't remembered calling him in a panic, but Lucy told her, reminding her that he would soon be here. Her hand trembles, and she answers in the strongest voice she can manage.

"Katherine, it's Pete. I called a few times, but Lucy said you were knocked out."

It's wonderful to hear Pete's voice. They've worked together for years. She relaxes and makes an attempt at a joke. "I'll have to remember these pills—" (She hadn't taken them, but it was all she could think of to say.)

He laughs a bit nervously. "Deborah wanted to call, too."

"Tell her it's all right."

"Holly's been asking for you—they've all been asking about you."

She would like to see her friend Holly, who works in Graphics. They are close, and in time, when she feels less raw, she might be able to talk to her about what happened.

What troubles her is that Pete has implied what she fears—the questions she'll be asked on her return.

"Have you heard from Sy?" he says. "Did he give you the rundown from the meeting?"

She is grateful that Pete is speaking to her as if she were back to normal. "Lucy mentioned that he was preparing an update on the presentation—he didn't want to disturb me by calling."

"Yeah, well, I thought you'd want to know if the ceramic tile for the cafeteria was approved and the answer is a resounding 'Yes!' Deborah said they hovered over the boards like a swarm of satisfied bees."

She smiles, hearing Deborah, a lover of literary fiction, saying something like that. "Swanson, too?" she says.

"Yes. The drawings went upstairs to Lucy today."

She's known all along that Swanson might reject her tile proposal outright as too showy, too modern—it was Tillie who'd warned her. She feels a moment of pleasure, of accomplishment— her working life is in order. "Such good news, Pete," she says, hearing the weariness in her voice, imagining Pete also can but is too thoughtful to mention it.

She'd taken a risk with the tile selection. Traditionally, Charter Oak had used only plain terra cotta in their facilities, but she'd wanted something different for Moses Rocket. After a long fruitless search, one day in Hartford's north end, she'd stumbled across a new tile dealership, a narrow storefront she might easily have overlooked. Through the front window, she spotted rows of cartons on the floor. Each with a sample tile on the top.

She walked in, and a man holding a set of keys stopped her. With a slight accent, he told her he was locking up. "I am late for an appointment."

Apologizing for holding him up, she handed him her card, saying she needed a commercial tile for the cafeteria of a facility she was designing. "I'm looking for something new, something different."

"Alright, yes. I might have something," he said, going into a back room, returning quickly with two tiles. "These are new to the market here in America. They are manufactured in Italy."

She brushed her fingers over the hard, lustrous, and subtly-textured surfaces, thinking they were lovely, perfect for Moses Rocket—one, a rich, deep red she would label *burgundy* for her client's benefit, and the other, a tasteful beige, she would label *oyster*. "Are these commercial tiles?"

"Yes. I have the specifications right here," he said, passing them to her. "I am sorry I have to leave; I am already late. You can come back tomorrow?"

"Yes. May I take them with me—the specs?"

"It is all right—I have copies, and you can take the sample tiles, too."

"Thank you," she said. "They are beautiful."

"Yes, they speak for themselves."

She got back to the firm late that afternoon and went straight to Doug Parks, the engineer who evaluated and approved materials specified for all construction projects. He was standing at his desk, preparing to leave for home. "A favor," she said. "I need an okay on these tiles by tomorrow."

"Nice," he said. "Where did you find them?"

"The North End."

Slipping the tiles and specs into his briefcase, he said, "You owe me one."

"Lunch at the Municipal."

He laughed. "I hear it's closing."

"No!"

"No one eats food like that anymore, but I salivate just thinking of their meatloaf sandwiches."

"It's a date."

She walked away, a bit sad and sentimental about the Municipal—a Hartford landmark—where she often lunched after shopping downtown.

All that night, she'd thought about the tiles and couldn't sleep. She caught up with Doug early the following morning, and he told her that the tiles met not only architectural building codes for commercial use but also the client's recently adopted building standards.

That same day, she returned to the dealership with a copy of the cafeteria blueprints. The man assured her he could supply her with enough tiles for the project. "That will not be a problem," he said.

She asked for his assurance in writing, and he said he would include a letter with his quote on price and delivery. She left the shop with a promise that he would send her enough samples for her presentation boards.

Pete's familiar voice, the good news about the tiles, brings her back to the life she'd had, and with what enthusiasm she can rally, she thinks of the two-foot pieces of wood cluttering her workstation, samples from the carpenter who'll be doing the millwork that require a color specification. "Pete, would you ask Deborah to send me the stain colors we'd been looking over? She'll know the ones I want. Tell her to give them to Lucy when she comes in to pick up her work."

He laughs the way he does when he's found a design solution. "Next, you'll want me to make a list—"

"Tell Deborah not to let Sy pick the color of the stain." As soon as she says it, she wishes she hadn't—it sounded petty.

"You know how things are—you better get on your feet and get back here."

Yes, she knows how things are, but she also knows she is not ready.

"Soon, I hope."

"We miss you." He hesitates as if there is something more he should bring up, that it might be better to do it now while she's recovering, giving her time to think about a different solution before returning to work. "You might as well know—"

"Modular carpet."

"Swanson gave Sy a lot of grief over the money spent on the analysis. He didn't like having significant proof in front of the whole committee that wall-to-wall is a bad idea."

"Sy told you?"

"Tillie told me when she called, asking about you."

Katherine feels as if something important has happened or been decided without her input. She forgets for a moment that Pete is not her adversary when she fires back, saying what he already knows. "Moses Rocket is an old building! With the exposed brick, the floors should look new—unspoiled." (She'd suggested new wood flooring at the start, but Charter Oak had vetoed that proposal.) "Traffic patterns in that building will be very specific—even carpet tiles will have to be replaced frequently. You know how bad wall-to-wall will look with watermarks, mud, gum, and the rest of what people bring in on their shoes, never mind what they'll spill!"

"Sorry, Katherine, I shouldn't have brought this up. Especially not now. There's plenty of time."

"Pete, I'm not an invalid," she says while realizing that "yes," she is.

Right then, she'd had an opening, an opportunity to reveal what she's kept from Pete, but *where to start and how to explain?* It was Tillie's idea that she and Katherine meet regularly, without Sy or Swanson. Their purpose is to get approvals from the Charter Oak team on the blueprints and other materials submitted by Cole & Seigel. All Swanson would have to do was sign off on them and submit them to Sy.

"When you have questions or if you need information that Will is not providing, call me on my direct line and send data requests to my email," Tillie told her. "I've developed a close working relationship with the committee members. They are sensible and want this project to move along to completion. Will knows I'll be scheduling hours with the committee, but he is not interested in the details."

"He's too involved with what the VPs want or don't want," Katherine added.

"Yes, that's a problem. The VPs scheduled to go don't want to leave the home office and move into an old mill building away from headquarters. They're putting a lot of pressure on Will and using any excuse to stall the project. But they're going whether they want to or not."

"Is upper management at Charter Oak aware of this?"

"I can assure you they are."

Having worked in the corporate environment, Tillie's last remark, her certainty, her emphasis, alerted Katherine to the possibility that Tillie (not Swanson) was now, in fact, the person in charge.

"So what you're saying is that most of what Swanson will be signing off on has already been approved by the committee. There will be no further changes."

Tillie laughed. "Let's say there will be less changes. And Katherine, you have to promise this arrangement stays between us."

Hanging up from Pete's call, Katherine thinks she should have met with him and explained this necessary intrigue, what some might call "a harmless surreptitious arrangement." Words like "trust" and "loyalty" have pestered her, and she has been telling herself for a while that she will at some point confide in Pete and is regretting now that she hasn't.

She reaches for the carafe, pours water into the glass, and swallows the pills. Instead of putting her right out (and she worries that her body is getting too used to them), they only leave her drowsy, thinking of Moses Rocket, a building she's come to love almost as if it were her own flesh and blood.

10

Lucy

Lucy opens the front door of the house and cries out, "What a glorious day!" The air is lighter, cooler, and fresher, with only a sniff of late summer. The sky is bright and a vivid blue. *"Oh, Luke, how I wish you were here!"*

She walks out, takes a few deep breaths, and steps into the sleek red Audi she'd bought just three weeks before Luke's passing. He'd wanted her to have it, insisted on it. "You always wanted a convertible, and we can certainly afford to get you one." His idea had cheered her immensely. Neither of them was aware of what little time they'd have to enjoy it together.

She drives the long way round to the Widow's Group, wishing her journey out on such a day was to some other place. The minister had called her after Luke's funeral and urged her to join the group of grieving widows. As politely as she could manage, she declined. He continued calling, and finally, she relented, agreeing to try one meeting. Out of habit, cowardice, even loneliness, she's attended regularly ever since.

Her route takes her past Silvano's Nursery, bustling with activity. People are pulling what looks like miniature farm wagons filled with glittering chrysanthemums. She feels a twinge of sadness, of regret, thinking of how Luke liked what he called their "weekend outings," searching for some unusual or exotic plant. She always did the driving. He liked to "look around," fascinated by how people landscaped their property, even in the most modest of homes.

She wonders what Luke would think of Silvano, who has become somewhat of a friend these last few months. He often stops by in the evenings on the days his men have been there, and they spend a few minutes together discussing the property. He understands how important it is to her that the grounds be kept up as Luke would have wanted them.

She usually offers Silvano some refreshments—lemonade, iced tea, a beer. They sit outside and talk quietly or walk the property together. She weighs carefully his concerns or some idea he's thought of to improve the landscape.

Sometimes they just talk, and he tells her how much he enjoys Ellen and that they get along famously. She imagines that they do. He's a patient man and undoubtedly allows Ellen to do most of the talking. Recently he's mentioned mums. "I am in love with mums," he says, telling her they are his favorite this time of year. "They are splendid. I'll bring you some—no charge—I do that for my best customers."

She'd refused, saying she really hadn't the time to care for them properly. He didn't push her to accept, and she liked that he didn't, but now she thinks that on the way back from the meeting, she may stop in and pick up a few pots for the front steps of the house.

Her depression or sadness or disappointment she feels this morning—whatever she might call it—has at its root a lack of sleep. Last night, she'd been awake at intervals, thrashing around in the bed, and when she did go out for an hour or so, the distress she was feeling woke her up. All this was triggered by a confrontation she'd had with Sy late Friday afternoon.

She'd reviewed the concrete cube's base building drawings and discovered an error in the square foot figures. A serious mistake. She checked them again before bringing them to Sy. "Paul will have to rework the prints," she said.

Sy shook his head and said he would look them over. Then as she was packing up to leave that night, he came back to her with the blueprints and asked her to make the changes over the weekend.

"Paul should do it." She sort of grinned. "Sy, you know the drill. His mistake, his responsibility," she said as if he should have known.

"I'm asking you to do it, Lucy. We'll need them for a project meeting on Monday morning. Paul was out with a client today and went straight home afterward. I called, but no answer."

"He can pick up the prints and work here or take them home tomorrow."

"A favor, Lucy," he said.

She should have refused, walked away, and was disturbed that it seemed she no longer knew how to handle this kind of pressure.

She'd taken the drawings home and worked on the corrections most of Saturday. The slightest noise distracted her—birdsong, the distant clamor from Pilgrims Corner, sounds she usually welcomed that made her feel less alone. Finishing, she felt one of those punishing flushes coming on. She threw down the drafting pencil and rushed outside. In the garden, she stood in the late afternoon shadows, waiting for her body to cool. She felt angry and sorry for herself.

In West Hartford village, she guides the car into the church parking lot. The Congregational Meeting House is a high, rectangular wood building with painted white clapboards and shutters like those on Luke's farmhouse. No wonder he'd chosen this place of worship, she thinks, arranging his own funeral as if he knew he was going to die. The same builder could have built them both, or the plans for it must have derived from the same book. The architectural details—moldings and panels—are identical, and all date from the mid-18th century.

Lucy walks toward the church and, for the first time, pauses and looks up. On top of the steeple is a weathervane, tinged with a greenish-blue patina. It is the same as the one that sways atop Luke's barn. She shakes her head impatiently, a bit weary, a bit fed up with coming here, yet she walks on and steps inside the church.

The interior is free of ornament, the walls white and plain, the high-backed pews dignified, the floors wide-planked and bare. No color anywhere but white, dark-stained wood, and a subtle glitter of gold and blue at the altar. She pauses, and her body is washed with a cross draft of soft air from the long open windows at each side of the church. They, too, are identical to the sitting room windows at the farm, where they also provide breezes, a practical, long-standing solution to a potentially stifling environment.

The similarities she finds here distract her resolve to move on from the life she and Luke had created, as it does each time she attends one of these meetings.

She descends into the newly remodeled ground floor, where the scent of fresh paint and new carpet lingers.

Several women have arrived before her. Some have formed friendships. Lucy is no closer to anyone here than when she started. She has nothing she wants to say—her grief for Luke is private.

She selects a chair with vacant seats on each side, sits, and nods pleasantly when the meeting starts; the final count today is fifteen widows.

More than last time. *Husbands are dropping like flies!*

The minister bustles in. He is a short, dark-haired man with a bit of a paunch, looking as if he's enjoyed a hearty lunch. He greets the widows, who cease talking and smile bravely up at him, grateful that he has arranged this meeting. He opens with a brief prayer. Lucy admits he has a lovely voice; the tone is gentle yet deep and genuine, as if what he says can and should be believed.

The minister begins with enthusiasm, introducing the new woman. Her name is Mila. The other women smile and quietly welcome her. The minister engages the women, concerned about how they are coping while Lucy pulls on the hair at the nape of her neck, thinks she needs a cut and begins checking hairdos. Most of the women have short poufy hair, but then she notices that Mila's hair is a tawny gray-brown color, tied back with a black ribbon. She's wearing black cotton slacks, a white sleeveless blouse, and a sweater tossed over her shoulders. A woman comfortable with herself, Lucy thinks.

Most of the other women are wearing knitted slacks with loose-fitting tops, beads at their throat or two-piece suits, shoes with low heels, and clothes they'd worn to the church service earlier. They, too, seem comfortable. She's never looked at these women so closely. For the first time, she realizes that they are all much older.

Suddenly, she feels a hot flush on her skin. She fumbles in her purse for a tissue, wiping the perspiration from her forehead. She despises this *affliction* that has taken over her body—it is almost evil. She unbuttons her suit jacket and lowers her head as if she's meditating. She remains absolutely still, aware of her rapid breaths and the women's chatter. She hopes no one notices. Once her heartbeat slows, she lifts her head, feeling thoroughly exhausted.

Thankfully, the widows are giving their full attention to the minister who's urging them toward refreshments, usually offered halfway through the meeting. Lucy remains seated, dulled, and slightly disoriented, with no desire for packaged cookies.

Alone in the circle, she feels a sense of defeat, of dread, that the flush might recur. She raises her eyes to a brightly colored poster. A large cat is dangling perilously from a treetop branch. "HANG IN THERE, BABY."

The self-help message blurs and reforms into a figure of Claire, Lucy's worst (but undeniably most interesting) former boss. "You look different," Lucy thinks, "you've lost your hair." Claire, dressed as Lucy remembers, wearing a short tight skirt, spike heels, and black net stockings, grins. "And you, Lucy, have lost your nerve."

Claire had been the senior architect in charge of all projects at the firm where Lucy interned after college. She had cropped bottle-blond hair, wore a ton of make-up, and smoked incessantly. Highly intelligent and enormously creative, she was consistently irreverent toward the young male architects and used locker-room language to ridicule the schemes they brought to her desk for approval. She was no kinder to the few females like Lucy. Some interns lasted a few days, a few weeks, and the most courageous, a few months. In the neighborhood where Lucy had grown up, there had been enough tough people that were smart like Claire. Lucy stood up to her, and because of that, along with Lucy's talents, Claire begrudgingly grew to respect her.

From the beginning, Lucy recognized that Claire got away with outrageous behavior because her observations were usually insightful and correct. Clients depended on her, believed what she said, agreed with her recommendations, and the firm's partners trusted her decisions.

Now Lucy wonders how she should have replied to Sy. He or Paul should have spent the weekend correcting the drawings. *How did she become such a pushover?*

"Use it or lose it" is Claire's departing message as her image fades back into the poster.

The widows settle back into their chairs with paper cups, napkins, and cookies. The new woman smiles as if she's noticed Lucy's discomfort. Lucy automatically smiles back, wanting to signal that she is fine and requires no empathy.

Gloria, one of the more vocal widows, says, "Listen up!"

The women give their full attention.

"My son brought me a dog!" says Gloria, almost quivering with excitement. "He never asked first. He said I needed companionship."

The women nod, understanding Gloria's initial outrage over the dog.

Lucy's heard at other meetings how daughters never visit or telephone, or when they do, they behave bossily, and how sons forget to send a birthday card because they're married to women who won't remind them.

"I can't leave Lizzie with anyone," Gloria says. "I'm as tied down now as when Dad was alive."

Some of the widows speak of their husbands as "Dad," "Pop," and even "Father." The women sympathize. One says, "You didn't ask for this dog, and your son should have asked you before he brought it home."

Gloria moans. "And now I'll have to put off my vacation."

From the circle of chairs, Lucy speaks for the very first time. "What about a kennel? Can't you leave Lizzie in a kennel while you go on vacation?"

"Dogs go insane in places like that," Gloria snaps.

Lucy feels embarrassed and vows she'll never say a word here again.

Gloria, though, has opened up the floodgates for animal lovers. Some had almost immediately replaced their husbands with a pet. Her new cat jumps on one woman's lap when she feels lonely, the woman insisting the cat knows.

One widow actually allows a dog to sit at the table, lapping food off a dinner plate in the chair where her husband used to sit.

The minister intervenes. "Everyone needs to focus," he says. He wants to discuss the idea of "living alone" versus "loneliness."

Lucy recalls the only time she lived alone during her marriage. Luke had left her for almost a week after they learned it was because of him they would not be able to have children. She'd tried everything. At one point, she gave up smoking and quit work because the specialist they were consulting with said stress could be a factor. In other words, the "fault" was hers. Now they test men upfront. She'd overheard one of the clients at Cole & Siegel talking in the women's room, as casually as if she were talking about having the flu, that she wouldn't go through any procedures until her husband's sperm was tested. No living soul besides her doctor (although Lucy suspected that Luke had confided in Ellen) knew the reason she and Luke were childless. What's happened to privacy? Dignity? Is this letting it all out better?

When Luke returned, heartbroken, they clung to one another and never spoke of the disappointment again.

The minister asks if anyone would like to share experiences of coping with grief and loneliness. Lucy has no ideas, no suggestions. She knows with some certainty that it is the effort she has put into the landscape Luke had created and the evidence of her success that has brought her a degree of acceptance, but she cannot share this with women she barely knows.

The winter after Luke's death came spitefully early and was both harsh and lingering. She saw him everywhere. Outside, at nightfall through the kitchen bay, he moved within the "limbed woods," as he called them, and the violet shadows on the snow. Inside the house, she felt his presence in a pair of slippers under a chair, as if he'd taken them off only moments before. His worn gray sweater, unexpectedly on the hook in the hallway, felt warm to her touch.

Once, she came into the sitting room, and his shadow fled into the hall. She rushed after it calling, "Luke! Luke!"

Mornings, she awakened to the scent of coffee and came downstairs expecting to find him, an early riser, at the table, his half-glasses on the end of his nose, sorting through seed catalogs. Finding the kitchen empty and cold, she wondered how she could go on without him.

After the first month of denial and disbelief, grief immobilized her. For hours, she might sit in a chair next to the window, looking out. Then one day, a bedraggled-looking squirrel appeared in front of her, its paws digging into frosted soil. The sight of the frantic creature disturbed her. She lifted the window and shooed it away, but it stayed in the spot where Luke used to set up the pole for feeders at the start of each winter.

That weekend she set them up. Then she cut off the runners from the strawberry plants and remembered to fertilize them. The vast array of tasks overwhelmed her, although she did what she could.

Evenings, she put off getting into bed alone and, at times, stayed up until one or two in the morning. She thought about moving into one of the other bedrooms. She thought about selling the house and moving back to Hartford.

She began spending a lot of time at the mall. She brought back silly, frivolous items she has since given away—a china dog that reminded her of Spotty, a childhood pet. Throw pillows with smiley faces on the covers. A silk flower arrangement she got nervy enough to place on the dining room table that seemed like a direct insult to the rest of the furnishings.

She drove to the mall after work and window-shopped for hours, searching for brightness, selecting clothes she might never wear, such as a beautiful white see-through blouse, an embossed belt, and a pair of paisley boxer shorts that made her want to giggle with the young woman at the register who picked the boxers off the counter with a bored expression that said women bought these kinds of things all day long. "Gift wrapped?" she'd asked. Too shy to admit the boxers were for her, Lucy had nodded.

Of course, she'd been in shock at the time. When she acknowledged that, she stopped her trips to the mall and began working longer hours at the firm. Anything was better than returning to the empty farmhouse.

At Christmas, she hosted a gathering for her co-workers. It was a lot of work and yet a lot of fun and distracting. She felt lonelier once they all left.

In January, she went to Vermont on a skiing trip, the first time since she was a girl when she'd go with her father, her mother preferring to stay at home. She rode the lifts to the steeper slopes, the sensation of passing through to another place where for a few moments, no memories of Luke existed.

Then an accident. She fell, skidding down a stretch of bare ice; fortunate, she was told not to have broken anything. She spent a week in bed, half-drugged.

Through February and March, she went to work and came back to the farm before nightfall. She felt apprehensive. The evenings were endless and full of despair. She told herself to start painting. From the house, she looked to the barn where her paints, brushes, frames, and canvases were stored in a studio space Luke had built for her that she'd never used.

She felt a degree of what she thought of as safety or certainty that came from remaining in the house. What could harm her here? She'd never been afraid while Luke was alive. Besides, what would she paint?

Eventually, the sun rose stronger, melting ice that dripped all morning against the windows almost as persistently as a rainstorm. She was somewhat surprised to find herself anticipating spring as she had with Luke. On the other three sides of the house, ice clung stubbornly to the eaves, and when it finally let go, it knocked against the clapboards with a noise like someone trying to break in.

Then warmer days came, and the bones of the old house stretched and snapped. The small brook nearby, freed from its roof of ice, spouted and splashed impatiently over rocks.

She recalled Luke going down a list of things to do and worried. How could she possibly keep up with the property as he had? Once, she'd mocked the yard he'd planted so carefully, and jokingly called it "the shrine." He'd given her a silent, hurt look.

She reached deep within herself for the force, the needed energy to manage the many small chores Luke had anticipated and actually looked forward to, bleaching out the mud prints from the back door rug, closing up the can of salt beside the granite steps, placing shovels, left upright like soldiers next to the clapboards all winter, into the shed. Small insignificant tasks that signaled renewal.

For a time, there was mud everywhere. As she walked from the house, her boots squished as if someone were following, and several times she glanced over her shoulder. *"Luke, where are you?"*

The wind blew warmer. She came outdoors with no coat or scarf, only his sweater, grabbed off the hook, and tossed across her shoulders. Finally, spring shivered into blossom. The brave snowdrops bowed their heads and melted back into the soil. Daffodils, forsythia, and shadblow bloomed.

She inspected the strawberries. Her efforts a few months before were rewarded. New growth emerged from the wasted-looking centers. In the asparagus bed, green fingernail tips scratched their way out from the brown soil. Rhubarb crowns were all coming back! She felt a brief and unexpected joy.

In some way, Lucy identifies with Gloria's excitement over the unasked-for dog, a new presence that requires Gloria's care and devotion, even love.

"Most of us are afraid, alone, or afraid of the feeling of aloneness," the minister says. The rest of the words he hopes will comfort this flock of women are lost to Lucy in the midst of sniffling and shuffling as the meeting breaks up. One woman says to no one in particular, "I do the best I can. What choice do I have?"

The new widow smiles at Lucy, and she's tempted to walk over and introduce herself, but the minister is in her path, bending to the woman who has just spoken and is now in tears.

Leaving the church, Lucy decides this is her last visit. No point in a new friendship here. She is out of place. She has nothing to share about children making her life difficult or any possibility of ever having grandchildren whom, the women say, make life worthwhile.

Driving back to the farmhouse, passing by Silvano's, she forgoes her earlier impulse to stop for chrysanthemums. She thinks of all the effort she put into coming back that had given her hope. What in the world has it brought her back to? The last thing she needs is pots of flowers she'll have to remember to water and toss out once they fade. She feels instantly sad over rejecting Silvano's friendly gesture. Sorry to disappoint him, but there is nothing she can do about that just now.

11

Rangy Barstow

"Mom! Dad!" he bellows, frightened that his eyes are open, but all they see is darkness. He attempts to sit up, and his head thumps against something hard. Then he remembers where he is, and he lies back, waiting for his pulsing heart to slow, and then he slides out of the huge culvert that has been placed for some reason, some need he is not aware of, in the cellar of his former home.

At first, the presence of the pipe alarmed him—he thought the workmen would be in and out. But it was put here months ago and likely abandoned before the cellar hatch had been nailed shut.

It is in the safety of the pipe that Rangy's spirit draws off from his body as he imagines wandering through the subterranean passageways, corridors, staircases, and open spaces of Moses Rocket. It is only then that his body manages some decent rest, his mind some respite from his worries—the fate of his cherished building and the consequences of his unintended action. He's done something terribly wrong and knows no way to put it right with the woman.

His actions have also shattered the pattern of how he used to spend each day. For months, he's slept inside the pipe during the daylight hours and, at night, prowled through Moses Rocket. He can't get caught inside the building. Not now, not after what he's done. If only she'd listened, let him explain. *Not my fault!*

Standing in a sparse light in the basement, hunger and a sense of incontinence overwhelm him. He finds his way to the door, unbolts it, and lifts the hatch. It is early enough so that the workmen who come to the site have not yet arrived.

He steps out to the yard, lowers the hatch quietly, moves quickly to the far corner that offers a bit of privacy, and modestly relieves himself. He rinses his hands and face from the bucket he'd hung on a nail outside the cottage early on after the water was shut off. The rain helps to keep it part-way filled. At other times, he fills it up with bottled water.

He straightens his clothing, adjusts his cap, and walks down a narrow path beside the row of houses that leads him to the street. He looks up at Moses Rocket, and as always, a feeling of sadness and helplessness overcomes him. He lowers his head and averts his eyes.

He goes in the direction of downtown Hartford, to the heart of the business district, and for the next few hours, he begs change from the people going to work. Rangy has money of his own, but he hardly ever spends it. It might run out, and then what would he do?

He gets enough change and buys a ham sandwich and cream soda from a vendor who's just opening. Although he craves a cup of coffee, he's too far from the *Omar* coffee truck. The hamburger restaurant is open, but he won't go in there.

He has a particular hatred and contempt for the brightly lit place that moved into where Kissman's used to be, the grocery store that hired him part-time when he was fourteen years old.

He used to carry bags of potatoes, crates of vegetables, and fruits up from the hatch out front. He stacked the produce exactly as Mr. Kissman showed him. He took a certain pride in his work then. But that's all gone, too. The street in front of Kissman's is littered with red and white cartons, yellow tissues, and paper bags. Employees wear striped uniforms and silly hats, and office people hurry out of the door, licking their fingers and picking food out from their teeth.

He passes the Municipal Cafeteria. Hardly anyone lunches there anymore. When he delivered for Kissman's, he used to admire the Municipal. Through the window, he could see men taking their time, reading the newspaper over a hot meal, a cup of coffee. People nowadays are too much in a hurry.

The Municipal had always seemed a special place. Dad had promised to take him. "The three of us, you, Mom, and me," Dad said. "We'll go to the Municipal for lunch someday, Rangy." The promise was held out and cherished. All Rangy had to do was be a decent boy, and they'd all go together to the Municipal. But they never got there. First, Mom got sick and passed away, and then Dad. All the years he worked at Moses Rocket before it shut down, he'd never been able to bring himself to enter the restaurant on his own.

Reading has always been hard for him. The letters are jumbled and backward. Doctors told his parents that he was less advanced in development than was usual for his age. But he was always curious, and Mom and Dad had read aloud to him from books the doctor and the teachers recommended. After Mom died, Dad used to read to him every morning from the newspaper before they left for work at Moses Rocket.

But he's also "gifted," Dad always said, in that he can repair machinery. If he was shown a picture or a diagram of how something is supposed to work, or if one of the men explained a mechanical issue to him slowly and precisely so that he understood exactly what the problem was, he was almost sure to find the solution. He was "quite an asset" at Moses Rocket, so he'd been told.

He goes into the alley behind Kissman's and sees a few cats circling in the spot for garbage pick-up. He pauses and looks into the green eyes of an abnormally large tom, a wild-looking creature, climbing over the trash. Then he hears a peculiar sound, one he's never heard before. He looks down, and something near his foot moves—he almost steps on it. *What is this?* He stoops to pick it up. A small animal with patches of matted fur just about fits in his hand, meowing pitifully, its eyes closed. *What are you?* Rangy wonders, thinking the tiny animal might be hungry. The tom cat is looking down on Rangy at the top of the trash pile. He can't leave the tiny creature in the alley, so he puts it carefully inside the pocket of his overcoat and moves on.

On his way back to the cellar, he stops at a convenience store. Ignoring how people scowl and move away from him, he purchases a pint of milk. Hurrying back to the cellar, he removes the creature from the shelter of his coat, placing it on top of the pipe so that he can get a good look at it. Suddenly in the midst of its bleating, he understands that he has found a kitten that cannot be more than a few days old.

As if he'd given life to her himself, he lifts the animal gently and brings it tenderly to his face. *"Kitty,"* he says, and then with a plastic spoon, he feeds her some milk.

Soon, Rangy again walks the streets of Hartford at night, although he still avoids Moses Rocket. He's amazed at how peaceful the city becomes once they've all left—the people who work in the big companies, the building men at the project site. There is hardly any traffic on Main Street. Only buses pass, the heads of a few passengers sitting upright, eyes moving over him as if he were not there, and sleeping heads propped against the windows like smeared paint. At this time of night, in his memory, the city is almost as it was when his life here was so different.

During his evening rounds, Rangy begins noticing the volume of stray cats. Hungry, frightened, and quarrelsome. For something to do, he catches the smaller ones and puts them into a cardboard box, bringing them home to his cellar. He feeds and cares for them. Although it is Kitty that has him by the heart—Kitty with her dark, thickening fur as if she'd been dipped into a vat of black dye, her slight body, and the miracle of her soulful blue eyes.

After his morning walks, alert for any sign of the woman he has hurt, he settles with Kitty into the pipe for a few hours. All day, the pounding from Moses Rocket reverberates throughout the cellar. The walls of his home, the beams above his head, and the floor beneath all shudder.

He holds Kitty next to his heart. He feels the quaking of hers.

He struggles to think of something, anything that he can do to stop the terrible noise.

12

Sy

He's always the last to leave the building on these nights when he walks through the design department. When he goes into Katherine's workstation, an unexpected sense of concern comes over him and a feeling of sorrow over what has happened to her. He heard from Jed that she is in bad shape, and no one is certain when she'll be returning to work on this project. It is important that he, more than ever, keep current, and he's made a note to meet with Deborah in the next few days.

He snaps on the lamp above Katherine's drafting board and goes through blueprints, noting changes and her remarks in the margins of the drawings, all dated and signed. He looks through the vendor samples she's requested, all of which are carefully labeled. He reads the phone messages Violet left for her and Katherine's last entry in the project notebook that she and everyone keep meticulously up-to-date. As always, her thoroughness and her attention to detail impress him.

She fusses over the notebook and insists that it never leaves her workstation. In essence, it is a complete project history from start to finish, an idea for record-keeping that Katherine introduced when she came to work at Cole & Siegel. It's been so successful that all the project architects signed on to create one for their own projects. Sy picks up the notebook in order to make a copy of Katherine's final entry for his home file.

He moves on to Henry's desk, to Deborah's, and then to all of the workstations, looking over material samples and blueprints. He's never forgotten Joel's advice. "You can get eaten alive in this business, Kid. You gotta look out for yourself."

He'd been in his third year of high school and had joined the Youth for Work Program that would give him credit for supervised work experience when his father suggested he meet an old friend of his, a building contractor. "Joel will put you to work," he said, dropping him off in front of a long, flat concrete building.

He was nervous, walking into a bare-bones space with cement floors and poor lighting. Ancient fixtures hung over a row of desks. The windows were clouded with dirt and smoke and looked permanently shut. The place smelled of smoke, too.

Tentatively, he stopped at the first desk and told the woman who was sitting there that he had an appointment with Joel. That was all his father had told him to say.

"Back there," she said, pointing to a small room at the building's far end.

Joel sat in a grubby, smelly room, separated from his employees by a wall of half-glass, half-wood. "So you're Sid Greene's kid," he said.

"Yes, sir," he said and put out his hand.

Joel grinned and shook it quite firmly.

At first, he could not believe Joel and his father were lifelong friends. They couldn't have been more different. Joel looked as unhealthy as some of his father's patients. With his dark and disheveled hair, thick eyebrows, and perpetual scowl, he looked more like a gangster you'd see on TV.

Cigarette butts spilled from a tin ashtray on his desk. Rolled-up blueprints were tossed into a cardboard box, and others were taped to a drafting board.

A chain of notes, phone messages, and reminders dangled from a light cord. "I don't let anyone clean up in here," Joel warned him. "I know right where everything is. You got that, Kid?"

He knew then that Joel would hire him, and he suspected that his father had probably arranged that with him beforehand.

Each morning, Joel arrived with two boxes of doughnuts—one for the employees and one that he ate out of steadily all day, drinking coffee and smoking. He was single and frequented the same restaurant almost every night.

He worked seven days a week. Once in downtown Hartford, Sy saw him walking into a theater with a woman on his arm. He only saw them from a distance and could not say what she looked like. He thought it better not to mention it to Joel, or to anyone else at work, for that matter. He'd already caught on that Joel was an obsessively private person.

How had his father known that a man like Joel would be good for him? He was the first adult outside of his family that he truly trusted. Joel was rough-spoken but kind. "What's the matter with you, Kid? You got rocks in your head like everyone else who works here? Pay attention! Pay attention!"

For a while in the beginning, he'd wondered why anyone would work for Joel—who would stick around given his management style that, at times, bordered on verbal abuse. But most of his employees had worked for him for many years. It was an informal, unpretentious place where you could be yourself, take a day off when you needed to, and borrow a few bucks off of Joel if you were short.

Would he have thought of architecture as a profession without Joel's influence?

"I got one golden rule for you, Kid. You get that diploma that'll open doors but forget all that artistic crap you'll learn in school. There's only one thing you got to remember. Always do what the man holding the purse strings tells you he wants."

He misses Joel.

There is so much he would have liked to talk over with him. He would certainly have given him some good advice about dealing with a man like Will Swanson.

Sy goes into the copy room. The chemical smell seems worse whenever the building is empty. It takes a moment for his eyes to adjust to the darkness, and he begins copying the pages he needs from the project notebook when he hears an unmistakable noise— the drag of the heavy middle door between the floors. It happens all day long, and no one notices, but now the sound is jarring. It's too early for the janitorial service, and whoever it is knows that Sy is in the building—the lights are on upstairs, and his car is parked out back. He should turn on the copy room light, hesitates, and hears Pete Larson talking to himself. Quickly, he separates the copies he's made from Katherine's original and realizes that his hands are shaking.

In reality, there is nothing wrong or against the rules about his having a copy of the notebook, but Katherine would surely question why it's necessary. Its sole purpose is that there is one source for all project queries. But having his own copy gives Sy a greater sense of control regarding the project. Also, he often works at home after Heather's bedtime, and it is convenient to have the notebook when questions come up.

The overhead fluorescents in Design flicker on, and for a brief moment, Sy feels less stupid, more normal, hearing Pete break out in song. *"I can't get no satisfaction, cause I try and I try, and I try,"* as if he were in his shower at home. Sy can't help smiling. He thinks about how the designers revere Pete and how he'll work with any one of them through the night, if need be, on their projects.

He wonders if Pete is working late on his own or is expecting one of his staff. He sees how ridiculous and bizarre it would look if one of them came in and found him pinned against the copy machine in the near dark. The whole department would amuse themselves for days with the story.

He'll have to risk getting up to the first floor. He shoves the copies into the project notebook, removes his shoes, crouches, and heads to the staircase, grateful that Pete's station is at the far front of the room.

At the top of the stairs, he slides into his shoes and goes straight into the men's room so that if Pete comes upstairs, he'll think Sy's been in there all this time. He washes his hands and splashes water on his face. He hardly recognizes himself in the mirror. His face is pale, his eyes feverish. This won't do. He's behaved stupidly. When he heard Pete come in, he should have turned on the copy room light, gone out, and spoken to him.

He walks back to his office, glancing into the workspaces of his peers that he never enters. It would be awkward, near impossible, to explain if one of them returned unexpectedly. Yet he manages to keep abreast of their projects. Lucy reviews all of the firm's blueprints, and they are kept rolled up in a box beside her desk.

Some nights he studies them in clear view of the front window as if he were examining those from his own project.

He decides he'll leave—Apple is expecting him, and Pete might come upstairs. Sy is not in the mood for even a friendly conversation. Then he realizes that he is still holding the notebook. He'll have to get here early tomorrow and put it back in its designated place on Katherine's desk.

Passing by the long front window, he pauses. The exterior lights outside the building soften the Japanese yews. A wind has blown hot all day, and a few branches feather the glass. He sees his daughter's likeness reflected within his own in the windowpane, and he thinks how sad it is that his parents have passed—they would have adored her.

She's at the age where she is beginning to notice his absences, his long hours. *"When is Daddy coming home? Will he read me a story?"* Julie tells him in the mildly emphatic tone she employs when she expects him to pay attention. He loves Heather and makes time for her—it's enough for now, *isn't it?* And at this hour, she's asleep.

Julie? Tonight, he won't think about his wife. His relationship with Apple is from the time before—something in his life, something in himself that is unfinished. He feels a simmering uneasiness but not enough to change his mind about leaving here and going to her. Since their unexpected meeting at Genesis, they usually spend an hour or so together a few nights a week.

And to think it was Will Swanson, of all people, who had brought her back into his life.

Six weeks ago, he and Swanson were in a meeting that had not been going well, discussing Katherine.

"She seems to think she knows what people want," Swanson said.

"What do you mean?"

"I mean the furniture and everything else to do with the design side of this project, putting everything on boards as if it's all decided."

"Will, that's her job."

"You listen to me, Sy. No one at Charter Oak likes chrome and leather, no matter what you people think. I want to go out with you and look at furniture, and without Tillie or Katherine," he added.

Sy was concerned about Swanson's interest in the selection of furniture and carpeting. Client involvement might tie up a project for weeks. Best to keep them out of showrooms unless they are brought there by an experienced designer like Katherine. But Swanson pressured him until he felt he had no choice. Sy brought him to Genesis, one of the older, out-of-the-way dealerships where it was unlikely that he'd run into anyone he knew.

Swanson was almost childishly pleased and excited. Sy told the receptionist they wanted to browse the office furnishings. She paged the manager, and Apple came into the lobby.

He was beyond stunned when she shook his hand but said nothing personal, almost as if they'd agreed on that beforehand.

"I want to look at office furniture," Swanson said. "Lounge, VP offices, and conference rooms."

"We're in the process of renovating the showroom, and what we have here is outdated. We do have current catalogs, though—what style of furniture are you interested in, Mr. Swanson?"

"Did you hear that, Sy? Do you realize that's the first time anyone in your business asked me what I wanted? This gal should be working on our project."

Leaving the showroom after a few hours of going through catalogs, Apple gave them her business card. On Sy's, she included her personal phone number.

He called her that night.

As if his emotions, sensitivities, and loyalties are like nails, screws, and bolts that he can sort into compartments, he doesn't confuse his devotion and love for Julie and Heather with his love for Apple. They are separate and distinct. From the beginning, Apple had lit what had been dark and lonely in him, and he could not give her up, not now. Not yet.

He wonders if the sandwich shop that her uncle owned is still there and imagines that it is.

He drives past Apple's apartment building and pulls into a parking space at the bottom of the street. Loosening his tie, he places it carefully over the seatback, unbuttons his shirt at the collar, and climbs out.

He passes several large, rambling houses, built early in the 20th century for insurance executives, each now converted into small condos or rentals, mostly for singles.

After his parents died, he converted the Poplar Street house in the same way. The ell side alone, where his father practiced medicine, brings a hefty income that he invests for Heather's education. *He's doing all right!*

Apple lives in one of the smaller rentals with a sitting room, bedroom, and bath—on the second floor of a gray Victorian. A galley kitchen with a stove, sink, and refrigerator leaves barely enough space to move around in. The rooms are situated at the back of the house, and a nice feature is a door in the sitting room that leads out to a wooden porch, a small yard below and a garden someone cares for, and a few old towering trees. On a mild evening such as this, the modest rooms seem comfortable and adequate, even though the entire space might almost fit into the family room of his home.

Looking out for him, he sees Apple at the windows in the same way that Julie or Heather might on the evenings he's expected home before Heather's bedtime. Apple opens the front door and stands in bare feet, watching as he climbs up the outside stairs. She is wearing a long cotton dress that lightly drapes her thin yet shapely body. She smiles, almost shyly, a bit teasingly, delight gleaming from her soft gray eyes.

He follows her into the sitting room, falling into an overstuffed chair. She pours wine, and he takes the glass from her, having no desire to speak. As if she knows, she doesn't ask, *"How was your day?"*

In the blue-painted kitchen, some nights she cheerfully cooks for him—simple dishes like pasta marinara, chicken sautéed in shallots and sherry, and black bean salsa. Delicious-tasting, low-fat food. "It's my Italian genes," she says when he compliments her. "I didn't expect to be a good cook."

He tells her he's sorry, but he can't stay long.

Her feet patter swiftly across the strip of white linoleum while she removes dishes with blue and white pastoral scenes from the white cabinets, placing them on a small square table.

Sitting across from her, speaking quietly, the door to the sitting room is open to the porch outside. Night breezes flow through the rooms, and treetops sway happily. It is as cozy a setting as if they were picnicking alone in a wooded clearing.

The hours he spends with Apple are precious and thrilling, more than he'd hoped for, and he swells with feeling—*how can he ever live without her?*

It was two years after that time he'd biked to Garden Street before he saw her again. He no longer spent hours in the waiting room of his father's office. He studied hard, wanting to get out of school as soon as he could. He'd already skipped a grade and planned to take college courses for most of his senior year. The rest of his time he spent at Joel's.

He'd become even more careful about his appearance, his choice of clothing, not wanting to draw attention to himself, wanting to look as if he fit in. Although he was aware of and accepting that with most of his classmates, he really didn't. He was on friendly terms with a few students in his advanced classes, and that was enough.

He might have missed Apple, gabbing with Joel all afternoon about what had happened that day at the building site—who'd delivered the wrong materials, who was goofing off on the job. "You got to check everything yourself a hundred times, Kid!"

He was almost seventeen, and most days, he rode the bus back and forth from work to home, and he was looking forward to having a car of his own. It was nightfall when the bus dropped him off. He saw the ell lit up and a few cars parked out front. He'd always been aware that his father worked long hours, but he felt something different that night, a deep sense of empathy.

Earlier that day, Joel had reminisced about his father. "Your old man is what I call a decent human being," he said. "Did you know he supported his family and paid his own way through medical school?"

Sy said that his mother had sometimes mentioned it.

"Your old man never looked for a fight, but he never backed down either. He always stood up for himself!"

He couldn't imagine his father, his gentle father, in a physical confrontation.

Sy was almost to the door of the house when he turned and walked toward the ell. He'd wait until his father was through with his patients so they could spend a few moments alone before supper. He felt curious, wanting to hear from his father something more about what Joel had told him—what it was like back then when he and Joel were growing up.

It was cooler than usual—a clear and beautiful night in late October, with a rim of pinkish color spreading along the horizon, and he'd walked obliviously beneath a shower of yellow beech leaves to the door of the ell. Florence, the new receptionist, looked up when he came in. "Oh, it's you, Sy. I was afraid it might be another patient."

People living nearby often came in without an appointment, and his father always made time for them. "How about locking the door?" Florence said. "Two emergencies today. Your Dad's finishing up with the last of the scheduled patients."

He liked Florence and hoped she'd stay. His father had shared her story over dinner the night he'd hired her. She'd worked for years as a secretary in the English department of a nearby college. During her interview, she'd assured him that after working with English professors, she could work anywhere. She said they were usually intelligent and kind, but she found them to be almost like children when it came to practical matters. She felt she needed a change.

His father told him later, when they were alone that Florence was considerate with the patients and got along with his mother, who they both knew could be somewhat aloof as well as fussy regarding schedules and the state of the waiting room. It didn't seem to bother Florence. She responded to his mother's queries pleasantly. "So peace abounds at last," his father said.

Sy locked the door and was headed toward the two-seater couch when he saw Apple sitting in a chair next to the window. She didn't look much older than the last time he'd seen her. Her hair fell in a soft curve, almost hiding her face. Her folded arms suggested anxiety. Not wanting to stare, he looked beyond her to the window where the yard's rocks and bushes were dissolving into purple-blue darkness. *Why is she here?*

The door to his father's office opened, and Mrs. Messina emerged with the nurse, who told Apple that Dr. Greene was waiting for her. She stood up quickly, looking frightened.

It was all there in her file. Apple was sleepwalking. She'd been found several times in the middle of the night, sitting outside in the yard, in wet grass, shivering with fear.

The physical exam found nothing overt. Her blood and urine samples were normal. She was physically healthy, perhaps a bit thin. A regimen of vitamins was suggested. There was a concern that something worrisome was on her mind, and a meeting with a psychiatrist, a woman colleague his father thought might be a good fit, was strongly recommended to Mrs. Messina.

The notes also mentioned that Apple spent two hours each day after school in her uncle's sandwich shop at the corner of Poplar and Court. His search for her would begin there.

A few nights later, Sy grabbed a windbreaker out of the hall closet. His mother called to ask where he was going, but he shut the door without answering. Lately, he'd distanced himself from her. This had nothing to do with love. In fact, he cared deeply and had always confided in her and enjoyed their outings to museums and offbeat films. He understood that she, too, was lonely, considering the long hours his father worked.

His experiences with Joel were changing him. He was trying to figure out who he was and what he should do with his life. A simpler truth was that he just didn't need his mother's companionship as he once had.

A local bus ran up and down Poplar until ten. If the weather turned cold, he'd take the bus home. He slipped into his jacket, lifted the collar, thrusting his hands into the pockets, walking steadily and alertly into a neighborhood about which his parents had always counseled caution, noticing that the size of the homes diminished the further along he went.

Joel had told him that these homes were built at a later time in the blocks between the settled Italian section at the lower end of

Poplar and the older, more stately homes at the upper end where his family lived. "Keep your eyes open, Kid."

Joel had taught him so much and how he'd loved hearing tales of disreputable contractors, shoddily manufactured furniture that had to be sent back, and materials that were not delivered to Joel's clients when promised. *Oh, the headaches, the heartaches of the business!*

Halfway to the sandwich shop, he began feeling a little foolish. What did he think he could do for her? What did he really know about her, anyway? And what if one (or more) of the neighborhood boys stopped him? But his need to see her, and yes, to know something more about her than what he'd found in his father's notes, impelled him forward.

He reached the shop and looked through the window, relieved there were no kids inside. A man was wiping up the counter, and he supposed that was the uncle. Sy took a deep breath and opened the door. The sound of the bell hanging from the ceiling caught him off guard. He made for the counter and sat on one of the stools. "Coke, please."

The man looked at him a bit suspiciously, maybe because he'd never been in the shop before. "What kind do you want?"

Sy didn't know what he meant.

"Vanilla coke, cherry coke, plain coke. Which one?"

"Cherry coke," he said as if that was his preference, although he'd never had one before.

Placing the soda down on the counter, the uncle said, "Fifty cents."

Sy promptly paid.

Too nervous to ask for a straw (his mother had always insisted on one for health reasons, and he'd gotten into the habit), he lifted the glass to his mouth and took a long swallow as if he were thirsty, wondering if he'd come at the wrong time to find Apple.

The shop was long and narrow, and he thought it might have been added on to the adjacent apartment building. These were the kinds of things Joel would have pointed out if they'd come in together. Overhead fluorescent fixtures lighted the front, but the back was dim, with only a yellowish cast from bulbs in the wall lamps shining feebly on three red vinyl booths. Suddenly, Apple appeared from the furthest booth. "Uncle V, can I play the jukebox?"

Her voice was soft and somewhat pleading, like a younger child's.

"Apple, you're supposed to be doing your homework. You want your mother to give me what for?"

"How will she know?"

The uncle laughed. "All right, all right." He went to the jukebox and fiddled with something in the back. "How many, Apple?"

"I don't know. I want to look first."

"C'mon, Apple. I'm busy."

"There's no one in here now, and anyway, I know how to fix it when I'm done."

The uncle walked back behind the counter and looked at Sy's empty glass. "You want something else?"

"Refill, please," he said, placing two quarters on the countertop. The uncle slid the refilled glass in his direction and called out to Apple. "Keep an eye out. I got to go downstairs." He pulled up a door on the floor, glancing pointedly at Sy. "You call me if you need me, Apple," he said before descending into the basement.

Sy quickly turned the counter stool in her direction.

"What songs did you play?"

"Still looking. My uncle keeps a lot of old records—"

"Like what?"

"You know—Ella Fitzgerald and Frank Sinatra—" Two of Sy's favorites.

"If I don't play mine, Uncle V will play his."

"What songs do you like?"

"Old rock n' roll—don't you?"

He shrugged as if he wouldn't commit to liking them or not. The uncle would return shortly, and his questions became more urgent. "Are you here every day?"

"Most days. That's my Uncle V. He owns the shop. I come after school, sometimes."

"To hear the music?"

"Uncle V lives next door. If I'm here, he can go home to eat."

"Do you wait on the customers?"

"No, my Aunt Marie is here then. That's her job, but I help out sometimes when it gets busy."

He suspected that her aunt and uncle were actually minding her. Her unusual sleepwalking behavior, wandering out of the house at night, must have concerned them, too. "You don't recognize me?"

"Have you been in here before?"

"No, I haven't. I'm Sy Greene, Dr. Greene's son. I saw you in the waiting room with your mother."

She blushed as if he might know why her mother had taken her there and spoke a bit shyly. "Are you in college?"

"High school."

"Me, too, but I'm only a freshman," she said, stepping back from the machine. "I've played enough till my mom gets here."

"Maybe I can come back sometime, and we can go for a walk."

She shook her head. "I'd get into trouble if my family found out."

"I wouldn't want that to happen," he said.

She looked at him more closely. Her eyes softened. She was so pretty and delicate then, like a full-grown doll.

"I only live a few blocks from here. Some days when it's light out, I'm allowed to walk home by myself."

Her reply made him think she'd like to see him again. He had his own phone and made a bold move, writing his number on a slip of paper. On his way out, he gave it to her. "You can let me know the days, and I'll meet you."

"Okay," he thought she said as he was leaving, hearing the words of the song she'd chosen before the door shut. *"Tonight you're mine completely, you give your love so sweetly, tonight the light of love is in your eyes, but will you love me tomorrow…."*

He wondered if her sleepwalking had to do with some boy, a crush she might have, affection not returned. He felt hurt and jealous.

He thought about her constantly.

Then a week later, she called him. He could hardly believe it, feeling excited and happy when they made plans to meet.

By early winter, construction work at Joel's had slowed, and so he came two, three times a week up Poplar and waited for her near the sandwich shop. They took a long route to Garden Street, where he left her. Perhaps fatefully, these walks were never discovered.

Returning home on those late afternoons, he wondered why he was so drawn to her. She seemed too young, and yet in some indefinable way, she seemed just perfect.

He is gentle with her when they lie together in the small bed on Harte Lane. He touches her as if she is fragile, a priceless object. Their love is different from a cheap affair like the ones in films. She undresses carefully, modestly, and hangs up her cotton jumper.

She folds her panties and bra, placing them under her folded t-shirt as if she is a young girl, again, undressing for bed. All of this is what he'd tried to imagine after he'd left her those nights at dusk so long ago.

13

Lucy

Lucy, dear Lucy,

Somehow, the note you sent while I was in Africa had gone astray, and I only received it this morning here in Boston. I wanted to call but thought better of it and decided to write to you first.

I am so sorry, Lucy, to hear of Luke's sudden passing. He was such a generous, intelligent, and loving person. All I could imagine (with tears flowing) is how you must miss him and how your heart must hurt. A colossal challenge, I'm sure, to go on without your wonderful partner, and I imagine you at your easel, brush in hand, helping you get through such a painful time. I never tire of the beautiful still life you gave me years ago—oh, we were so young then!

My year in Africa was challenging, exhausting, and exhilarating. Third-world housing (I detest that term; it sounds elitist). Site planning. Engineering. The design of whole villages! Putting to use so much of what we learned at MIT.

Remember how few of us women were in those classes—we've done all right! So good to get away from kitchens! I'm exaggerating, but you know what I mean.

Oh, Lucy, what more can I say? Please forgive me for this note so long after your loss, but I wanted you to know of my concern and sorrow.

I miss you, Lucy. When you can, come see me in Boston. Until then, take good care.

Always in fond friendship and with love,

Eileen.

Lucy reads Eileen's note twice before she slips it into her briefcase.

Since it arrived, she's read it many times. She was excited to hear from her friend and yet sad, realizing that time was passing and that Luke was gone. It also brings up a sense of failure in her working life. The hint in Eileen's letter of her experiences and achievements on such a grand scale makes her work at Cole & Siegal seem small and not all that exciting or meaningful.

That evening when Silvano stops by, she shares Eileen's letter with him. "She is brilliant. She had a full scholarship at MIT," she says, although she doesn't tell him that she had also been awarded significant scholarship funds during her college years.

Lucy rarely talks about herself. What she has done with her superb education seems, in her opinion, insignificant compared to what Eileen has accomplished.

"Will you go to Boston and meet with your friend?" Silvano says.

Lucy wasn't sure when she would go, nor could she explain why. Silvano doesn't pry. He never does.

Frequently now, she finds herself looking out for him. His quiet nature and gentle voice soothe her loneliness.

At times, she wonders why he has come, and if she were to ask, and she knows this is something she would never do, he'd say that he wants to make sure his men are following his instructions on the garden's upkeep.

At some level, they both realize that there is more to this, stopping by unexpectedly and his staying to chat with her. She thinks perhaps he is lonely, too. He told her once that he was single and had never married, as if wanting her to know that he had no previous attachments. Once in passing, he'd said something like, "I'm fifty-six years old and too set in my habits, I think, sometimes."

She takes these remarks, or reflections, as exchanges but doesn't quite know how to respond or what she might share with him.

Luke was her lifetime partner, and at this point in her life, she's bewildered by how to relate to another man.

Silvano has a number of siblings, nieces, and nephews; a few work at the nursery. Occasionally, when he stops by, he brings one of the younger children with him, a six-year-old boy named Theo, who enjoys running around the property as soon as he gets down from Silvano's truck.

Theo is very observant, letting his uncle and Lucy know what flowers have bloomed and which ones have faded since his last visit.

"This one is a handful," Silvano says with some tenderness. "Some nights, I take him out for a ride. It gives my niece and her husband a break. He likes coming here, and I hope you don't mind."

"On the contrary," Lucy says. "I love it when he comes."

She keeps a supply of various kinds of cookies for Theo. It is a little guessing game between them. He has large, intelligent eyes like Silvano and is both thoughtful and curious, biting into the cookies, thinking hard about what they might contain.

At times, she imagines him in the kitchen with her while she is baking them.

Silvano suggests that night, as he is leaving, they might drive to Boston together. "You could visit your friend, Eileen."

Taken by surprise, she blurts out, "But what would you do?"

"I often go by myself to the MFA or over to Isabella Stewart Gardner's home."

Lucy smiles. "Yes, imagine her life!"

"We might go to dinner after?"

The Keeper

She nervously says, "Maybe we could, sometime."

Thoughtfully, he leaves without saying anything more.

14

Katherine

Of all of the rooms in this ancient farmhouse, some planned, some haphazardly added, this square room, with light from windows on three sides, is her favorite, and from here, she can look out for Mac.

In the latter part of the 18th century, her mother's family, the Wicks, built this part of the house, always referred to as "the original rooms," with wide plank flooring, 18" moldings, paneled doors with wrought iron hinges, latch door handles, bolts and pulls. As if they were spaces in a museum and a memorial to ancestors who'd first lived here, they have been cared for by ensuing generations and faithfully maintained. Luke used to laugh and brag with a proud glint in his eye (he'd done the research for the Historical Society, unearthing facts and stories confirming what he'd always believed) that the Wicks were quintessential New Englanders. "Proud farmers, ministers, doctors, teachers, and statesmen, progressive in their instincts," he would say and add with amusement that the cautious and thrifty Wicks spared no money when it came to "function," being one of the first families to install bathrooms inside the house.

Katherine looks around at the old and odd furnishings that he would never have thought to replace. This room is brimming with an atmosphere of what she thinks of as familiarity and comfort.

Worn and sagging sofas, linen pillows, and faded rugs with worn-off fringe, the perfect look (or "fit" might be the correct word) with everything else that is visible, like the huge roll-top pine desk and above it, photos of various Wicks of different generations, and the walnut table with a tall, wooden lamp and its yellowed shade, sitting placidly on a lace doily.

On the walls, there are also framed hand cross-stitching, commandments of behavior like "Honesty is the best policy" and "Honor thy father and thy mother." Anyone would feel safe in this restful room where time seems to have come to a halt more than a century ago. She is not particularly sentimental or reverent about this room or its "artifacts" but is aware that she would never replace what is here. Its continuity is "a mark of respect," her mother had told her, although she was too young then to understand exactly what she'd meant.

She is anxious to see Mac and wonders what's keeping him. Maybe her old rival, Veronia.

Mac has rarely come east since his children were born. When they were small, he refused to put them on a plane, and Veronia always journeyed to California. Mac had often told her how Veronia adored her grandchildren, and the kids found their grandmother "interesting and fun," missing her when she returned to her home.

When Veronia had surgery four years ago, Mac came alone to care for her. During his visit, he and Katherine spent a lot of time renewing their long ago close and trusting relationship. When he was leaving, she wished he didn't have to go, although she never told him. But her feelings reminded her how they'd separated years before after a sensitive and difficult conversation about where their relationship was headed.

She recalls being in a state of panic when he left that first time. She called her best friend Margie, her college roommate, and told her what had happened.

"I don't know what to do. I don't want to go back to living at home."

"You sound heartbroken."

"I think I am, but he was just a friend."

"Really?"

"Yes, a lifetime friend, Margie. That's all it was."

For a brief moment, Margie said nothing as if she were thinking of the right way to say what she was thinking about Katherine's long-time relationship with Mac, and then, as if changing her mind, she said, "Why don't you come to New York?"

Margie was leasing a rent-controlled apartment from a reporter on assignment in London. "I think he's leasing it from someone else, but it doesn't make any difference—it's a great location, there's room for you, and the rent is cheap."

As soon as she arrived in the city, a small architectural firm housed on East 63rd Street interviewed Katherine. "Was she organized? Was she willing to work on many tasks?" The salary was low, but needing experience, she accepted, grateful that the job was full-time and with medical benefits.

She met with clients, drew plans, selected materials, found her way to supplier showrooms, and put up with her boss yelling and swearing *a fongul* into the phone after he hung up with clients. She loved the job and enjoyed rooming with Margie and walking to work. The city was noisy, exciting, interesting, and, at times, overwhelming. Briefly, she'd been happy.

One afternoon, while shopping for a client, she met a man named Jake Tremont at the Knoll showroom. "I'm on a quest for a podium for a church I'm renovating in Greenwich Village," he said.

"Sounds interesting."

"Yes, but difficult to find exactly what I want," he said with the same intensity. "I believe a mixture of the antique and the modern is the only valid approach for any design."

She was in her twenties and had no idea that she was attractive to (or worthy of) a man like Jake Tremont, although when she and Margie went out together, without too much effort, she found that men were interested in her. She was on the thin side, had "good skin" (Margie used to say), and thick wavy hair.

In her mind, she was far from any raving beauty.

What she had then that attracted men was her personality—that was what they told her. She was fun, curious, and socially comfortable.

Jake was ten years older. He was handsome, tall, and muscular, his dark hair cut stylishly, combed back from his face, accenting what she thought was a "noble profile." His name had a roguish quality, like in a romance novel, that fit him so well she wondered later on (healing her broken heart) if he'd made it up.

They left the showroom together and chatted out on the street for a few minutes. "Think about whether you'd like to have dinner with me sometime. I'll call you at work," he said, tucking his suit pants into his boots. In a cavalier manner that she wondered he might not be aware of, he waved to her before taking off on his motorcycle.

She'd never met anyone like him. The way he spoke was almost foreign, sophisticated, serious, and maybe self-absorbed—which didn't bother her. He was not her first lover, but compared to what she thought of as "episodes of experimentation" in college, he was proficient, gentle, and considerate. Recalling past disappointments, she was ardent, appreciative, and responsive, doing her best to please him.

He lived in a beat-up trailer that was parked in the yard of a Brooklyn brownstone. She was put off and taken aback when he first brought her there, but to her surprise and relief, the inside of the trailer was neat, sparsely furnished, and clean. "It has everything I need," he said.

"It's really nice," she said, admiring how modestly he lived.

He'd told her that a woman named Jenny owned the building and raved about its beautiful and authentic interior. Jenny was away at the time, so he brought Katherine inside, and she swooned over its spaciousness—the large, open rooms with original wood floors, high ceilings, ornate moldings, built-in cupboards, and light.

Such wonderful light!

From the second floor, they looked down on his trailer, the yard a small and leafy oasis, the trailer seeming like an intruder in such a desirable space.

In the beginning, she was not at all concerned about Jenny, and it was only later that something he said felt worrisome. Finally, when she asked him about her, he explained that Jenny was a good friend—he'd known her for years.

Katherine believed him. After a few months, she told Margie she was in love.

"Careful."

"No, don't ruin it!" She clapped her hands over her ears like an adolescent who's been warned about the facts of life—what could happen, the risks.

In January, Margie and her boyfriend, a lawyer she was deciding whether or not to marry, went on a Club Med vacation to the Bahamas. Katherine thought it would be nice to invite Jake to stay with her. "We'll have the whole place to ourselves," she said.

He was reluctant at first, but then he said he would, bringing a large suitcase filled with what he said was necessary for his comfort. A coffee press, whole grain bread, soap without chemicals, and even a laundry bag.

He kept his clean clothing folded inside his suitcase. She made fun of him in a loving way about all this, and he replied that, like most people, she might be confusing order and practicality with obsession.

For almost the whole week, he cooked—he mostly avoided restaurants—they were a waste of money and a harbinger of germs. After two nights together, he gave up sleeping with her after a session of lovemaking—he was too used to sleeping alone.

She was put off and a bit let down.

When next they made love, she found the pressure he applied to her breasts irritated her to the same degree it had aroused her during their first cozy encounters inside the trailer.

She worried the relationship wouldn't last and yet, during those anxious moments, couldn't imagine life without him. His sharp good looks were perfect, his features in proportion as if he'd arranged them himself, and she thought she could be content looking at him for the rest of her life, even though it annoyed her when he became jittery and nervous hearing sounds from the other apartments, or how he barely spoke to her when he was thinking of his projects, or how he seemed to be waiting for her to finish a tale she was relating to amuse him about the architect she worked for so that he could speak so that she would do the "listening." By the end of the week, she was aware that their attempt to live together pleasantly had exhausted them both.

On what would turn out to be their last night together—a surprise birthday celebration—he left the apartment to pick up the special cake he'd had a baker make for her. He'd been gone for almost thirty minutes when he called. He was in a phone booth. He was miserable. He was getting in too deep and wasn't ready. He hated himself for telling her like this—but in a few days, he was leaving for Montreal—he'd been offered a job there and had accepted. "I've been desperate all week, wanting to tell you and struggling at the same time to figure out what was right for us. You'll be better off without me, Katherine."

Of course, she was shocked and terribly hurt and spoke hastily without thinking of what she'd been aware of for some time. "Is Jenny going with you?"

Silence at his end, and she hung up, afraid he'd say that she was, and she'd beg him not to leave her or ask him to give their love more time.

Later that evening, standing at the front window, the lamppost cast a moody light over the street, like in the black and white forties movies he was so fond of. Snow frosted the decorative iron railings and the narrow steps up to the apartment door. A few leftover Christmas wreaths swung against the windowpanes, making a scraping sound as if trying to hold on. *He'll be back, he'll miss me, and any moment, he'll ride up the street on his motorcycle.* A loud knock on the door, and a man's voice shouted, "I know you're in there!"

She opened the door. It was her downstairs neighbor. He shoved a square white box at her. "They rang my bell when you didn't answer. I knew you were up here. I heard you walking back and forth. Everything all right?"

She nodded, said thanks, and shut the door.

Frosted with coconut, the cake was artfully adorned with chocolate-glazed architectural symbols—the most remarkable cake she'd ever seen. She stared at it, actually admired it, thinking how considerate he'd been to order it for her. She felt a brief pang of tenderness for him before covering the box and throwing it all into the trash. She wept bitterly, and, like a teen filled with angst, she listened to soulful music that only deepened her despair.

She asked herself unrealistic questions (she thought later on). *Why had she met him? Why had he left? What had she done to make him leave? And the worst. Had he been with Jenny the whole time?*

Of course, he had!

Prior to Jake, she'd never behaved in this way with anyone, throwing herself heedlessly into a relationship, nor would she in any afterward. For a very long time, she hurt terribly, and her wounded pride embarrassed her. She'd been naïve and, for a while, held onto the notion that her heart was broken and that he was the only man she could ever love.

But something more nagged at her.

She'd committed fully to someone she barely knew, someone untrustworthy. She hadn't listened to her inner voice like Luke had taught her to do whenever she was conflicted. "You don't need me to give you an answer, Katherine. Just listen to your inner voice."

If she had, her inner voice would have told her she should have been more cautious.

She thinks of Mac and is aware of how much she needs him. How much she has always needed him. *What is it that she is hoping for when he is here?*

A car comes up the drive, and Katherine looks out and sees Ellen's dark green Honda. *"Oh, no!"* she whispers, wanting to have this first meeting with Mac all to herself.

Katherine's relationship with her aunt has never been easy. After her mother died, Ellen came to live with them. Katherine resented her, blaming her, as children sometimes do, she supposes, for her mother's absence.

Ellen is carrying a bundle under one arm, and in her hands is yet another casserole. She's been bringing them two, three times a week. She is shaking her head and talking aloud, and more than any kindness her aunt performs, this somehow touches Katherine, finding some vulnerability of aging in her former combatant.

Ellen now has her own key. She was so upset when she couldn't get into the house, declaring that it had never been locked up in her lifetime, that Lucy gave her one, with a warning that for now, considering what happened to Katherine, the doors would stay locked. Lucy was surprisingly stern, telling Ellen not to disturb Katherine and to always remember to lock up before leaving. Ellen was put out but did what Lucy asked.

Katherine hears Ellen placing the casserole in the fridge and then her marching footsteps in the hall toward the sitting room.

Triumphantly, she holds a long, narrow pillow out as if it is something that Katherine has asked her to bring. "Look what I found! It's perfect! Small enough to fit in that oversized briefcase you cart around." (Katherine feels it is useless to try explaining again that it is sizeable because it often holds samples for her clients.) "You can slip it out and place it for support in the small of your back. They'll all be too preoccupied to notice if my recollection of business meetings is accurate."

The pillow, evidence of her disability, momentarily surprises Katherine.

She examines it closely. Narrow and oblong in shape, covered in a plain, canvas-like material. She thinks of what it might be like to actually use it, adjusting it before the start of a meeting in conference rooms at Cole & Siegel, at Charter Oak, at a dealer's showroom, and how it would suggest weakness or, worse, provide an opening for people to ask about what happened, to offer sympathy, condolences, to comment on her condition as if she'd been changed in some way.

Her back muscles are weak and spasm after ten minutes in a chair without support. The spasms are certainly a warning Katherine must take seriously if she wants to get back to her apartment and to work.

She has been lying in bed, working on the bid sheets for the Moses Rocket interiors. They were in her briefcase, and she passed a message to Pete and Sy through Lucy that she was working on them. But even though she's stopped taking the pain meds that had caused drowsiness and disinterest, it's been difficult to concentrate on the pages of computerized specifications.

Crime victim! Like someone pointing a finger, calling her names. Not the jargon she's used to, such as *space standards, dimensions, workstations,* words whose meanings hold little terror other than successfully meeting her clients' expectations—a challenge in itself.

The pain in her back has now swiveled down to her left leg. She's angry that she is an assault victim and angry over Ellen's gift.

"What's wrong, Katherine?"

"Nothing," she says, shifting her position, looking disdainfully at the pillow, deciding she will get the back brace Doc Cousins recommended that can be worn discreetly under her clothing. She remembers to thank Ellen, and her aunt's face brightens that her gift hasn't been rejected. "Do you want to try it out right now?"

She shakes her head. "Maybe later, Aunt Ellen."

"Where should I put it?"

She swallows a somewhat crude thought and says she'll take it upstairs and try it out later.

"Where's Lucy?"

"Getting dressed. She's going to lunch with her friend Margaret."

"What takes her so long? I can be ready to go anywhere in five minutes."

"I remember."

Water rushes down a pipe and reaches the first floor. A loud knock erupts from beneath the floorboards. "That god-awful pipe makes such a racket!" Ellen cries. "Luke should've had it fixed!"

"He didn't mind the noise. He said it made him feel at home."

"Fiddlesticks! He didn't want to break through the plaster."

"He didn't know what he'd find. It's expensive to modernize the plumbing in a house this old. We talked about it once—"

"He could well afford it. We both know he didn't want to change a thing in this house, and there are some things he should have, for Lucy's sake."

"What do you mean?"

"That wood stove, for a start!"

Katherine can't dash out of the room with some excuse and feels cornered.

"Listen to me, Katherine. This morning I woke up at three o'clock. I was surprised—you know I always sleep right through the night," and Ellen goes on, not expecting Katherine to answer. "It occurred to me that if I keeled over tomorrow or met eternity in my sleep or fell down the cellar stairs and broke my hip—my worst fear because I have a low pain tolerance, and it's anyone's guess how long it would take for someone to find me—it wouldn't matter to a soul."

"For heaven's sake, Aunt Ellen!"

"Don't look at me like that. It's almost a relief. Attachments mean burdens and responsibilities. It's less confusing, emotionally, to live alone. I enjoyed my job at the bank. I like routine and predictability and wouldn't change anything about my life." She motions toward Lucy upstairs. "I never wallow in regrets."

Good for you, Katherine thinks, and in the next instant, she wonders if Ellen's life sounds too much like her own. *Oh, where is Mac?* "I need to stretch out for a few minutes before Mac comes," she says. "I'll go lie on the bed until he gets here."

"Why don't you rest on the sofa? I've got to leave."

"Too lumpy." Katherine picks up the pillow and limps up the staircase, holding on tightly to the railing, pausing as Lucy is making her way down. They smile politely like strangers do when they pass each other in a crowded, awkward space.

"Going back to bed?"

"Until Mac comes—he must have been delayed."

Ellen calls up, "I'm off. It'd be nice to see Gerry McNulty again, but tell him I couldn't wait all day and give him my best. I always liked that boy! And Katherine, don't forget what I told you. Don't hurry back to work—no one's indispensable. Believe me, I should know."

Her words reverberate in the high hall like an aria, seeming to float among specks of gleaming dust in the light of the staircase window. "I like being alone," Katherine says to Lucy.

"I'm still getting used to it," Lucy says, looking strained and tired in her bright pink shirt.

It occurs to Katherine that her being here and the care Lucy has given her has not only been kind but has disrupted Lucy's life, her routine, and how she's managing. She should be making more of an effort to engage with her.

During her first days here, when Lucy guided her to the bathroom, brought food upstairs to her on a tray, and helped to change her clothing, Katherine felt angry and resentful and could hardly bear it when Lucy touched her. Worse, each time Lucy came into the room, her sad expression reminded Katherine painfully of Luke and what they'd both lost.

15

Katherine and Mac

Finally, Mac is here, and she goes downstairs to the sitting room to meet him as quickly as her damaged body will allow. Breathing heavily, she sits on the couch nearest the door, not wanting him to see her limp across the room, feeling nervous, waiting for him to come inside, as if he were only dropping by unexpectedly like he used to, hanging around, talking to Luke or Aunt Ellen, as if the farmhouse was his home, too. She'd like to think that nothing has changed between them, yet so much has.

Throughout the years, they've talked regularly, and he often sends photos, mostly of his children, but it must be four years since she has seen him in person, and she can hardly believe that he has come all this way just because she called him in a moment of panic and terror.

He's dressed as always—jeans and a cotton shirt with the sleeves rolled up. The high-top sneakers are something new, seeming (and an image comes to mind from photos he's sent) as if he'd come out to play catch with his children. Suddenly, she is full of remorse, her eyes brimming with tears, thinking she's never gone to California even though he'd often asked, refusing him the pleasure of seeing her again and introducing her to his children. *Why? Why had she disappointed him so many times with cursory excuses he must have found trivial and perhaps not entirely true?*

She thinks back to a time when they were eleven or twelve when all she had to do was mention some new and most likely forbidden adventure, like standing up on the bridge overlooking the railroad tracks, waiting for the speeding train, and the blast of air and energy when it came, the bridge shaking mightily as if it could collapse beneath them. Soot dusted their faces, their hair, and bare skin so that they had to wash up in secret at a nearby pond before returning home. She always felt exhilarated after their trips to the bridge, but Mac didn't like it, yet he wouldn't let her go alone.

Somehow Aunt Ellen discovered what they were doing. She informed Katherine's father, and they blamed Mac, and he never denied being the instigator. Katherine was grounded, and her father said she could no longer have Mac as a friend. "I thought that boy was trustworthy," her father said.

Katherine refused to give him up and carried on in a way they had not seen before. Luke was sent up to her room to calm her down.

Sobbing in Luke's arms, she told him it was all her fault. Thus Mac was vindicated, and Luke thanked him for protecting her but added that it would be wiser in the future to talk her out of such activities, and Mac promised he would.

She also remembers how, without a word, he left her for California. It was a terrible shock, a hard thing to get over, to forgive. She thought she was being brave and honest regarding their relationship. *Was she?*

Or was she somehow frightened by his declaration (for that's what it was)? He'd approached her with such earnest devotion, leaving her feeling as if she'd lost control somehow. When he left, she was angry, hurt, and then bereft.

"Mac!" she calls out the window. "The porch door is open."

As he always had, he comes in with a big smile and a cheerful expression. He looks down at her, and she looks up at him. What is there to say? "Sorry, I'm late, Kat."

"I—I hardly recognize you—when did you grow a beard?"

"A little while back."

"I like it. You look like a New England sea captain" (and you look more resilient, she thinks).

She feels the happiness he brings on being here and takes a closer look at him. His thick hair seems a few shades lighter. *The infamous California sun?* She thinks he is not overtly handsome but a tall, good-looking, strong-looking man. Unlike Lucy, who avoids making eye contact with her, and Ellen, who faces her but looks above her head or over her shoulders, he looks directly at her, at the swollen black and blue welt below her eye, disfiguring the face he treasures. "Kat," he says, leaning over her chair and softly kissing her bruise, and she feels for an instant like a hurt child, glad and grateful for this tenderness.

"It's all right, Mac. I look worse than I feel." (Not true.)

There is, too, a noticeable difference, some knowledge in his eyes, his expression, and the manner in which he speaks and looks at her that is new, something that she would be unlikely to detect during one of their lengthy phone conversations, especially as she does most of the talking.

He smells of soap, a clean, masculine scent, and she wonders if he has ever used the bay rum aftershave she'd sent him at Christmas.

It was a last moment kind of gift and maybe too intimate, she worried at the time, but she sent it anyway.

He pulls an ottoman to a spot in front of her chair and sits with his legs sprawled to one side, his face in profile.

Years ago, he sent her a black and white postcard, a photo of two old-time movie stars—Clark Gable embracing Loretta Young—with the words "I did it!" scrawled on the back. There had been no formal wedding. The image of him married, belonging to someone, connected in a binding agreement, did not fit with her idea of the person with whom she'd once spent so much time with in her youth. Nevertheless, she hoped he'd be happy.

She'd sent them one of those over-the-top wedding cards citing the blessings of marriage and all the obstacles they'd have to overcome in life but that the "togetherness" of it all, "the sacrifices," would be worth it, enclosing it with an expensive gift, a beautiful crystal fruit bowl. Apparently, Sally wasn't the kind of woman who sent "thank you" notes. Mac never mentioned the gift, so Katherine thought it might have gone astray or been overlooked somehow. She also sent gifts when the children were born, most likely a teddy bear, which was her traditional gift for friends with babies, but again received no acknowledgments.

She realized that Sally might resent her relationship with Mac, but she wouldn't give him up, although she stopped sending gifts or cards and continued her friendship with him by phone and email. She assumed he communicated when Sally wasn't around but never asked, not really wanting to know.

When Luke and Caroline were still small children, Mac called her late one night. His voice slurred as if he'd been drinking—not like him at all. "Sally and I have separated," he said. He'd just signed the divorce papers and sent them to Seattle, where Sally was now living on a houseboat. He was reluctant to talk about what had happened. "The children are safe with me, Katherine."

Almost as if she had not made the call to him the night Lucy brought her here from the emergency room, waking up in her childhood bed, barely able to move, believing she was going to die, that her body was letting go, feeling the tremors in her hands, choking on her words—I need you—and his shock, asking her where she was calling from and what happened, and the only words she could get out were that she needed him before the room darkened and the phone fell out of her hand. She now asks quietly, "How long are you here for?"

"I'm taking a flight back tonight. The kids are covered for two days, and I've got a client flying in from Denver."

Expecting to have at least a few days of his company, his companionship, so seeing him now, just for the last few minutes, makes her feel so much better. She's disappointed and childishly upset. *He was mine, first, before Sally and the children.*

"Katherine, I am sorry. But I don't like leaving the kids for any length of time."

"They must be eight and ten by now."

"Caroline is eleven, and Luke is almost thirteen. I would have brought them with me now that they're older, and I will another time, but they're caught up in programs they enjoy in the summer months. Veronia is also disappointed I can't stay longer."

"Veronia! How old is your mother now?"

"Seventy-two."

"Seventy-two! Is she well?"

"She's fine, except for cataracts. She keeps herself busy. She works now only when she's interested in the part she's offered and has taken up gardening, even joined a garden club—can you imagine?"

No, Katherine can't but doesn't say it. She thinks it might have been kind, if not for Veronia but for him if she'd stopped in to see her once in a while. Suddenly she laughs, pictures the two of them as children, and the fear she had of approaching the door of her new friend's house. "Remember the day you told me she was a movie star?"

"Actress," he says.

"I'd just lost my mother—I wanted you all to myself. How could I compete with an actress?"

"You never had to compete with anyone." With that, he stands up and stretches.

It seems intimate somehow, this flexing of arms as if he'd just gotten out of bed—masculine and familiar. She realizes that women must find him attractive.

"I spent yesterday on a plane, and I was inside with Veronia all morning after church. Come on; it's a shame to sit inside on an afternoon like this. I'd really like to walk around the property."

"My leg—I'm sorry, I can't..."

"Lucy told me a little, Kat."

"The x-rays show nothing's wrong." She looks up at him. "Do you think this limp, the pain, and the discomfort, are all in my head?"

"No, not with what you've been through—it must have been terrible."

"Yes, it was—it is—" she says.

"You know we'd make quite a couple now," and he turns his head.

She sees the damage to his right ear. Instead of a continuous curve at the bottom, there is a piece missing, as if someone took a small bite out of it. "My god, Mac! What happened?"

"Remember that motorcycle accident?"

She answers truthfully. "I'd forgotten."

"The doctor wanted to make it whole again—I don't know. I was afraid it would look fake."

He grins and says, "I had nightmares it would detach, break off like a potato chip or something."

She shakes her head. "I just can't picture you on a motorcycle. You were always so cautious."

"Oh, I changed for a while," he adds with some lightheartedness as if at this stage of his life, it's better to make jokes about some experiences he's had. "After the accident, just the thought of getting on the bike made me break out in a cold sweat. I felt foolish around Sally's friends, who were experienced bikers. She hated that I was giving up riding and had me meditating, eating raw vegetables, and engaging in group therapy to 'conquer my fears,' as she put it, and was angry when I sold my Harley."

She is eager to hear whatever he wants to tell her.

"What really happened between you and Sally? I never asked. I—I didn't want to pry."

"One night, she'd dragged me to one of those staged group sessions that I hated. In the middle of a hug from someone I didn't know—it seemed to me that people I'd met two minutes before would suddenly stand up and embrace me, actually cling to me as they might do with an old friend or a lover—I couldn't stand it, and I walked out.

"I waited for Sally outside, but she never showed up. That was the first time she took off. We hadn't been married for that long."

This new knowledge of the pain he must have endured with Sally touches her. *What drew him to her in the first place?*

"At some point," he says, "I think it was after Caroline was born, Sally became unhappy. She felt tied down, bored, bored with me, too, I thought, and regretted having the children. I didn't know how to fix the problem. Then she became friendly with a group of bikers and wanted us to join them, so I got a bike and learned to ride."

"What about the children?"

"Good friends of mine, an older couple, Tom and Marci Baker, used to mind the kids when we were out riding.

"For a while, Sally seemed content. She loved the biking culture, and her friends started hanging out at the house, mostly when I was at work. I didn't much like them or how they behaved around the children.

"They played loud music, and sometimes they acted stupid, teasing the kids so they'd cry. I put a stop to that. I made very good money, and they knew I wasn't stingy with Sally. I was aware that they drank and used pot and warned her that the funds would dry up, so they were more careful when the kids were around. Usually, when her friends came over, I took the children out somewhere nice for kids, like the zoo.

"After I had my accident, Sally wouldn't give up her friends. I said I'd use the money I got from the sale of the Harley so that she could have her own car. She didn't want a car and latched onto one of the single guys and began riding with him. I knew things between us were bad, but I honestly didn't know what to do.

"At the time, we were renting a furnished house. I used to call every day around lunch to check on the kids, to see who was there with Sally.

"One day, she didn't answer the phone, so I thought maybe she was outside with the kids or had taken them for a walk. I left her a message to call me. When I didn't hear from her, I called again, but she didn't pick up. I left work in a panic. When I got to the house, I came in and called out, but it seemed no one was there. I went into the kitchen and found the children in the playpen. Luke was too old for one, but they were both in it. They looked up at me and said nothing as if they'd been warned not to make a sound.

"That's the feeling I had when I saw them. They looked tired, frightened, and hungry. 'Where is Mommy?' I said to Luke. That's when he started to cry."

Mac stops and looks at Katherine. "Can you imagine? She left Luke and Caroline in the house alone."

"No, I can't," she says, feeling sad for Mac, for the children.

"I picked them up, one in each arm, took them out to the car, and left, bringing them to Marci and Tom. They said we could stay with them for as long as I wanted.

"Marci was wonderful. She gave them a warm bath and put them in the pj's I'd left there for when they stayed overnight. Luke refused to speak. We all tried.

"Then Marci asked what they wanted for supper, and Luke, speaking for the first time, said, 'Pancakes.' I've always remembered how that got to me, a child unprotected, abandoned, wanting something so simple.

"Once they were in bed, Tom and I went back to the house. There was no sign of Sally, and I had no idea where she was. I picked up a few stuffed animals the kids liked to sleep with and a metal box containing their birth certificates and medical records.

"I left everything else there—clothes, toys, furnishings. I know it sounds crazy, but I wanted nothing from that place. I was finished with Sally. This will sound stupid, but for a long while, I thought about setting fire to that house.

"The next day, I went on a shopping spree with Marci for everything the children might need. Then I shopped for myself. The day after, I took Luke with me to buy toys—Caroline was much too young to go with us. Then I enrolled him in a progressive daycare that Marci recommended, and he loved it.

"We stayed with the Bakers until I found a house in a neighborhood nearby. Veronia came and stayed with us for over a year. When she left, Marci and Tom took care of Caroline for a few more months until she was old enough to go to the same school as Luke."

He turns away and shakes his head as if to rid himself of memories of what had happened that day. "You know how you imagine the worst that can happen?"

She doesn't answer, waiting for him to go on.

"Sally leaving the way she did, leaving them in the house alone and unprotected, was the worst thing I could think of—something that happens to other people. I had terrible nightmares—*what if I hadn't come home—what if one of her kooky friends came by and took them somewhere—what if someone had hurt them?* You can't imagine the things you worry about with kids. I felt I'd put them at risk and lost confidence. I got so bad that Marci and Tom suggested I meet with a therapist.

"Luckily, I found the right person, and that eventually helped."

Katherine feels a sense of shame. All these years, during marathon calls, telling him about her petty work problems, gossip, and failed relationships, he'd listened and empathized. Yet, when his whole life had fallen apart, he'd never told her. Why? She wants to ask, but this isn't the time, and why should he have to explain anything to her?

"Luke and Caroline—they're terrific. They are what kept me from hurting Sally or myself. They needed me."

"Yes," she says. "Oh, Mac, I'm so sorry."

"It's all in the past, Kat. No more sleepless nights wondering if I measure up to someone or some things I don't understand." He touches his altered ear almost fondly. "It's a keepsake, a reminder."

She can't help but smile. "Will you ever get it fixed?"

"Maybe, maybe someday."

He should have looked more peculiar, but his ear is not what she looks at or thinks of. He is Mac. Her best and closest friend. Her solid and dependable soulmate. Her almost lover.

He coaxes her into leaving the house, and Katherine holds on to his arm stiffly, like convalescent and caregiver, like a long-married couple. They slowly cross the wide lawn and walk beneath the maples Luke had planted on that side of the house, past a plot of strawberries that Lucy had dutifully kept up after Luke's death, up a slope to the path circling the orchard. Pausing at the stonewall, she sits down on a flat rock jutting out from the wall. Beads of sweat spot her upper lip, and she blots them with a tissue.

"This wall had crumbled, so Luke rebuilt it by himself." She pats the rock affectionately. "This rock was too heavy to move, so he built the wall around it. He used to say it reminded him of a church pew and that there was no better place for it."

A wild myrtle vine has worked its way around the rock, growing thickly through the stones. The air is gentle with a warm breeze. Everything smells fresh and pleasing.

"Do you live in one of those houses built into the side of a hill with no foundation?" she says.

"Sally wanted to, but the mudslides scared me off. Once we had the kids, I wouldn't consider it. Occasionally, I did put my foot down."

"And she paid attention?"

"As I told you, I was the breadwinner."

A breeze stirs the ferns. Birds scavenge in the undergrowth.

"Katherine, enough about me. There isn't anything more I want to tell you—it's all in the past."

He picks up her hand and holds it in both of his. "Do you want to talk about what happened to you?"

In this special place with Mac, her attacker's unpleasantly foul scent comes to her again strongly. Lately, she's beginning to remember more details, like how dark it had been in the underground garage and how a sign reminds you to remove sunglasses. But instead of her thoughts going forward to whom it might have been that had hurt her, they revert back to Wallace. She feels a sense of relief believing he is the one, despite what Detective

Hays has told her. Although it is irrational, it is simpler, easier to picture Wallace, his small and furtive darting eyes and slight, wiry build, and she even imagines him smelling like the stench of rotting garbage. The idea of someone random who she has never seen frightens her too much. She won't tell this to Mac. She wouldn't know where to begin or how to explain or justify her suspicions. "I don't remember exactly," she says. It is a small fib that won't ruin her time with him. He is probably aware that she is holding back, but he doesn't show it.

"When do you go back to work?"

"The end of next week."

She looks so worn, so exhausted, the welt below her eye still raw and angry. "That soon, Kat?"

"I am tired. But I'm anxious about the project, and it's better if I get back there."

"Why is it better?"

How can she express her fears? Her weariness in the preceding months, double-checking everything regarding the interiors, the schematics that ultimately will be recognized as hers, whether or not she's initiated them. "What would I do, Mac? I'm going out of my mind, worrying. I'm in the middle of this project, a wonderful old building along with the rehab of small houses, cottages really, that were very well designed and constructed, but the architect in charge is mainly interested in pleasing the client and finishing on time."

"What matters now is you. Why don't you take a few months off, come out to California before—"

"Give up my work? Give up Moses Rocket? I couldn't!" Her fingers move nervously against the fabric of her skirt.

Her leg begins to tremble, and he notices. "Hey, it's all right. Of course, you have to do what feels right for you."

He looks away for a moment and quietly says, "I've never forgotten how beautiful it is here."

Her life is a wreck, and she's relieved to talk about something else.

"Luke brought it back to the way it was when my mother was alive. My father never had the time or the interest."

"Luke wrote to me about how your father had sold off most of the land before he went to Florida."

"He relished making deals. At the dinner table, on the rare nights he was at home when we were kids, he used to tell Luke about his investments and stock market killings as if he were trying to teach him how the world worked—"

"How his world worked."

"Without any warning, he called Luke and told him he had been approached by a developer wanting to buy the farm's acreage. They had a terrible argument, my father declaring that nothing could stop development, that land values were dramatically increasing, and that he would sell off before everyone else. And he did, making a great deal of money."

"Luke was a successful lawyer. Why didn't he buy the land?"

"He wanted to, but my father told him that for what he was getting for it, Luke couldn't afford it. Then Luke refused to do the legal work for the transaction.

"While Luke never forgave him for selling, my father never forgave Luke for 'having to spend good money' for what Luke could have done for nothing. Ironically, a short time later, my father had his stroke. After his death, Luke and I were left with a small fortune.

"I wanted Luke to have it all so that he could go to the developer in hopes of buying back the parcel. But my father had told Luke the truth. The value of the land, sliced up for development, was much more than Luke could match."

Mac shoves his hands in his pockets and surveys the orchard, the towering pines above. "What a shame for Luke."

"I found a diary he'd kept, recording what was bulldozed. *Today trashed the floor of wild violets; today the fronds of cinnamon fern and princess pine; today the secret places of jack-in-the-pulpit mother had shown me as a boy.*'

"The names of the streets—Mayflower Terrace, Alden Circle—disgusted Luke. He was used to names like 'Finch Street' for our neighbor John Finch, the farmer who owned land near us. Luke complained to the town council that the street names proposed for the development were inappropriate. There was nothing they could do. Nothing they would do.

"Lucy and I were worried. Neither of us had seen this side of him before—a get-even, almost mean temperament. Nothing had ever brought it out, not even giving in to my father about law school when Luke wanted to study botany.

"From the day heavy equipment came in to begin excavating, Luke watched over the construction. He used to call me and ask me questions about building codes. He reported any violation—the proper amount of road frontage for building sites, a foundation a few feet too close to a wetlands area—and the developer had to investigate each allegation and correct each infraction before the construction resumed. 'Thirty-four houses, paved drives, fenced yards, and expensive landscaping rose out of a parcel that had been woods and farmland since 1640,' I remember Luke saying with rage and with tears in his eyes.

"Oh, he was bitter! He mocked the architecture, the concrete foundations, the vinyl siding, and the plastic shutters. His only comfort, he told me once, was the sight of this white, center chimney farmhouse with its steeply pitched roof and shutters of the old kind made of wood that could be closed against a storm."

"Still and all, this is an enviable spot—an oasis—yet a lot for Lucy to take care of."

"She's hired someone to do most of the work."

"She intends to stay then?"

"Of course."

"I've always thought of her as a 'city girl.' Luke mentioned one time that she wasn't all that happy to leave their home in West Hartford."

"It must've been hard. She designed an addition, a painting studio that I don't think she had a chance to use before they sold the house and came here. Luke made her a new studio upstairs in the barn—"

"It's funny, the things you don't know about the people you think you know so well."

"I've always assumed she'd stay. I hope she will. Before what happened to bring me back, I didn't spend much time here, but now I can't imagine never coming back to visit."

"Remember the cattails? The way we lighted punks up near the shallows?"

"Yes, I remember."

She's feeling very tired, and what he's remembering seems so long ago and, after all, they were children, but she doesn't say what might hurt or tarnish his memories.

"Did you know that Veronia became good friends with Luke, and Lucy, too?"

"You told me once he was her lawyer."

"Much more than that. Veronia had saved for years, expecting me to want to go to college. I'd already been accepted at my first choice—remember? I told her I wanted to wait a year. She argued that if I didn't go now, I'd lose my place. She kept pushing and wouldn't stop. Uncertain, I said some awful, hurtful things I didn't have any basis for about her and my father, ran out of the house and came here. You had already left for school. Luke must've known how lost I was feeling without you.

"He and I went for a long walk. He didn't say much—he just listened, giving me the room to talk about how I was feeling. I realized I'd overreacted and went home to Veronia, apologized, and a week later left for school."

They pause beneath a huge old beech tree. She wonders if there is a woman—someone significant—in Mac's life.

She pictures his children and some unknown female catering to them, and Mac dazed and unaware, happy that they all get along together. "How is your new job working out?"

"At the last minute, I decided not to take it. I started my own business—Internet Tech Security Specialist. My clients, mostly company execs, are all over the country." He laughs. "I set up an office the kids call 'The Command Center.' I work on projects until they get home from school and spend the next few hours driving them to basketball, soccer, baseball—"

"What about when you travel?"

"Marci and Tom take over. And when I can, I bring the kids with me. They love going."

"You were way ahead on computers."

"I suppose I have a good reputation."

"You're too modest."

His voice takes on some contained energy.

"You know the best thing about my new business is that I can do it anywhere. Sometimes I get homesick for the change of seasons, and California has grown to seem unmanageable now that the kids are getting older. I guess I would like a more traditional setting for them, and I've never really liked cooking a turkey on a spit at Thanksgiving. We'll probably move before Luke starts high school."

"Where will you go?"

"I was coming East this fall to introduce the kids to New England."

She remembers the only time he came East was when the children were much younger. She'd been in Paris with a man she was fond of, more of a friend than a lover, as it turned out.

"Veronia is getting older, and it's harder for her to travel. She adores them and likewise." He smiles and adds, "They both love to ski."

"Do they see Sally?"

"Not really. It's awkward for the three of them. And she doesn't like having to visit them with conditions."

"Conditions?"

"That's right. I got full custody when we divorced, and the judge agreed on only supervised visitation for her. Although she is sober and off drugs, I will never leave them alone with her again."

She can't quite take in that he might return to New England with his children. *How wonderful that could be!* As they walk back to the house, she thinks, again, that it was selfish to ask him to come all this way for what turned out to be a few hours—although she feels so much better for having seen him.

Back in the sitting room, he takes her into his arms. "I'm so sorry this terrible thing has happened to you, Kat."

Feeling safe and loved, she thinks about how he does everything just right. She wouldn't have wanted this cherished holding of her until this moment. In his arms, she wants to weep, purge herself of the terrifying moments in the van.

"I wish I could stay longer," he says.

"No, I understand." She thanks him again. "Oh, Mac, I shouldn't have asked you to come all this way."

He lets go of her gently. "Of course, you should have, and of course, I would come—did you think even for a moment that I wouldn't?"

She watches him walk toward Veronia's car, his back straight, his head to one side, one arm swinging as if he's pushing himself through the air. His right arm is lifted, and his hand is spread over his damaged ear. "A habit," she thinks. He reaches the car, waves, and shouts that he'll call tonight before he goes.

She knows he is leaving for California because his children need him at home, and after all she's learned today, she understands that, of course, they do.

Still, she wishes he could have stayed a little longer.

He has a life distinct and separate from hers that seems, for the most part, to satisfy him in ways that are meaningful, despite everything Sally did to destroy him.

She stands at the porch's open door. The car passes by, and he turns his head to look at her, to shout goodbye. "I'll see you soon, Katherine."

How she loves him! "Mac! Wait!"

But the blue of his shirt is a winged flash as if a bird has soared through the green landscape, and then he is gone.

Back in her room, she picks up the card that has been lying all this time on the nightstand. First thing in the morning, she calls Dr. Rablen's office. She doesn't expect to spend months in therapy. A few visits until she feels stronger and more confident. That is all she needs.

16

Rangy Barstow

Early on a Sunday, Rangy picks up Kitty and puts her securely into the wide pocket of his overcoat. She meows and meows, and he comforts her.

"You be quiet. I'll let you out when we get there," he says, like a caring parent soothing his child.

The sound of him unlatching the door brings forward the army of cats he has collected. Some hiss, others meow and scratch at the door, and others only stare at him. They all want out of the cellar. He thought he was saving them from hurt and the large toms, but all he's done is confine them. He should let them all out of this dark cellar, or maybe a few at a time?

He's afraid they'll hang around outside, meowing to get back in for food. They'll draw attention. They have all grown. They frighten

Kitty. He wishes now he'd never brought them here. He really hadn't thought it through like Dad always taught him he should.

He has to move fast and braces himself, opening the door. "Scat, scat! Get away!" he cries, and a few run into the cellar's far corners. One climbs up Rangy's leg, trying to attach himself. Rangy throws him off and quickly shuts the door. He feels awful, but he doesn't know what to do with the poor creatures.

It is a dry, warm, and sunny morning with a soft wind, a day of promise, and Rangy makes his way toward the oldest cemetery in Hartford. At this time of year, ferocious weeds crop up, and he likes to clear the plots before the sun is at its hottest. His pace quickens, and Kitty quiets, her tiny face peeking out, her eyes blinking, unused to such bright light.

Once they reach the cemetery, he lets Kitty go free. "Go on. Go play. You know I have work to do," and she scampers away.

With all of the losses and the changes he has endured, the cemetery is one of his favorite places. Split in two by the highway a number of years ago, it is mostly neglected.

Fortunately, his family lies—he won't think of them as *buried*— on the high side of the road that remains attached to the city, on a soft rolling hillside with old trees shading the resting places of the Barstows.

As always, Rangy stops first at a long-abandoned stone house, a caretaker's cottage. He walks around to the back to a rusty tap that is hidden behind an area of overgrown brush.

He realizes then that he was so worried about the cats he'd forgotten to bring a cup with him. He turns the handle and puts his hands under the spout, catching some of the slow-flowing water onto his palms and drinking it as fast as he can. It tastes a bit rusty, but it is cold and the only water he has access to. He wishes (as he does each time he comes to the cemetery) that he could get inside this small and pretty building. It would make him a perfect home. If only there was someone to ask, someone in charge who'd let him use the house in exchange for watching over the graves. At one time, he used to come here with Dad. An old man lived in the stone house then. He wasn't too friendly.

Once when he was a boy, when Dad was cleaning up around the gravestones, Rangy saw the old man come out of the house and go around to the back. Rangy followed him, wanting to tell him that he liked his house and if he could see what it was like inside. But when he did, the man hollered and told him to "Go away!" He got scared and ran back to Dad, and he said it was best to leave the fellow alone. And Rangy always did. Then when he and Dad came one time, the cottage was locked up, and it didn't look like anyone lived there anymore.

Rangy returns to the front of the house, appraising the gray blocks of stone that make up the walls, the lower front and side windows shielded with black iron bars, the high row of unbreakable windows that vandals have not shattered, the panes dark with soot that almost conceal the colored glass pictures they protect. Rangy has always been drawn to these jewel-like figures with golden rings above their heads, the sheep, the birds, and the flowers.

Where could he find a place like that?

It's been so long since he's had a real wash. He's lost another tooth in the back of his mouth, and another is coming loose. He'd always brushed his teeth. Without water, it's impossible for him to do what he's been taught. No clean water to shave, either, although his whiskers are sparse, a blessing now that he thinks of it. He's gotten chased from the washroom at the bus station where he sometimes goes, warned not to return. People look at him strangely and frighten him.

People's reactions have always been incomprehensible to him, like when he goes into the library to use the men's room. There is one woman at the front desk that smiles at him, and he hurries past her to use the facilities, but there is another one there at times that won't let him use them. "You're not allowed in here," she says in a loud voice so that he turns away, embarrassed and ashamed. "I've told you that before!" He wonders what is wrong with him and why people—strangers—can be so mean.

He walks on a familiar path toward the mounded earth of his ancestors. As if they could rise up and disappear, he first counts the weather-beaten, hardly readable stones and is not certain why he would, and maybe he's afraid they could be stolen, and it does make him feel better when he finds they are all here. The first Barstow in the 1700s to the infant child with only a flat rock for a headstone to the most recent grave, that of his father's. *Dad!* he cries. He misses his father terribly. His cry brings Kitty back, and he picks her up, cuddling her against him until she squirms herself free to chase a butterfly.

Rangy takes a plastic bag out of his pocket and picks up the cans and food wrappers left by the vandals, dropping them in the bag. He pulls up the weeds around each Barstow grave. While he wipes dirt off of the stones with his coat sleeve, he thinks of how he might stop work on Moses Rocket. His first try failed miserably. *He'd gone too far, too far.* But it all happened so fast, and he only wanted to speak to the woman about Moses Rocket. *She wouldn't listen.* He inspects the bite mark on his hand. He must find her to say sorry. He's even gone back to the site when he thought it was safe enough, but her car was never there. He hopes that nothing bad has happened to her.

After an hour or so, with no solutions to any of his dilemmas, Rangy feels satisfied that at least the burial plots are well cared for. He looks around and can almost weep for the overturned stones. The streaks of paint sprayed on some of the other gravestones. The high choking weeds. He can't resist lifting out a large clump of mottled grass on one of the mounds, still soaked with overnight dew. He flings it out to the paved road, and it lands on the highway, where the wheels of a slow passing truck grind it into the tar.

On the truck's side panel, there is a large picture of a cat. In the background, there are more cats dressed in bibs, holding knives and forks, their tongues hanging out.

To his mind, it is a terrible picture, a disrespectful one. Again he is reminded that he has to find a solution for all of those cats in his cellar. There's more than he can feed. He's even used some of the money Dad left for him. He also fears his time in the cellar may be running out. One day the workmen might lift up the hatch to remove the pipe. *Where can he go?*

By late morning, he is hot and tired. He has no wish to return to the cellar. No wish to wander the city. No desire to roam the Moses Rocket building. He looks yearningly at the stone house and thinks it might be cool inside.

Suddenly, he runs up to the massive door and pushes his body against the solid wood panels, using all of his considerable strength to try and break in. But the door won't give. Probably the reason vandals have not destroyed the stone house—they can't get inside either.

Rangy takes off his coat. He picks up Kitty, returns to his family's burial plots, and lies down in the space in between his parents' graves. Kitty's a little sleepy now and curls up next to him, closing her eyes.

Rangy pulls his coat over them both.

Anyone passing here wouldn't notice that beneath the heap of what looks like discarded rags lies a man called Rangy Barstow, and it is unlikely he'll be disturbed. The boys that desecrate the gravesites usually come at night, and by that time, he and Kitty will have gone.

17

Sy

What a night! Heather woke them up with a horrible scream. They jumped out of bed at the same time and ran to her room. Flicking on the overhead light, they found Heather sitting up in bed, sobbing so hard she couldn't catch her breath or tell them what was wrong.

Julie picked her up and told him she would stay with Heather until she fell asleep. It is now five-thirty, and Julie only came back to bed an hour ago.

He slips out of bed, and on his way to his office where his clothes are hung, he thinks he'll work from home today, give Julie a break—she must be exhausted. He feels, too, that he owes her something, some explanation for how he behaved last night, but then he remembers that the monthly project meeting is scheduled for today. He has to be there to bring his colleagues up to date on Moses Rocket.

The Keeper

David Siegel, Jed's partner, is semi-retired, but he will be attending the meeting. A rumor's been spreading through the firm that David had some exciting news to report. He is on the board of various companies and non-profits and socializes regularly with Hartford's elite. Most everyone at Cole & Siegel is aware that David is a man who knows what is going on in the city, and the firm is often the beneficiary. Sy suspects that David will enlighten them all today, and most likely, it is a new business.

Sy selects clothing for the meeting that is casual, signaling that his habits are those of a young, up-and-coming architect. He rarely wears a suit, and, in fact, the only one he owns, he's never worn at the firm.

He showers and dresses hastily, going downstairs. He wants to leave the house before Julie wakes up.

After work yesterday, he'd met Julie and Heather at her parents' home for dinner. His mother-in-law Sylvia made one of his favorite meals—beef bourguignon. She enjoys cooking, and he truly appreciates the meals she prepares that are very much like what his mother had served. He assumes that many women of their generation didn't worry too much about cholesterol, salt, red meat, and desserts.

The conversation at dinner was light-hearted and pleasant, focused mostly on Heather and the enjoyment of a mouth-watering apple tart spiked with Calvados.

Afterward, they all helped with the clean-up, even Heather, and then Julie and her mother went for a long walk while Sy and Ben sat out in the yard, watching Heather racing around the yard, attempting to catch fireflies in the jar her grandmother had given her.

He tries not to think of Apple when he is with Sylvia and Ben, imagining how disappointed and heartbroken they would be knowing he was involved with another woman. The thought saddens him.

Ben is a highly regarded therapist, a kind and gentle man who Sy deeply admires. Ben reminds him of his father and what it was like being with his father, entrusting him with problems or worries. For some time, Sy had wanted to bring up Will Swanson, hoping Ben would offer some insight into Swanson's behavior or at least get some advice on how best to work with him, but it was a tranquil evening, and he was feeling such joy hearing Heather's shouts of happiness in the semi-dark, he decided not to bring it up.

Unfortunately, Julie spoiled the visit. As they were leaving, heading to their respective cars, Julie stopped him and asked if he realized this was the first evening he'd spent time with his daughter in almost a week, emphasis on the word *daughter*, he noted, and she would have said more, but he became angry and stopped her with harsh words he immediately regretted, reminding her that he had responsibilities, a family to support.

He'd been cruel. A bully. *A jerk!* The worst thing was that he realized he was hurting her but couldn't stop himself, and almost out of breath, he finished with, "What more do you want from me, Julie?" and walked alone to his car.

As soon as Heather was in bed, he apologized a bit stiffly, promising that after this project, he'd spend more time at home with Heather. It wasn't enough. She refused to discuss it any further last night. It was just as well. He felt so guilty, so tired, he might have blurted out the truth, confessed that he was having an affair with a woman he couldn't give up. Thinking what that would do to Julie, to Heather, to his in-laws was terrifying.

Julie is honest, intelligent, and sensitive. She'll want a reasonable explanation for why he'd lashed out (and that is exactly what he did), and he thinks *"fair enough."* What worries him is that during the rational and thoughtful conversation, he knows they will have, she is perceptive. *Would she ask if he was seeing someone?* He assures himself that she won't. He has never once before been unfaithful.

He cannot give up the pleasure, the thrill that he experiences when he and Apple are together.

Moreover, he knows Apple is vulnerable.

He recalls the notes he'd found in his father's patient files, an innocent young girl sitting out in the dark yard, alone and frightened. He never did learn why she sleepwalked and thought it was possibly a phase she went through.

When they are together, they rarely mention the intervening years in their lives. Some part of him would like to know what she's experienced, but, at the same time, he doesn't really want to know there may have been someone important in her life that she might have cared for deeply.

All this brings him to what happened the last time he saw her when they were teenagers, and he feels a bleak despair for the years she's been absent from his life.

He'd behaved cowardly that night and afterward was too afraid to go back to her neighborhood or to her uncle's shop, fearful of meeting up with the rough boys they'd encountered.

He and Apple were sitting together on the first floor of The Salem Funeral Home, a few blocks from where she lived. The building, a large house, really, had been empty for some time and was up for sale.

Apple had left her uncle's shop and was supposed to go straight home, but once they met, she insisted on bringing him here. They had nowhere else to go and were constantly aware of who might see them and report back to her parents, or Uncle V. They climbed into the house through a back window.

It was December. "I can only stay for a few minutes," she said.

"How do you know about this place, Apple?"

"Everyone in my neighborhood knows about it. This is the biggest house around here. It's been empty for ages. My mom said people are superstitious. Nobody wants to live in a house where— you know—"

"You've been in this house before?"

"No, but I heard the boys talking about it at Uncle V's."

"Why? What do they do in here?"

"I don't know."

"What if they come now?"

"Nobody will. Uncle V says that Italians always go home at suppertime."

She was so trusting, so young. He wondered what he would do if the boys showed up.

It was colder in the house than outside. A streetlight shone through the windows, putting her face in silhouette. He could smell the scent of coffee from her uncle's shop on her clothing. Their stretched-out legs matched for distance on the floorboards. Might she grow taller and tower over him? That thought worried him, too.

"What are you getting for Christmas?" she said.

He was startled and answered honestly. "Christmas doesn't matter much to me."

"How come?"

How could he explain? Religion wasn't discussed in his home. Unlike some of his friends, he never had a bar mitzvah. Even when he was small, little was ever said about Santa Claus. His parents, though, were always thoughtful, always generous. He remembered one time as the holiday approached that he'd asked for a chemistry set. It was expensive, and they wanted to know if this was something he was really interested in exploring. He wasn't certain. They asked him to think it over to be sure he would use it. A week later, he decided he didn't care about it one way or the other and told them he'd changed his mind.

It would be hard to tell Apple that his family wasn't into what his mother called "rituals."

"My Mom thinks Christmas is too commercial," was all he said.

"Well, I love Christmas, and I love getting presents! Our whole family gets together and takes turns celebrating at each other's houses. There are all kinds of food—and a lot of cookies."

Again, at that moment, she sounded so young, and of course she would. He was almost three years older, a senior in high school, and a trusted member of Joel Shopenhauer's firm.

He smiled at her and said, "It sounds like fun, Apple."

How he loved looking at her. The way she combed and parted her hair brushed across her forehead. Her petite nose and mouth, her unusually white skin, a pallor that crimsoned easily.

Overall, she was delicate, although her eyebrows were thick like Mrs. Messina's but lighter, much lighter, in color.

The wool mittens on her lap, knitted with reindeer and snowflakes, were those of a much younger child. He would have been satisfied to hold the hand closest to him, saying and doing nothing more.

Right then, he decided to give her a present. It would have to be special, something she hadn't thought of. The silver chain at her neck glinted. Was that the one she'd been wearing the first time he saw her?

"What did you ask for, for Christmas, Apple?"

"I'm still deciding," she said and sighed. "It's kind of nice in here. A lot quieter than at Uncle V's."

Why did she sleepwalk? What was wrong with her? If he asked about it, she would know that he'd seen her medical records, and she would be embarrassed, maybe shocked, that he would do such a thing and might not want to meet with him anymore.

She stood up and said, "I'd better go, Sy. My mom gets worried if I'm not home on time. I'll get into big trouble if she ever finds out I've come here."

They walked slowly through the shadowed rooms across the wooden floors as if their footsteps could be overheard, hearing an occasional creak that scared her as they moved toward the back of the house. Suddenly, they heard voices, and she grabbed his jacket sleeve, the first time she'd ever touched him. It felt as if his heart had actually flipped in his chest. He took her hand with confidence. "We'll go out the front door," he said. But the double oak doors were locked. He searched for a key above the molding at the top of the door. "It's not here," he said.

"Maybe it's just kids from my neighborhood. They all hang out at Uncle V's. They won't bother me."

He wouldn't say so to her, but he was frightened. "We don't know who it is, Apple. We have to find someplace to hide."

They heard the sound of glass shattering. *What if someone started a fire in the house?*

From Joel, he knew there had to be a fire escape, a way out from upstairs, and pulled her toward the staircase.

"No! I'm afraid to go up there—"

He thought of what the boys might do if they found Apple with him. He could hear Joel's voice. *"They're gonna drag you back to Uncle V's and beat the shit out of you, Kid!"*

"Trust me," Sy said, and Apple took his hand, and they ran up the staircase together. There was a lot of noise coming from the back of the house, and he wondered what the boys were doing.

"My mittens! Sy, I dropped my mittens!"

"I'll find them for you later, Apple. C'mon!"

The rooms on the second floor were empty, with nowhere to hide, so they retreated up to the third floor.

It was one large open space with a number of long wooden boxes stacked at one end. "Coffins!" Apple sobbed. "They're not coffins," he said, although he thought they probably were, the plain kind for people who couldn't afford anything nicer.

"Apple, listen to me. We'll hide at the far end, behind the boxes. We'll be safe!"

He didn't feel safe and tried to think what he would do if the boys found them. He wished he hadn't let Apple talk him into coming here.

Suddenly, a bright light flooded the room, and they heard some commotion outside. "Cop car out front!" one of the boys cried.

"We're out of here!"

Sy heard the police searching the house. One of the policemen came up to the third floor and shouted, "All clear." He opened up one of the boxes and then went right back down the stairs.

The house grew quiet again. Apple was lying next to him, crying softly. He put his arms around her, wanting to hold her there, just the two of them in the empty house.

Fifteen minutes later, they found her mittens, slipped out the back door, and he walked her home, watching from a distance until she was safely inside.

For a while after that, he thought about her a lot and hoped she'd call him again, but she never did, and knowing her family would never approve of an older boy showing interest in her, he made no further contact.

She was his ideal of flawless beauty, perfection, and innocence, but he never acted on it in any meaningful way. He left home at the end of the school year for college to take courses over the summer.

He started to date and had girlfriends, but none of them felt special like Apple. This went on for a few years, and although the vision of Apple faded somewhat, he never forgot her entirely. He remembers that a few years back—he and Julie were already married—he was attracted to a designer at the firm that reminded him of Apple, and that prompted him to send a note to Garden Street, hoping that if she didn't live there any longer, her parents might pass it on to her. She never answered, and he thought she'd forgotten him.

He hadn't seen her again until the day he brought Swanson to Genesis.

Sy usually takes coffee with him before leaving home, but today he wants to be out of the house before Julie comes downstairs. He has no defense for his late hours. He has a home office, and before Apple, it had become routine for him to have a leisurely supper with Julie and Heather, bathing his daughter, reading her a story, and then he worked for a few hours.

His desire, his need for Apple, has changed him so that, at times, his life with Julie now seems programmed and lacking in spontaneity. The rub in all of this is Heather. *How could he ever abandon her?*

In the car, he listens to the news and hears during a break that there is a traffic jam on Route 84.

He leaves the highway before the busier downtown exits, wending his way through back streets, gray, grimy, littered with debris and lined with broken-down chain link fences in front of nondescript buildings advertising resources not available in other parts of the city—tires, auto repair, heating and air-conditioning, even a pawn shop.

He imagines bringing a dozen bulldozers to this area and flattening everything, although he knows that could never happen.

The area is too settled to change. People are used to it as it is. They need what is here. And the expense would be too great.

He pulls into *Dunkin Donuts* and goes to the drive-by window, ordering coffee and a toasted bagel. He parks the car and takes a bite. After his first swallow, he feels full and drops the rest back into the paper bag.

The coffee has cooled enough, and he takes a few sips and leans back, feeling like someone heading for a day's work at a job for which he has little enthusiasm. The excitement he'd once felt, the thrill of managing his first big project at Cole & Siegel, has come to seem like pure drudgery.

Yesterday during his meeting with Swanson, he got written confirmation to hire one additional staff on the project. "Make certain your firm hires that girl we met at Genesis," he said.

Sy doesn't like admitting, even to himself, that since the day he brought Swanson to Genesis, he's felt something akin to a deep hatred for him. It began when Apple was going back and forth with furniture catalogs to the bookshelves and the table where they were all sitting.

Each time she reached up to one of the higher shelves and her dress inched up in back, Swanson grinned, never taking his eyes off of her. Sy got up from his chair and said to Apple, "Tell me what catalogs you want, and I'll get them down." Swanson never said a word.

At work, he finds a small box marked "Special Delivery" on his desk. He opens it quickly and removes the carpet samples Swanson had insisted on considering, in colors that might work in a client's living room but are all wrong for a corporate office. He is sorry that he'd given in to Swanson's request. He should have backed Katherine at the start regarding carpet tiles. He puts the samples back into the box and, looking as if he is performing some sinister covert action, locks them into the file drawer of his desk and heads toward the conference room.

Pete is standing at the door. "Good morning, Mr. Greene. I got some good news for you. I spoke to Katherine this morning, and you'll be glad to hear she's returning to work."

He brushes past Pete, saying, "Hey, that's good news, Pete. We'll catch up later," and joins the others at the table.

He intends to bring Apple's name up in the meeting when it is his turn to update the others on his project. He won't mention Katherine's absence. It would be wrong, in bad taste, particularly with Lucy in the room, and there is no need to mention her—every one of them knows the lack of a key person creates problems.

The firm's partners are sitting side-by-side at one end, and the meeting begins, as usual, with the architects passing out copies of their project summaries. Pete jokes about putting them into File 13 as soon as he gets downstairs. They all laugh politely. For the next hour, the PAs bring their colleagues up to date.

When it's his turn, he admits he's behind schedule on Moses Rocket. "I met with Swanson yesterday, explained the problem, and he gave me the okay to hire one additional full-time person."

"Do we have that in writing?" Jed says.

"Yes, Jed. I've got it right here."

"Okay with you?" Jed says to Pete.

Pete shrugs. "I'd like to wait for Katherine."

"If Charter Oak is willing to pay for additional staff to get the project on track, we should hire someone right away," says David. The tension in the room heightens. "For the last six months, Charter Oak has been in negotiations to lease 20 floors of a building under construction downtown. I heard from a reliable source they are preparing to go ahead—it should be announced next week. We intend to bid on the project. Jed and I agree that it is crucial that anything Charter Oak wants on Moses Rocket should be done. We want Swanson to report back that we're cooperative and responsive. We want this new project and should get it. We're the largest firm in the area, and a lot of talented people work here."

The meeting winds down with everyone in a decidedly cheerful mood. New business, particularly on a project of this size, means job security and no temporary lay-offs that sometimes occur when business slows. Sy follows Jed out of the conference room and asks if he has a moment.

"Urgent?"

"I wouldn't have thought so before the meeting."

"I've got a few minutes before lunch with David. "Let's go to my office."

Sy begins with the truth, saying he had no choice, that there was no way to keep Swanson happy without breaking a few rules. "He wanted to look at furniture and pressured me to take him out to dealerships alone."

"When was this?"

"Before Katherine—"

"Why didn't she go with you?"

"He insisted on going alone. He made a point of excluding her and Tillie."

"You tell Pete?"

"No, I didn't."

"Why not?"

He is risking something here but goes ahead as honestly as he can. He feigns embarrassment, sounding as if Pete is, at times, unreasonable, too protective of his staff. "I thought it would cause more trouble than it was worth."

"You should have told Pete."

"You're right, Jed. In hindsight, I should have told Pete and Katherine."

"That's the way we work here."

"For weeks, I avoided taking Swanson out. I made excuses, but he kept insisting, saying I should charge the hours as a meeting between the two of us. Finally, it seemed simpler just to take him."

Jed is clearly annoyed. "So, what does he want now?"

"He wants the woman who helped us out at Genesis hired on the project."

"Who is she?"

"Her name is Apple Messina."

"Apple Messina?" Jed looks as if he has a bad taste in his mouth. "Why don't you talk to Pete now?"

"I tried to talk to him, Jed, and I can't get anywhere." (A slight falsehood. He'd suggested a new hire, but not specifically Apple.)

"Has she got any experience? Where did she work before?"

"I don't know much about her. I thought Pete could take it from here, requesting her resume."

"We've never hired anyone because a client thought we should."

A deception on Jed's part, Sy thinks. The firm often makes accommodations. A number of interns, mostly summer help—friends and family members of Jed and David's colleagues in the city—have been hired without the requisite interview. He understands that it is the way things are done, but he's sometimes felt badly for the students from the local college, sent to interviews by counselors in the career services department for positions that have already been filled.

Jed is clearly annoyed. Sy wonders if he should risk repeating Swanson's remark about Apple. "I think she impressed Swanson."

"How so?"

"He said she not only seemed cooperative but had the kind of face and figure a man could stand to look at during our too-lengthy presentations."

"He said that?"

"He did."

"Swanson's one pain-in-the-ass client."

Sy has no idea if Apple can afford to work without benefits. There has never been a discussion of money between them. "We might hire her on a contract basis only for this project."

"Get Pete's approval first. Tell him we talked."

"I'll set up a meeting."

Jed stands up and looks directly at him. "So she's a looker?"

"Apparently, Swanson thinks so."

Back at his desk, Sy regrets repeating Swanson's sexist remark to Jed. It was a desperate act, and he won't let that happen again.

He's too agitated to deal with Pete in person, with the hassle and the confrontation it will cause when Pete hears that he went directly to Jed. He sends him an email with the information regarding Apple and how Pete can get in touch.

That same evening, out on the small porch with Apple beside him, sipping a glass of *Pinot Grigio*, with the sweet fragrance of a summer night rising from the garden below, he tells her she can give her notice at Genesis. She'll be hired at his firm, and a man named Pete Larson, the architect in charge of the design department, will be contacting her.

She gleams with happiness, looking at him with gratitude and affection.

He appraises her pale loveliness and thinks she'll never suspect how much thought, energy, and strategy it has taken to get her on board. For a brief moment, he wonders if the designers will welcome her, if they will put her at ease, and consoles himself with the thought that they might feel less threatened or competitive with someone who hasn't had much experience. She is cheerful and pleasant and should fit in, given a little time, and he intends to watch over her.

The following morning, on his way to meet with Swanson (with David's news on his mind), he thinks that if Charter Oak accepts the bid from Cole & Siegel, two, maybe three senior people will be required. He imagines that the jockeying at the firm has already begun. His preference has always been for new construction, and he hopes he'll be assigned to the project. It would be an opportunity to design interiors specific to a client's needs.

In that regard, he wants Swanson to report back that he's been cooperative, that he is talented, suggesting creative solutions to the difficulties that will undoubtedly arise in a project of this size, and that he is a competent manager, knowing how to complete a project on time and within a fixed budget.

Sy pauses for a moment at the door of Swanson's spacious corner office. The man is leaning back in his chair, seemingly relaxed and thoughtful, his hands behind his head, looking out at Hartford's rooftops, chimneys, pipe vents, and a newer, taller building in the distance. Sy would give half a month's salary to know what Swanson is thinking. There is no question over the degree of pressure Charter Oak's VPs exert on him.

Recently, upper management has become more openly indignant about moving into a renovated building. Swanson might be concerned that he'll have to leave the home office and go with them—he's admitted as much.

Should he walk in or knock first? He looks at the time and walks in. "Good morning, Will."

Swanson sits upright, swiveling his chair to face him. As usual, he is dressed as if he stepped out of an ad for corporate executives—gray suit, white shirt, and a signature Brooks Brothers tie. He is clean-shaven, his graying hair freshly trimmed. "You're here early," Swanson says.

"Right on time, Will."

He takes the box of carpet samples out of his briefcase and sets them on Swanson's desk. "These just came in."

He leans forward, looks them over, and says, "Nice. The pile is as high and as dense as the one in my own living room. What about the other colors?"

"We're working on it."

"We?"

"The carpet rep and I."

"How is Katherine?"

"Apparently, she's feeling much better. She's expected back any day now."

"Glad to hear it."

As if he's learned in all of his years in the corporate structure to mask surprise, alarm, anticipation, maybe disappointment, or even pleasure, Swanson is, as usual, cool, contained, and unreadable. He compliments Sy, a rare gesture of appreciation. "Now I have carpet samples equivalent to the cost of carpet tiles," he says.

Sy feels he ought to warn him again, at least subtly, that the choice he's been forced to make due to pressure from upper-level executives is not a good one. "I know you are aware that in six months—"

"I don't give a damn how the installation will look in six months. We won't get one of these VPs to move if their offices don't look the same as the ones they're sitting in right now. How many times have I told you they want carpet they believe they deserve at their level in the company, the same that is laid in the home office?"

Swanson pushes his chair back a few inches, all of his friendliness withdrawn. "Have you got the specs with you?"

Sy hands him a copy, too angry to speak.

"Purchasing will want it," he says with a dismissive look, a signal to Sy that the meeting is over.

But Sy has given Swanson what he'd wanted, what he'd hounded him for, and it is time for him to get what he requires, and he speaks firmly.

"Will, I need the names of the VPs on the block floor plans."

Swanson shakes his head firmly and avoids looking at him. "The VPs are adamant and won't budge. They want their offices at the perimeter. They feel they deserve that much, moving out of the home office to work in an old factory building."

"This was agreed to at the start, Will."

"Nothing was agreed on. It was being considered."

Swanson is wrong and probably knows it, but if Sy doesn't leave right now, he's afraid he might lose it. He's fed up with all this jockeying with Swanson, the back and forth, the ups and downs of this miserable little project, just a building rehab, after all. He's tired of losing sleep over each and every encounter with Swanson. For a brief moment, he sees himself as Katherine and the others on the project might, and he supposes he has set a precedent, giving into Swanson's demands when he could find no other solutions and, at the same time, fulfill Jed's mandate "to move the project forward and keep it under budget." He stands up and picks up his briefcase. "I'll have to bring this to Jed's attention."

"Fine with me," Swanson replies.

Sy detects some new authority in his tone, possibly suggesting that if Cole & Siegel wants the new project, they'll have to cooperate with any and all client demands on this one.

Unexpectedly, Swanson grins. "When does Apple start?"

Sy can hardly control himself. "Not sure yet." He won't discuss Apple with Swanson. He won't! Swanson will find out from Tillie soon enough that she's already been hired.

Out in the hallway on his way to the elevator, he's relieved that he's no longer in the same room with Swanson, breathing in the same air. He looks down at the traffic pattern on the carpet—smudged, soiled, and worn—and thinks again that he should have pushed more for modular carpeting, and now it is much too late.

Another sleepless night, so frequent now, and in the morning, as he's leaving the house, an unpleasant exchange with Julie. He brushes her off, saying he has an early meeting with Jed Cole.

He arrives at work and has no choice but to stop and speak to Violet. "Is Jed in his office?" he says.

"You're all fired up, Sy."

He ignores her remark. "Is anyone with him?"

"As far as I know, he's in there alone."

He goes straight to Jed's office, knocks lightly on the door, and walks in.

Jed stands up. "I'm just leaving—what's up?"

"Sorry, Jed, but I have some bad news."

"What now?"

"Swanson won't approve the block floor plan for the VP offices in the center of the building. He's insisting the offices be moved to the perimeter."

"For Chrissake, it's been in the papers!"

"He says the VPs won't budge. I told him the decision came down from the top, and they had no choice."

"Everyone at Charter Oak agreed."

"I reminded him that he'd approved the blueprints for that area."

Jed studies Sy with barely disguised disappointment. "I don't want to go to Charter Oak with this. Not now, while they're considering our bid for the new project. You go back and tell Swanson that we'll fix it so that the VPs can have anything they want as long as they honor their agreement to offices in the center of the building."

Looking ahead, imagining the VP's demands, Sy almost stutters. "You're saying, 'anything they want?' What about corporate standards—"

"I don't give a rat's ass about standards—at the end of the day, nobody will."

18

Katherine

Early morning on a Tuesday, Katherine is at the front door of the farmhouse, pacing back and forth on the wide and creaky floorboards. She is on her phone, ordering a taxi to take her to her apartment in Hartford. It troubles her that her voice is shaky and uncertain, as if she were older than a woman in her fortieth year.

Lucy comes down the stairs and overhears Katherine on the phone, asking if there are any women drivers available. She's hurt that Katherine has decided to leave without talking it over with her. She waits until she hangs up, and there is disappointment in her voice when she says, "Kat, I can drive you. There's no need for a taxi."

How can she tell Lucy that she only decided to leave a few hours ago? And the reason she hadn't told her first thing this morning was that she didn't want to have a back and forth about whether she should go at this point in her recovery.

"I have to get used to life on my own again, Lucy. I realize I was traumatized by what happened. Now I want to think of it as an unfortunate setback, something that could happen to anyone, something I have to get over. It's time," she says as if she's about to do something that takes a great deal of courage and that Lucy should understand.

The matter is settled; there is nothing more to say. They stand in the hallway in an awkward silence, listening for the taxi. When it arrives, they walk out of the house together. The driver gets out and opens the door. Katherine looks him over but doesn't respond to his greeting.

Lucy sees that Katherine is hesitant about getting into the taxi. "Kat, please, let me take you."

Katherine smiles bravely. Lucy has been so kind, and Katherine knows that she has not been an easy patient.

"Thanks, Lucy, thanks for everything."

Quietly, Lucy says, "Call if you need me."

"Yes," Katherine says, "I will."

And Lucy thinks, *no, you won't!*

At times like this, when she feels ineffective, Lucy talks to her husband Luke, bringing up old wounds, old frustrations, and disappointments. *Where are you, Luke? Where are you when I need you?* Her heartfelt questions need some answers, and she waits, looking over the beautifully landscaped property as if he might appear. And she feels sorry for herself, thinking *about all those hours she'd spent alone while he worked in the gardens, time that they could have spent together!*

Katherine stays alert for the short ride downtown. As if the driver understands she is not interested in a friendly conversation, he doesn't make any attempt at small talk.

As they approach the city, the contrast between the farm's tranquility and the city's noise, its gray and black-seamed spaces of light and shadow, seem unfriendly and unfamiliar.

Katherine wonders if she really will be able to manage on her own. For an instant, she thinks she might ask the driver to turn the taxi around and take her back to the farm.

He stops in front of the high rise she moved into thirteen years ago when it was newly built, a massive concrete structure with large, square windows. At the time, people in the architectural and design community that she worked with objected to the building's workmanlike structure that did not fit with Hartford's Greek temple and church-inspired architecture.

Unfortunately, when a few pieces of granite slid off the building's face, everyone declared it was jinxed and suggested it might be unsafe, warning her against living there. She paid little attention.

In some mysterious way, the building suited her, and the idea that no one had lived in the rooms of the unit she'd purchased pleased her to no end. Maybe because she'd grown up in such an old house with a well-documented history of those who'd lived there—and where she'd felt, at times, like a visitor.

In the confines of the elevator, she's edgy, relieved when the door slides open into a hallway darker than she remembers, narrow and impersonal, and slightly stale smelling.

She opens the door to her eleventh-floor unit—one bedroom with a galley kitchen, an overly large living room with a square recess where her drafting board fits nicely for the work she habitually brings home. It looks as if no one lives there permanently.

The décor is not much different than the offices she designs. Oak floors, a square of gray commercial carpeting in the large living room, Mies van der Rohe lounge furniture, knock-off Breuer chairs, oak tables from Sweden, lamps that look more like torches at the end of spears, and a drooping ficus she has never had the time to properly care for.

She thinks of the apartment as a convenience, little more than an extension of her workstation at the firm, and has no inclination to decorate it with personal items. The walls are painted off-white and are bare except for museum prints—Klee's abstract, "Picture Album," a hieroglyphic composite of symbols, and a Matisse cutout, "Memory of Oceania," a picture of warm tropical hues, suggesting a figure on a sailboat, shimmering water, and Tahitian light, the only visible connections to a past life spent in New York City at the start of her career.

These prints are unlike any she might specify in Hartford. The Klee is too abstract, too dark, and too moody. Matisse is perfect, a masterpiece, like all of his work. But Katherine had learned early on that abstract art had little appeal for Hartford's corporate population. Employees at Concord Mutual, where she'd previously worked, and at most of the facilities she presently designs, prefer restful landscapes. At one firm, the staff had hassled her about the magnificent Matisse graphics, prints she'd specified to hang outside of their workstations, complaining they looked "like something their kids could draw."

In the kitchen, she fills a pot with water to soak the almost-dead ficus when her phone buzzes.

She takes it out of her pocket. She doesn't recognize who is calling but decides to answer.

"Katherine, how are you?"

"Jack!"

She is so pleased and happy to hear the voice of her old friend and former boss, Jack Heft. It's been a while since they've connected. "How are you? And where are you?" she laughs.

"Have you forgotten? I've been working in Chicago for months?"

She doesn't remember but doesn't say so.

"I only got back last night. I heard what happened to you, Katherine. I'm so sorry."

It is just like him to lay it all out in a few brief sentences, and they know each other too well for her to hide or cover up how she is feeling. "I'm scared, Jack."

"Of course you would be." The tone of his voice hardens. "Have they found this guy?"

"A nice detective calls every so often to tell me there is nothing new."

During these phone calls, Detective Hays also presses her about recalling further details, and understanding that it is his job to do so, she replies kindly that she's told him everything she can remember, and that is all she says. She wants to go forward, and remembering what happened makes it more difficult for her to do so. Detective Hays probably realizes that, but he seems reluctant to let her case go into some kind of "unresolved" file.

"Kat. Are you back to work?"

"I only left Lucy's this morning—I still need some downtime."

"When can I see you? We'll go out to dinner, to some nice quiet place. I want to see for myself how you are."

It's too soon. She's too shaky, too awkward. "I'll call and let you know, Jack."

He doesn't press.

"I'll be around for a while. If I'm not here, leave a message. I want to talk something over with you—when you're ready." He tells her to take care of herself.

He made it so easy to talk, to pass on dinner. He wasn't intrusive. "I'll be in touch soon, Jack. I promise."

They met years ago at an American Institute for Architecture meeting just after she'd returned from New York City. They had a drink together and a lively debate over design approaches for older buildings, his particular interest. At the end of the night, he offered her a job. She left Concord Mutual and moved to his much smaller firm. His innovative projects were often photographed and written up in trade journals, and, as his senior designer, she established her reputation in the city.

Eventually, she wanted exposure to different work experiences and larger projects, and when Jed Cole offered her a senior position at his architectural firm, she left Jack on good terms. They meet for dinner occasionally and discuss their current projects, their frustrations, and their collective vision for design.

Suddenly, she feels lighter, more at home, glad that she actually picked up the phone and spoke to a colleague, a friend, in private, as if nothing has changed.

She reasons that it would be nearly impossible for anyone to break in. When she first moved here, Luke had insisted she install a peephole, a deadbolt lock, plus locks with chains on the front and back doors.

"I'm safe here," she says aloud and lies down on her bed, and falls into a deep sleep.

In the coming days, she sleeps a great deal. She has groceries delivered and eats adequately, simply. Both Lucy and Violet send her a few delicious meals from a place called "Abi's Gourmet." Lucy calls regularly. Katherine is warm and friendly. After a brief conversation, they hang up.

Katherine thinks she has wounded Lucy by leaving so unexpectedly and that perhaps she hasn't shown enough gratitude for how Lucy had cared for her. When she can, she'll do something to make up for it. She was fortunate to have someone like Lucy, a trusted family member, to nurse her back to some degree of health, but staying at the farmhouse, a place she'd avoided since Luke's death, was a daily reminder, and it had been difficult.

It will take a while for her to feel confident enough to drive or enter the garage. Her first journey out is a short walk to a nearby hair salon. For her appointments with Josie Moss, her physical therapist, and Dr. Rablen's office, she takes a taxi.

Both of them are very encouraging and pleased with her progress. Dr. Rablen gently cautions her that therapy has been helpful but not yet transformative. "We have a ways to go," he tells her. He counsels patience.

She practices walking in the apartment without a noticeable limp, wearing low-heeled shoes, thinking of how she'll dress on returning to work, and clothing that will conceal the back brace she'll have to wear. She's lonely but discourages visitors. She tires easily, especially when she thinks about the future.

Most of the women she knows are married or have been and have children. Others, like her friend Holly at Cole & Siegel, are pregnant. This past year when she turned forty, she admits it had been unsettling. She read articles with terms like "old eggs." She'd always believed she had plenty of time, but when age forty was right in front of her, she worried that she'd slipped up and been careless with her life.

Feeling depressed, she'd resolved to reframe the experience as uplifting. In the magazine section of the Sunday paper, she'd read through an article titled "Fitness After Forty." The writer recommended an exercise where a woman visualizes herself as a lithe spirit in the shape of a torpedo soaring through the portal of 40 as if it were an open door into a cool light space to new possibilities, new adventures, and empowerment.

Katherine vowed she'd get a head start, keep herself in shape—before it was too late. She watched what she ate, gave up red meat and sweets, like the jelly doughnuts she craved, and plied herself with fruits, vegetables, and whole grains. She exercised—aerobics three times a week to get her heart racing for the recommended twenty minutes. Yoga once a week to fine-tune muscles and coax her body into a state of relaxation.

She enjoyed the yoga sessions and wished she could go more frequently but was always too caught up with the work she brought home.

As the day of her birthday approached, a sense of gloom and reluctance loomed over her, conjuring up the black balloons she saw in florist shop windows with "lordy lordy look who's forty" printed all over them. Some nights, she woke up out of a sound sleep, and the uncertainties she could dismiss during a day at work collided in her head at 3 A.M. Through a small round window on the wall beside her bed, she watched the moon through its varying cycles, and it was somehow comforting.

Her fortieth birthday fell on a typically bleak, raw January day. The firm was throwing a party for her that night. It was supposed to be a surprise, but she had known about it all along. Her friend Oscar had told her, saying he hated surprises. She felt the same and thanked him for alerting her.

She adores Oscar. He's talented and a lot of fun, and they occasionally go out to lunch together. He confides in her regarding the frustrations he experiences with the man he is living with presently. He'd like to settle down and get married, but he has yet to find the right partner.

Dressing herself that morning, she decided against wearing the black pants suit she'd laid out the night before and put on a new red wool dress, spiked heels, and a pair of large sterling silver hoop earrings. Leaving for work, she'd appraised herself in the full-length mirror on the back of her closet door. "You don't look a day over thirty," she said, and the mirror responded with, "Really?"

She answered back, "Forty is not old!"

That evening, determined to be a good sport, she laughed at the cards, the jokes, the *over-the-hill* banner Violet had strung up, but with an increasingly panicked feeling, verging on hysteria. She gulped glasses of champagne and began to slur her words. She got teary-eyed when Jed presented her with a fourteen-carat gold drafting pencil and said they were fortunate to have her on staff. She was relieved when it was over and not the least upset when Oscar announced to everyone in earshot that "hitting forty sucked." That was exactly how she felt.

She'd been in no shape to drive, and Oscar said he'd take her home, making her laugh the whole time, distracting her with gossip and stories about friends and co-workers.

When they got to her apartment, he parked out front as if he was an entitled celebrity, clicked on the flashers, got out of the car, walked her into the lobby, and kissed her tenderly on each cheek. One long hug, and he was gone.

There was a delivery for her—a bouquet from Mac— pink roses, dried delphinium, Queen Anne's lace, bursting out of a large basket. *"We are always the same age inside."*

Someone more famous than me wrote that.

Love you, Mac.

Soaking in the tub, feeling profoundly lonely, missing Mac, her brother Luke, regretting that she'd refused Lucy's invitation to go out for dinner, regretting she hadn't a lover to celebrate with, she wept and wept.

Pete is expecting her back at work sometime next week. She is feeling much better physically and wants to resume her old life and get back to working on Moses Rocket, a distraction that will help in her efforts to move ahead from what has happened.

After breakfast the following morning, she decides that she doesn't want to spend another day alone in the apartment with nothing to do. She'll go to work and get a head start.

She puts on a cream-colored suit that hides her back brace and slips into a pair of modestly stylish flats.

In the lobby, she tells the security guard she's headed for the parking garage. He nods sleepily at the monitoring cameras in front of him.

She tells him again, more firmly, and finally recognizing her, he sits up. "I've got your back," he says. "No worries."

She goes down to the garage, enters, and though it is different from the one where she was attacked, it holds the same terrors. She carries her briefcase and keys in one hand, a can of pepper spray in the other. She's purchased several on the advice of Detective Hays.

Noises from a piece of blowing paper, a dull thud when a car door is shut, and even the sound of voices frighten her. She's unable to run or fight off anyone. Reaching her car, she's out of breath and slides in as quickly as she's able.

She's so eager to leave the garage that she forgets to pause at the exit and look both ways. From somewhere, she hears a horn blasting and looks around nervously. A car pulls up next to her, and a red-faced woman shouts, "You idiot! If you can't drive it, park it!"

"Now that's a first step back to reality," she thinks with a rueful laugh.

Smoggy air drifts toward the capitol's golden dome and smells of rain that could be on the way.

Men stride into buildings in suits and dark flat shoes, and some women are still wearing sneakers with their suits, but fewer than before. High heels are in vogue again, like the ones she'd been wearing when... She steels herself not to think about what happened.

At a stoplight, she glances into the car's mirror. Her skin has healed, but she's applied too much make-up, especially over the welt that she convinces herself is hardly noticeable. She pulls a tissue out of the box beside her and wipes off most of the blush.

She drives slowly, staying in the right-hand lane. Trucks and cars pass by. From one, children dressed for a day of swimming give her the V sign. She waves back and smiles, remembering tedious backseat rides from her own childhood when that would do for a distraction.

Mac's children come to mind and the holiday photo he sends each year. She wonders what they are like and when he'll bring them East for a visit. At moments, she finds it hard to believe the circumstances that left him caring for the children on his own. She'd known that he was divorced and the children were living with him, but he'd never shared the details with her until this last visit. She thinks back to how kind and thoughtful he'd been during the brief period of time they'd lived together years ago and knows that his children are in good hands.

Leaving the highway, she steers the car towards Moses Rocket. The sandstone blocks on the exterior have been refinished. She's envisioned them looking like the weathered rock at the side of the highway. That's what she expects, and when she turns the corner, she is shocked. The building looks as if it's been painted in shades of pink. Stunned and disbelieving, she sees Mike Raymo out front, taking a delivery. She pulls up in front of the brick cottages and walks across the street toward him.

He waves and smiles, shouting over the hammering, the sawing, the rock and roll music. "Katherine, good to see you back. Wait there till I get these windows parked."

In direct sunlight, the ruddy-cheeked stone blocks look their worst. She feels a hammering in her chest and tears up in anger and disbelief. When Mike joins her, she says, "The stones, they're so pink!"

He shrugs as if, of course, they are all wrong, but there is nothing he can do. "Iron oxide," he says. "Predominance of iron oxide."

"What did they use to clean it off?"

"As far as I know, it was power washed."

"Not blasted?"

"Can't. Sandstone's porous. And too soft. You've got to be careful with sandstone."

"Has Sy been here? Has he seen this?"

Used to the commiserations and confidences of the people with differing agendas on a project, Mike shrugs again. "He stops by every few days. He didn't say anything about it to me."

In her opinion, Sy has not been careful with the sandstone. He's been careless! He must have signed off on the job and left the rest to Mike, who follows instructions from the firm's architects to the letter. The building is a horror. A mistake that can't be rectified.

As if it's possible that Mike can do something to salvage, to correct what has been done to the building, she pleads with him. "But don't you see, Mike, that they went too far? Sy should have had a portion of stones at the back of the building cleaned off first."

Mike is a gentleman. He works as hard as the men he supervises and is well respected. In his own way, he is fond of Katherine and enjoys working with her. If he lets down his guard on the site (he rarely does), he will confide to Katherine something he feels she might appreciate his opinion on, like some architectural detail that had been overlooked. He trusts her and knows she will follow through, correcting mistakes. When he learned of her attack, he felt it deeply. He won't bring it up with her because it is too personal. He sees how unwell she looks, not only physically, but there is something off with how she's reacting to the change in the building, although he won't remark on that either. He tries to smooth things over. "This is what you get when you wash off a hundred and fifty years of grit, but give it some time, Kat. The stone will darken."

"Not in our lifetime." Though later, when she calls Jack Heft to ask if anything can be done, he assures her the color, in time, will fade. She'd persisted, asking if it would soften in their lifetimes, and he'd laughed and said it depended on how long they'd be around. She hadn't been in a mood for sarcasm or jokes and quickly got off the phone before she said something she'd regret later on.

"Listen, Kat, I've got to go up top before it gets any hotter," Mike says, pointing to the roof. "But first, can I walk you through the building? There are some nice interior changes you might want to see."

Yes, of course, she would, but she shakes her head no. A shooting pain down her leg warns against it. "I don't have time this morning."

"I'll take you through myself anytime."

She's too upset to thank him properly.

Back in the car, she spends a few moments rubbing the cramped muscles in her leg. It is not the first time this has happened. It starts with a muscle spasm in her back, a warning that if she doesn't sit down or, better, lie down, she will soon experience painful muscle contractions. At home, she uses a hot pad and *Motrin* to ease her discomfort, and that is where she should go, but it seems like giving up, and she convinces herself that her leg does feel a little better now that she's sitting down. She'll return to work as she'd planned.

For a moment, she looks up at Moses Rocket and thinks, *How can you love a building?* How many times has she used that word casually or even a bit passionately to Pete, to Tillie, to Henry, to Deborah?

Probably "love" is not what she feels or means at all, but maybe more of a profound sense of commitment, a respect for a building's age, its history.

Structures of all kinds have their own spirits, personalities, characteristics, whatever you want to call them. Moses Rocket was gutted and reassembled and seemed patient through each stage of renewal as if all of the violations would be worth it. Now, with its rouged face, the building has lost its charm for her, its authenticity.

She thrusts the key into the ignition, worrying about other changes to the project she is not aware of. She is too upset, too disconcerted to notice a figure lurking near her car. He is about to rap on the window but at the moment the engine starts up, he leaps back quickly and slips away unseen.

19

Sy

The bi-monthly walkthrough with Swanson at Moses Rocket is scheduled for 11:00, when he and Swanson will don hardhats, and Mike Raymo will lead them into the building. Sy always feels anxious in the hours beforehand. There is no predicting Swanson's moods. He has been downright cheerful at times, complimenting Mike for the changes that have been made. At other times, he has hardly spoken, seemingly displeased with the whole operation.

During the walkthrough, the construction crew will behave like sailors on a ship when an officer walks by, uncharacteristically quiet with the work they're engaged in, focused on their tasks, and there is less shouting, less noise, with the radio turned off. Once Swanson had complained it was too distracting; it gave him a headache. "How can anyone stand that racket all day long?" he'd said to Mike, who understandably shrugged off his question, saying, "What are you gonna do?"

If Swanson asks questions today, as always, Sy will write them down, keeping a careful record of what has been discussed, as well as Mike's patient responses, explained in terms Swanson can easily understand.

Swanson mostly seems disinterested and impatient, as if making an appearance, taking his valuable time, is all that's really required. He actually joked during one session that if anything went wrong, the finger of blame would be pointed at the two of them. Still, he stays alert enough to recognize where he is in the building so that when it's time for a general inspection by the committee at Charter Oak, he'll take over, leading them along, speaking knowledgeably.

The walkthrough almost always takes about an hour, after which Swanson quickly departs to have lunch with a few of his fellow VPs.

Sy can't help thinking of Joel and his management of one of his ongoing construction projects. He'd be at the site every morning and again before the men's quitting time. He was demanding, decisive, efficient, and often tough with the crew, and yet he worked just as hard, sometimes right along with them, to keep things moving. Sy remembers that at the successful conclusion of a project, there would be a great celebration with all the workers and their families, and Joel at a mike, making jokes and expressing his appreciation.

Joel would never have put up with Swanson's antics, mood changes, and unreasonable demands that keep everyone on edge. Sy understands that while he is in charge of the Moses Rocket project, he hasn't the same leverage. On this job, there are layers of control—both at his firm and at Charter Oak. Joel was a one-man show.

He admits he is often at a loss as to how he might handle Swanson and tries to think what Joel would do. He recalls his final week at Joel's, the night they sat in his office after the others had left. Joel seemed different, relaxed, and friendly, speaking softly, with none of his usual bluster, telling Sy that he had to learn how to be tougher with clients when the need arose.

Sy wished now he'd paid closer attention to what Joel had been trying to tell him in such a fatherly way, but at that point he was already moving on. He was going to be an Architect and wouldn't have to deal with the problems that Joel had encountered. *How naive he'd been!*

To this day, he misses him. In his final year at grad school, Joel was diagnosed with lung cancer, stage four. The disease had spread, and nothing could be done, and Joel had only a matter of days before his life would be over.

Sy had visited him at St. Joseph's Hospital, and coming in, he saw an old man lying so still and quiet on the bed that he thought he'd come into the wrong room. Joel seemed different, small, and shrunken. His bushy brows and thick dark hair had turned wispy and almost white. He looked delicate, a term he would never have used before regarding Joel, and it was only when he spoke that he sounded like his father's good friend and the man who'd mentored him. "When I see your old man, Kid, I'll give him your regards."

They said their goodbyes, and Sy remembers leaving Joel and walking shakily out of the hospital to his car. He got in and leaned over the steering wheel, trying to hold in his emotions, but he couldn't do it. Overwhelmed with grief, feeling a huge sadness, the choking tears flowed.

As soon as Sy comes into the lobby, Violet calls him over to her station. "The walkthrough at Moses Rocket has been canceled," she says. "Will Swanson's assistant, Tillie, called. She said Swanson had some kind of emergency."

"That was all she said?"

"That was it, so you're off the hook."

In his office, the first thing he does is call Mike Raymo.

Mike laughs. "So it's off for today! What a shame! My guys were really looking forward to it."

"I bet. Listen, Mike. I'll let you know when we have a new date."

When he hangs up, he feels such a sense of relief he won't have to deal with Swanson that he decides to call Apple and let her know they can spend a little more time together tonight, and he'll bring dinner. But then he remembers she's not back from Springfield yet. *How he misses her!*

Feeling disappointed but wanting to have what he thinks of as a "little celebration," he calls Julie and tells her not to cook dinner.

"We're eating out tonight! I'm leaving early, and I'll pick you and Heather up at six. Choose some nice quiet place where we can all relax."

When he arrives home, Julie meets him at the door. "I'm sorry, Sy. Heather isn't feeling well. She's already asleep upstairs."

"What's wrong with her?" he asks with concern.

"A little fever. She probably caught a bug. I gave her an aspirin, and she's out for the night."

"I'll go up and change my clothes and check on her."

She starts to walk away, and he feels the tension between them, and her withholding and feeling bad, he reaches out. "Hey, how about I order us a pizza? It'll be nice to relax and watch a film together. We haven't done that in a long while. What do you say?"

She looks up at him as if she's about to ask him something.

He sees her drawn, tired out, and sad expression. "Julie," he starts.

"No, please don't say anything, Sy."

"I'm sorry," he says. "I know I've been irritable—it's this damn project."

She leaves it at that, leaving him to worry if she knows about his relationship with Apple, although she says nothing more. She's so truthful; if she did know or had any suspicions, wouldn't she ask him outright?

Mulling this over, he goes upstairs to Heather's room. She is, as Julie said, in a deep sleep. He brushes his hand over her forehead, relieved to find it cool.

He showers quickly, dresses, and goes downstairs. He finds Julie on the living room sofa, and she is sound asleep.

Quietly, he goes into the kitchen. He picks up a wine glass and a bottle of red, finds a bag of pretzels in the bread drawer, takes it all into the family room, and flicks on the TV. Soon, he, too, is asleep for the night.

20

Katherine

She drives to Cole & Siegel and parks at the rear of the building, entering by the door that will take her down to the design department more easily.

She prepares herself to greet her colleagues, aware that her status and how people will see her have changed. She is a victim, and it will take all of her composure to assure herself and them that she is just the same and maybe even stronger for what has happened. Yes, she's experienced a wholly unexpected setback, but she is moving on from it and is eager to continue her work.

What really weighs on her is what has been done to alter the building's exterior. She can't stop thinking about it, aware that it's not anything that she or anyone else can fix.

Again, she wonders what other changes have been made during her absence.

She starts down the stairs, hoping that she appears calm and professional—she has always been very good at disguising what she feels—and that her colleagues won't notice her slight limp or how tightly she is holding onto her briefcase.

She reaches the landing, walks through the short hallway into the design department, and to her surprise and relief, no one is there, as if, for some reason, there's been a work stoppage. She goes straight to her workstation, puts her briefcase down, and sits at her desk, alarmed at how much energy it has taken to get there.

Her desk, drafting board, and file cabinet are smothered with building samples, project reports, blueprints, notes from her staff, and phone messages. The clutter is disconcerting—she always clears her desk each night before leaving. Where to start?

She goes through the stack of phone messages from Violet. There are quite a few from Sam Winston, the modular carpet rep. She doesn't have the heart or the energy to call him. He put a lot of effort into providing her with samples in time for the presentation in the colors and patterns she'd requested. She'd like one more meeting with Swanson to try and convince him that a modular carpet is the best choice for Moses Rocket. Suddenly she feels weighted, exhausted. She sits up and takes a long, deep breath and lets it out slowly, leans back in her chair, and to her dismay, her eyes start to close on their own.

"Kat, you're here!"

She sits up, finding Oscar looking down at her. "Oscar! It's so good to see you." As always, he's beautifully dressed in tailored slacks and a dark grey silky shirt, clothes that are frowned upon by some of the stodgy senior officers at the firm.

"We expected you back on Monday."

"Well, I'm here today."

"I can see that! You know we planned a celebration for your return next week—nothing fancy, just pastries and coffee." He leans over her chair and hugs her warmly. "Welcome back—I missed you."

"I missed you, too."

"Can we catch up over lunch?"

"Maybe not today, Oscar. Have you seen Pete yet this morning?"

"I heard from Violet that he's been delayed. I'm not sure when he'll be in."

"And Deborah?"

"She should be back after lunch. Oh, and Henry called in. He'll be a few minutes late—something came up with one of his kids."

"It seems the whole department is out somewhere."

"It's been crazy busy down here. Listen, Kat, I've got a meeting with Archie. We'll talk later," he says with raised brows, and she suspects that he is readying himself for another row with his boss. "Good luck upstairs," she says.

The Keeper

Archie Kendall was the first project architect the partners hired when they started the firm. He is retiring, and this is his final project. He'd begun when there were fewer designers and fewer choices for fabric and furnishings. He's fussy, difficult, and controlling, and the designers don't like working with him. Pete might have given the project to one of the more experienced designers, like Deborah, but she was tied up with Moses Rocket.

When Oscar leaves, she calls Sam Winston. He's tried to get in touch so often that he must be under pressure at his end to know the results from the flooring presentation. He doesn't answer, and she leaves a message that she's back to work and eager to hear from him.

She looks down at the wall-to-wall mustard-colored carpet on the floor, a pattern like dried mud, wondering how such an ugly product ever got into the marketplace. It was installed here because it was cheap and could take abuse and is soiled with every imaginable stain, despite the efforts of the cleaning service. After a month of traffic, this is how wall-to-wall carpet will look inside Moses Rocket—she can't let that happen.

The room is so unusually quiet that she can hear voices from upstairs—Lucy, Oscar, and Archie Kendall are in what sounds like a testy discussion. Music drifts from the copy room, where the interns stifle their boredom by listening to Grateful Dead tapes. She detects an odor seeping from the blueprint machine and thinks that must be what's causing her headache, her queasy stomach.

She hears Henry Briggs arrive at his workstation across the aisle from hers. Talented, modest, and hard-working, he's the other senior on the Moses Rocket project and is responsible for millwork drawings. She gives him a moment to get settled.

"Kat, how're you doing?" he says, as casually as if she's been out with the flu.

"I'm doing okay. Thanks for your card."

"Good to have you back."

His voice rises and crackles with frustration. "I've had it working with Sy."

They often commiserate, but before she can ask what's going on, the muscles in her back begin to throb. "Excuse me for a minute, Henry."

"Have I upset you?"

"No, no, it's okay. I'll be right back," and she heads to the women's room. She feels a bit weak and needs to sit down somewhere private. She's close to tears thinking that this coming back early isn't quite working out as she thought it might. She can't do her job in this condition. She goes into the women's room and sits in a chair. Her back spasms.

She stays very still, and without meaning to, she drifts off to sleep. She stirs and checks the time on her phone. She's been out for almost 20 minutes.

Carefully, she stands up and walks over to the sink. One wrong move and the back spasms will start up again. She wets a paper towel, dabs her face, and walks slowly back to her workstation. Henry is waiting in the aisle. "Kat, you all right?"

"I guess I'm not," she says, trusting that Henry won't repeat that to anyone.

"I wonder if you'd help me clear out my workstation? I'd like to take material on the project to my car. I need to catch up, and it's better if I do it at home, where there's more room and a place to rest if I need to. Unfortunately, I'm not supposed to lift anything heavy or awkward."

"Sure, Kat, I'd be glad to help." He pauses, understanding that she is in no condition to return to work.

"Why don't I put everything in my car and follow you home? I'll carry it all up to your place and lay it all out so you won't have to lift a thing—you just have to tell me what to do."

"Oh, Henry, thank you," and she begins pointing to what she wants to take with her.

When they're finished, she calls Violet. "Oscar told me you were back in."

"I'm sorry, Violet. I was distracted and forgot to let you know I was here."

"It's a little soon, don't you think?"

"Yes," she says, almost hating having to admit it, and it feels like giving up when she tells Violet she'll work from home for a few days. "Henry will be out for an hour or so, helping me carry materials. There's more room at home to spread out."

"Sounds like a smart idea."

Hearing no pity, no sympathy, only common sense from Violet, Katherine feels a little better and that maybe it is wise to get caught up with work where she's not likely to be interrupted or, as she told Henry, if she feels the need to rest.

It really helps that Henry had been assigned to the project from the beginning, and it doesn't take long at all to organize the materials they've brought back. When they finish, she offers him coffee, but he only wants water.

He reminds her on his way out that if she needs anything, she should call. "I will, Henry," and thanks him again before locking the door.

She goes into the kitchen and takes two *Motrin* with a large glass of water. In her bedroom, she changes into sweats, clicks on the heating pad, and lies down on the bed. She sleeps all afternoon. On waking, she gets up slowly, goes to the kitchen, and scrambles two eggs. Afterward, she showers, intending to sort through all the messages and notes, but feels exhausted and goes straight back to bed. She turns her cell off—Mac might call, but she can get in touch tomorrow. The last thing she notices is how black the sky is through the oddly placed window on the wall beside her.

She sleeps soundly until six the next morning. She doses herself with cups of strong coffee and starts to review the blueprints Henry has taped down on the drafting board. She begins with the most recent. There have been numerous changes to the plans, and she wonders why Sy is allowing these revisions on work that had been signed off on weeks ago. She wonders if Tillie is aware of the changes.

She needs to talk with someone about what is going on and thinks Lucy might have some answers. She calls, asking if she would stop by after work.

"Are you okay?"

"I'm all right. I want to talk about the project."

"I'll bring us dinner."

Lucy arrives at six with a meal of pesto chicken and a miniature apple galette. The scent of garlic mingles with the buttery brandied fragrance wafting out of the small pie. "Smells delicious, Lucy."

"Abi's Gourmet. My nightly dining place."

"The food you and Violet sent over from there was delicious." She thinks of the meals Lucy prepared during the weeks she stayed at the farmhouse. "You've always been a great cook—you seemed to enjoy it?"

"Used to be. Don't have much interest these days."

Lucy is still grieving, and Katherine hears in her voice the sadness of Luke's death, but she can't go there with her. She won't allow what she thinks Lucy wants or possibly needs—a blow-by-blow description of the shock of finding Luke or, more accurately, finding Luke's body. They've never talked about it. She might have lent some comfort, but she only survived Luke's death by putting all of her energy into her work. What could she have done for Lucy, anyhow? Hours of sitting together reminiscing about him? It's better for Lucy to grieve with the other widows at Luke's church.

"I've set up folding trays in the living room. What else do we need?"

"I've got everything in these bags—disposable china plates, napkins, and cutlery. No clean-up after."

"Wonderful! Let me grab wine glasses."

"Got them, too," Lucy says brightly.

It takes a few moments to settle in, sipping wine while the food warms in the microwave. A sense of comradeship unexpectedly takes hold of Katherine, finding in Lucy's expression an appreciation for seeking her out.

Lucy notices the stack of work Katherine has brought here. "How did it go yesterday?"

"The stone blocks on Moses Rocket—have you seen them?"

"I haven't been to the site for a while."

"The building is ruined. I told Mike they should have been washed by degrees."

"Did he agree?"

"You know Mike. He shrugs and changes the subject."

Lucy sips her wine, a look of commiseration and, for a moment, a look of absolute contentment on her face, discussing with Katherine the building they both admire, the project Lucy felt should have been hers.

"There's so much work to catch up on, Lucy. You know what it's like when you miss a few days on a project—but a few weeks? I gave up, thinking it would be better to catch up at home. Henry helped me clean out my workstation and brought it all here. I've tried sorting through it, but I can't make heads or tails out of these recent changes. I thought maybe you could fill me in."

"We're behind, no question. Since you've been out, what Swanson signs off on one week, he rescinds the next. Yet he memos Sy weekly—often daily—proof that he's carefully managing the project. He complains about almost everything—the schedule, the budget, the plans that aren't drawn—"

"What do you think is wrong, Lucy? Why is this project floundering?"

"It's not one thing or one person. Although I do believe Sy is terrified not only of making mistakes but of displeasing Swanson."

"He had no strategy up front on how to deal with him. In the beginning, I tried to give him some background on how insurance companies function. He wasn't really interested in what I had to say."

"I've worked with tough clients, Kat, but Swanson is in a class all his own. He's not easy!"

"He's more of a hindrance. I remember when Deborah and I gave the flooring presentation on copy rooms and vending areas. I was explaining the wisdom of using materials that could be easily maintained. Suddenly, he interrupts, asking about furniture for a VP lounge area."

"Not hearing a word you were saying."

"I tried to continue, but he interrupted again. 'There's something here I can see you people don't understand—'"

"I detest the way he always says 'you people.'"

"Wait—deadly serious, he says, 'these facilities are not for artist types but for ordinary people who have to work every day for a living. How about getting down to earth and using furniture people like.'"

"What was Sy doing all this time?"

"Nothing. When Swanson stopped speaking, he just signaled me to continue, and I used that old trick of design jargon, saying something about the 'eccentricities' of the building."

Lucy giggles. "Did that get Swanson's attention?"

"Not really. He said there would be no further decisions made until he went over all the VPs concerns. The meeting ended like so many others—no approvals, no decisions. In a way, it's to Sy's credit that he's gotten this far," Katherine says.

"I think Swanson is stalling."

"But why, Lucy?"

"I'm not sure—there's a lot I'm not privy to. But at this point, if management at Charter Oak is considering our firm for the new project and they ask Swanson about his experience with us, I don't think he'd support our bid."

There is much more Lucy could tell Katherine, but she's reluctant to do so. It will only upset her to hear the gossip that a designer may have been hired to work on Moses Rocket, someone who might even replace her. Petty gossip, yes, she can fill her in on some of that.

"Last Friday, I had to go down to Neil for some blueprints. Sy, Swanson, and Tillie were there, having Henry go back and forth to the old conference room for samples as if he were a carpet salesman."

"No one brings clients downstairs."

"They looked like kids let loose in a toy shop."

"Where was Pete?"

"I don't know." Lucy laughs. "Oscar kept walking back and forth in front of your workstation, giving them nasty looks—"

"Swanson was in my workstation?"

"No one was helpful, Kat. No one wanted them downstairs. Deborah stayed in your workstation the whole time. They weren't in there that long, either. They weren't," Lucy repeats.

Katherine is struck by Lucy's pained look. She should say something. Although she's peeved and troubled over what Lucy has told her, it's not the end of the world—no one has to treat her with kid gloves. "You would have done a much better job with Swanson, Lucy. In time, he would have trusted you enough to take your advice."

Lucy looks closely at Katherine. "You think I would have done a better job?"

"Absolutely."

"That is what I told Jed when I asked for the slot."

"Too bad he didn't listen to you."

21

Lucy

She's about to leave for the night but stops to chat briefly with Violet. Mostly they discuss Katherine. Violet is fond of Katherine, admires how hard she works, and her concern that she gets well is genuine. Talking with Violet gives Lucy an opportunity to share her worries over her sister-in-law, knowing that what she tells Violet will remain private.

Jed Cole comes out of his office, shouting, "Lucy! I'm so glad I caught you." He looks at his watch. "I've got to meet Nan and some friends for dinner, and I'm late already."

He looks distressed. She assumes he wants to speak to her in his office, tells Violet she'll be right back and walks over. "I'm setting up a last-minute meeting for tomorrow morning," he says. "If you're free, I'd like you to join in."

"Sure. What time?"

"First thing—our main conference room."

She would like to know what the meeting is about, but he seems so rushed that she lets it go. "Anything I should bring?"

"Just yourself, Lucy," and he disappears into his office. Lucy asks Violet who else will be attending the meeting. "Wait a sec, and I'll check. Okay, the conference room is reserved for Jed, Sy, Pete, and Felice. I'll be adding your name."

Felice is the recently hired Human Resources manager. Lucy thinks this meeting might be about the new hire in the design department.

The next morning, Violet catches Lucy on her way in. "Just so you know. The meeting started a half-hour ago."

"But I'm right on time?"

Violet shrugs. "I don't know what's going on."

Lucy walks into the conference room and is greeted by Jed. "Here's Lucy," he says as if he were anxious she might not show up. The others greet her with smiles. There is a pot of coffee on the table, empty cups, and used sugar and cream packets. Jed motions that she sit in the vacant chair next to his and swivels to face her. "How're you doing?"

She hears something a little false in his cheery tone and wishes she could think of something clever to say. "I'm fine, Jed."

"Lucy, we need your help. The Moses Rocket interiors are almost at a standstill."

"I'm all caught up with what has been given to me so far," she says, turning to Sy. "Up here, we're still waiting for approved block plans from Will Swanson."

"I spoke with Will this morning. He's meeting with the VPs this noon, and we should have all approvals by the end of the week."

Jed starts again. "Lucy, we've got a client who's dissatisfied—"

"With my work?"

"Of course not—sorry, I should have told you last night, but I was running late. This meeting concerns Will Swanson. He's a hard case, as you well know, yet we need to work with him and finish up this project smoothly."

"I don't understand why you're telling me. I have very little contact—"

"Our concern is Katherine. I hear she's come on too strong in her dealings with him."

Lucy feels her body warming and, for a moment, says nothing. Nor does she move, fearing the start of a flush.

Jed doesn't seem to notice her discomfort. "We thought you might have a talk with her—none of us want to upset her."

"The project means everything to her—particularly now. I've never seen anyone work as hard as she has to bring a building back to life."

"I have no doubts about her willingness or her abilities, Lucy. It's her relationship (and Lucy gets a whiff of "her attitude") with Swanson that concerns me. I understand how difficult he's been—I've said myself that he's one pain in the butt client."

The others nod in agreement. Lucy is aware that they are relieved to have Jed take responsibility for what is being said and are content to be onlookers.

"Frankly, our concern is not only Katherine's physical condition—"

"She's strong, Jed, and she's recovering."

"I understand all that, Lucy." He sits up a bit in the chair as if he's tired of walking on eggs and gets right to the point. "You've spent the most time with her since the unfortunate incident. What can you tell us regarding her emotional state?"

"I don't know what you mean."

"I mean, is she up to the job? Can she handle it? That is what I need to know. We'd rather have her recuperate fully at home and not spend time in the women's room downstairs."

Lucy looks at Sy and then at Felice. For a moment, there is silence, and then Sy says, "Katherine has been through a hell of an ordeal."

"Yes," Felice says. "I wonder if she's seeing a counselor? I really think she should."

"I think I can speak for Katherine," Pete says. "She is more than ready for any challenge regarding this project or any other."

"I don't know if anyone can speak for Katherine," Jed says. "Nan told me that if she were assaulted, she'd never be the same. She'd be afraid for a long time. We all have to go alone to meetings downtown. We've made arrangements for better security, as you've asked, Pete, but Katherine needs to be well enough, emotionally strong enough, to give this project her full attention. There's too much at stake if we're going to have a shot at Charter Oak's new building downtown."

An insinuation—no—an outright statement from Jed that things are not going well on Moses Rocket, and the fault lies with Katherine.

Manipulation confuses Lucy and always has. Her breath quickens while she sits quietly, commanding her body to relax and not let her down.

Jed clears his throat and removes his glasses. "Lucy, I and the whole team would appreciate it if you'd have a talk with Katherine as soon as you can. Feel her out. Let me know if you think she can manage. Believe me when I say that I—all of us really—have her best interests at heart. We all want her to get well."

In shock, Lucy stands up, looks at each of them in turn, and in a quiet voice, says, "I'm sure you all want her to get well." She looks at the wall clock. "I'm sorry, Jed, but I've got another appointment."

"Thanks, Lucy. Talk with her as soon as you can and get back to me."

She sits at her desk, white with fury. She hears the raspy cry of a Phoebe outside. The slender white bones of the birch are all she sees in front of her, the bird hidden from view in the leafy branches above.

During the meeting, she sensed an unstated disappointment regarding Katherine and her professional behavior at Charter Oak. She suspects there is some impending decision, something afloat regarding Katherine and the completion of this project. It may have to do with the new hire. But what is particularly wounding for Lucy is that she's been asked to engage in an act of duplicity with a beloved member of her family and with the expectation that she will cooperate and do what Jed has asked.

She should have defended Katherine more vigorously and put Sy on the defensive, for surely he is responsible for telling Jed that Katherine was too forceful in her dealings with Swanson. And who would have reported that Katherine had spent time in the women's room? Not Henry or Deborah—that's for sure.

Lucy should have warned Katherine that she might be replaced. She should have told her the night they had supper together. Lucy puts up her hands, covering her face. She'd seen no need to tell Katherine, to worry her. *"Come on, Lucy! You didn't want to ruin the pleasure you'd felt talking over the project with her for the first and only time."*

The flush comes. Held back earlier by sheer willpower, it is so strong that moments later, the front of her blouse is soaked. She's dizzy and feels nauseous. She picks up a sheet of specs for millwork and a red pencil as if she's making corrections, waiting for the minutes it will take for her body to recover, to cool.

When it does, she reaches into her desk for keys, shoves the specs into a drawer, and locks it. She rolls up the blueprints on her drafting table, puts them into the file beside her desk, and picks up her briefcase and purse.

Stopping at the reception desk, she tells Violet she is leaving.

"Not feeling well?" Violet says.

Lucy is tired of explaining her movements. "I'm out for the rest of the day."

The weather has turned unexpectedly warm again, and the car's interior is stifling, smelling "new," unpleasant chemical odors of leather, rubber, and carpet. She flicks on the air-conditioning and rolls down the front windows. Driving away, she scarcely glances at the building behind her.

She enters the forest preserve on Route 4, shaded by trees on both sides and drives more slowly, turning down the fan. Usually, she drives through this length of road preoccupied with drawings for her various projects, client approvals, and scheduled revisions. Today, feeling soiled and complicit, she wants to think of nothing, only to breathe in the clean, fresh air.

The only reason she'd been called into the meeting was her connection to Katherine. That much is clear. But the idea that Jed or anyone at the firm believes she's a person who can be sent on an errand of disloyalty—did Jed realize what he'd asked of her? Was he aware of how superficial, how phony he sounded when he said he was concerned about Katherine? She should have told him to go straight to hell!

She laughs aloud at the pretense, the falseness, the pettiness. Tears sprout, but she won't allow them. She is going through "The Change" she's denied and dreaded. Pretty soon, she'll cry when someone says something nice to her, and she'll end up like her mother, drowning in the past, something she'd always resolved would never happen to her.

She pulls into the rest stop at the end of the preserve, turns off the ignition, and adjusts the rearview mirror. Her face is pasty white. A few freckles spin over the bridge of her nose. She swears they're rotating and blinks a few times. Her hair looks like hell. She looks like hell.

That meeting has made clear to her, in some sad and awful way, how she is seen by others—especially at the firm. Patsy. Errand girl. Words her father had used with disdain.

Is she being hysterical? Full of self-pity? Perhaps.

And what is she going to tell Katherine? She's aware that her sister-in-law can be too direct at times and relentless when it comes to her perception of design integrity. She most likely has unintentionally offended Swanson during meetings at Charter Oak.

Well, Lucy, get it all out! Ball like hell now! And when did you start this swearing? Pretty soon, you'll be saying fuck in regular conversations!

Lucy weeps. Her pride is deeply wounded. How can she recover from this humiliation?

"Luke, I miss you, I miss you."

Oh, she is paying for her life with Luke! The protection he afforded. She still gets out of bed each day to talk to him.

Despite Ellen's advice, she has not given Luke's clothes away.

She wears his pajamas to bed—blue with white piping, white with navy and red stripes, a baby yellow pair this morning, rubbing the cotton against her face, remembering their first night together, unmarried, at a posh hotel, when he'd walked out of the bathroom his hair wet from the shower, looking absurdly young and shy, surprising her with his gentle proficiency. *Oh, he was a wonderful lover!* It is more than a year now, and Luke won't fade from memory, so how can she let go?

She no longer cares where she is or where she's supposed to be. Dazed, she looks through the windshield into a thicket of green. She's never been to Ireland and has only seen pictures, but she'd always listened with curiosity and interest to her father's descriptions of his homeland.

For a moment, she wonders how the varying greens in the photographs he'd shown her would compare to what's in front of her. She thinks of the sorting of colors before she paints. *When she used to paint.* "You haven't set brush to canvas since moving to the farmhouse!" She also thinks about how her friend Eileen would be disappointed if she knew.

Oh, her whole life is a fucking failure! There you go, Lucy! Not like you at all! But, oh, how good it feels to say such a forbidden word!

Her skirt feels tight as if it's caught on something. She shifts to ease the tug. She touches her softly rounded stomach and inspects the stretched waistband of the skirt as if it is the first time she's seen it this way. Her blouse is wrinkled, partly untucked, and tight across her chest. She's always watched her weight and might be five or so pounds over what is normal for her, yet she can't deny that lately, her clothes do not fit properly. And they are the wrong colors. This particular suit is too blue. Everything in her closet now that she thinks of her wardrobe is too something—too yellow, too red, too purple, too matched! Once, she'd loved fashion and had her own distinct style and was discriminating about what she wore. *What happened to change all that?*

She can no longer breathe in these clothes. How can she be taken seriously by anyone at the firm, or anywhere else for that matter, in ill-fitting, cheery-colored outfits? And these shoes with their smallish heels—when did she give up on regular high heels, kept now at the back of the closet? She has nice legs and has always looked good in them. How did she progress to sweats and those lumpy sneakers she wears around the house? She used to wear jeans, flats, and a shirt of some kind.

She thinks of how nicely Silvano dresses in everyday casual clothes as if he cares how he looks or maybe how he thinks she might care how he looks. The last evening he'd stopped by wearing a gray sweater, slacks, and a white shirt, his hair and mustache trimmed, his skin tanned. He looked so attractive!

She feels tired, worn out, and stays in the forest preserve for a long time.

Where to go from here? She sits upright and turns the ignition, and heads to the mall. Stepping out of the car, she notices that her feet look swollen in pinched, outdated shoes, and they are uncomfortable. She marches into a shoe store and stops the first salesperson she sees, a good-looking, eager young man. "Do you have loafers? Penny loafers?"

"Penny loafers? I don't think so but let me check with the manager." He returns quickly, his face showing relief that he can be of help. "No, ma'am, we don't, but Millers has them."

"I'm fifty-two years old, and I'm not a 'ma'am!" she wants to tell him but quietly thanks him and follows his directions to the shoe store, wondering if it's her imagination or did he speak as if she might be hard of hearing?

She finds Millers and sees in the window exactly what she's looking for, what used to be called "penny loafers." Fortunately, they have her size, and she wears them out of the store.

Clothing is something else.

Habit takes her into the largest department store to the Misses section, where she usually buys her clothes. She feels a sense of panic, walking through the aisles, confused with the choices. She won't risk another flush. A hasty search and she realizes she has a closet full of such clothes and won't buy more of the same, going up a size to boot! In fact, she intends to clear out her closet and start anew!

She might try one of the smaller shops she's always been too timid to enter, where the mannequins are spare, and their outfits are meant for the young women that thrive at the mall—who else could fit into them?

She tramps down one side of the mall and up the other before going down to ground level. She finds nothing appealing in the windows. She passes a newly opened gourmet kitchen shop. She loves browsing and loves gadgets for cooking. She'd wanted to take a course in French cooking, but evenings she's too tired to go back down to Hartford. Besides, who would she cook for now?

In the store's front window, she views her reflection and thinks she looks ridiculous in her robin's egg blue suit and cordovan penny loafers.

The Keeper

Maybe she should just go home, call Katherine, tell her what she'd been asked to do, and warn her that a woman has been hired that may replace her on Moses Rocket. *Not yet! Not yet!*

She passes a yogurt stand. It's after the lunch hour, and she's had nothing to eat since coffee and toast at breakfast. *Stay focused,* she tells herself, and strides on. The loafers are comfortable—in that sense, a good choice. She thinks perhaps she needn't tell Katherine anything. Why should she report back to Jed? Let him come and ask, and then she can tell him he'll have to speak to Katherine if he wants to learn if she can "handle" her job. *Here, Lucy, here is where you draw the line!*

Halfway down the corridor, she comes upon a store with a faceless window mannequin wearing a pair of khaki pants and a white shirt with a casually draped sleeveless olive-colored sweater. On its feet is a pair of loafers similar to the ones she's purchased. It's a new store—The Safari Shop. Inside, there is piped-in music of the big band era, music her father had loved.

She inspects the clothing that can be worn by a man or a woman. The colors are muted. The blouses and shirts appear roomy. Waistbands are firm, not elastic. She sees an alcove with clothes specifically for women, and that's where she heads. The skirts vary in style from mini to pencil, and those that are gored, flowing about the thighs—something for every figure. She likes the bright white cotton blouses, too, that would look so well with straight slacks, and she imagines dressing in them with a scarf around her neck. These clothes would also look fabulous with some of the interesting jewelry she has but never wears because the pieces never seemed right for her primly matched outfits.

A salesgirl wearing dark blue khakis and an oversized checked shirt that conceals her undoubtedly young and slim figure approaches. One look at her newly blossomed beauty and Lucy's confidence withers. If there was a way to leave the store without being abrupt, she would. "Welcome to Safari!" the woman says. "If you need help, my name is Amy."

Here come the tears of gratitude, Lucy thinks, but the young woman's frank and friendly expression encourages her. "My name is Lucy. And yes, I do need help. I—I want a whole new wardrobe."

An hour or so later, Lucy leaves Safari, uplifted. She likes the clothes she chose with Amy's guidance. It'll be fun to wear something new, to select a necklace to go with the plain dark brown, slightly below-the-knee, gently flared dress. The three-quarter sleeves will show off her many silver bracelets.

She's almost faint with hunger and goes back to the yogurt shop. She sits on a nearby bench with her bags and eats her yogurt with pleasure, feeling invigorated.

On the drive back to the house, though, her abated anger rises. New clothes—a new image—might be a beginning, but at the end of this day are not enough. She needs and wants now to do something to appease the hurt, the outrage coursing through her. She may as well admit it—she wants retribution!

The Keeper

She heads the car back down Route 4 toward Cole & Siegel. From the outside, the building appears as lifeless as all of the other cheaply constructed professional buildings in the area. She parks in the back and goes straight to the side door—there are some advantages to being one of those privileged few with a key. (She's heard some talk about updating the policy with a new gadget that would open the door using a password, no key required.) She steps in quickly and stands for a moment in complete darkness. *What are you doing here, Lucy?*

She goes into Sy's workstation, aware that he has an appointment tomorrow morning with Swanson, Tillie, and the committee at Charter Oak to discuss what they all call "the concrete cube," but wants to be certain, and there it is, the meeting noted on his calendar.

Downstairs, she unlocks the door to the main computer room, switches on the lights, locks the door, and sits at the computer designated for the Moses Rocket project. She moves all files for the concrete cube from the main file (this will also remove them from the project team's computers) to a new one so that if anyone is looking for drawings on that building, they will not be able to find them. Naming the new file "carpet specs," she buries it in a completed project and leaves.

In the copy room, she finds Sy's request for blueprints for his meeting. Just as she thought, they are in the outbox for him, and she takes them upstairs to her desk. Then she removes all blueprints with the latest changes for the concrete cube from the box beside her desk (older ones won't do Sy any good for his meeting tomorrow) and takes them, along with the ones from the copy room, out to her car, tossing them into her trunk.

In the confusion tomorrow she'll offer to help. She'll look at Sy directly and tell him she knows nothing about the prints. She is clueless and equally concerned that they are missing.

In the meeting this morning, it was sneaky and cruel of him to talk to Jed about Katherine when she wasn't there to explain or defend her actions. And Pete! Lucy's disappointed in him, too. Even though he supported Katherine, he should have told her a new person had been hired for the project.

There is too much subterfuge in this world she inhabits, and it makes her sick!

Almost to the farmhouse, it occurs to Lucy that she's made a pathetic attempt at revenge, and in a day or so, she'll have to retrieve the file she's hidden.

Turning into the farm's driveway, the motion lights come on and spill across the lawn, revealing lovely swathes of symmetry, of movement—Silvano's men have cut the grass. The property looks well cared for. At least she's managed that for Luke.

Carrying bags from The Safari Shop into the house, she wonders if anyone at the firm will notice when she dresses differently. On the other hand, she no longer cares.

Tomorrow. Tomorrow, she'll make an appointment to get her hair cut. She'll make it for an hour during the workday. She'll let

Violet know. What can they do? Fire her? She has no need to work for money. It's a small resolution, she thinks, for how to change the way she's been living. Maybe, the first of many.

Weariness takes over. Inside the house, one lamp is on in the sitting room, as if someone has been waiting up for her. Turning it off, she climbs up the stairs. She wants a bath and wants to scrub herself clean and new. But she's too worn, too shaky.

She manages to undress, slip into Luke's pj's, and fall into bed.

22

Rangy Barstow

He is downtown, sitting in the park on the shady bench he thinks of as his own. It is so quiet here, especially this time of the morning when people are at work inside the nearby office buildings. He likes it when the wind blows, washes over him, and the air smells so good.

He is preoccupied with a dilemma over what to do with the cats he has rescued. Any day now, the men on the building site will break into the cellar for the pipe they've left, and they'll find out that someone has been living there with cats. He has no doubts at all that they'll round them up and have them put down.

Some have grown large and terrify Kitty. When Rangy goes out alone, he locks her inside one of the cellar cabinets so that she can't be harmed.

Again, he thinks maybe he should just let the cats out of the cellar, but he's been feeding them for weeks, and they'll probably return when they're hungry, attracting attention.

He hasn't had anything to eat, and his stomach is making a lot of noise. Reluctantly, he leaves the park and walks the few blocks to *Omar's food* wagon for coffee and a buttered roll. It is such a nice morning he thinks it would be a shame to go back to the cellar and decides he'll take his food back to the park and eat it there.

On the way, walking his usual route at the rear of what used to be Kissman's, he passes by the row of trash bins, and notices one has lost its cover. He's about to pick it up and put it back on the bin when he sees a transistor radio sitting on top of the rubbish. He thinks no one would throw it away if it were still working, and he almost moves on, but then, on second thought, he thinks how people throw out so many useful items all the time, even nice pieces of furniture that he might take for his own use if he had someplace to put it. Quickly, he picks up the radio. It is small, like Kitty, and fits nicely into the inside pocket of his overcoat.

Back at the park, he eats the roll with great enjoyment, taking his time with the coffee. When he's finished, he tosses the paper bag and the cup into the trash like Dad had taught him, eager to inspect the radio.

Up close, it looks almost new. He presses a small round button that he hopes will turn it on and hears a woman's voice. He's so pleased the radio works that he hardly listens to what she's saying, but when he hears her mention something about "cats," he gives her his full attention.

She's calling from the town of Windsor, saying she lives in a large home on old tobacco land. Her life's work is sheltering homeless cats. Not one has ever been put to sleep. Those she is unable to find homes for, she keeps. She sounds like a nice person, and Rangy feels as if she is speaking directly to him. He's delighted he's found a solution for his cats, and he returns to the cellar.

Two nights later, Rangy begins moving the cats out of his cellar. The area around Moses Rocket is dark and still, and the only sound is an occasional ambulance speeding to St. Joseph's Hospital. He'll be at his task for quite a few hours. Fortunately, it's a Friday, and the workers won't return to Moses Rocket until early Monday morning.

There are a few cardboard boxes in the cellar, and he takes two of them that still have their covers intact and begins to round up the cats, one at a time. It's quite a job. They heave and scratch and yowl. Once he seals the box for the move across to Moses Rocket, they are quiet, making mewing noises. He tells them that soon they'll be free and in a new home in Windsor. "A nice lady is going to take care of you from now on."

Outside, it is almost as dark as it is in the cellar. He wonders where the stars have gone to. The moon? Yet he feels grateful for the cover, aware that he can't take risks of any kind. *Foolish, Rangy, you've been foolish.* What if the woman had recognized you when she drove by Moses Rocket the other day? He saw her pulling up, and when she got out of the car, he could tell that she was all right, and that made him feel a little better.

He'd never meant to hurt her at all!

It has taken hours to bring the cats to Moses Rocket. Only one escaped, a motley gray tom. Now he has only the bag of food to lug over. At a quarter past four in the morning, he is finished and scurries back into the cellar. *Oh, he is tired!*

Of course, he's kept, Kitty. She's gentle and companionable and doesn't drive him crazy, scratching at the door to get out at night. He picks her up, and she purrs against his ribs. After all this time, all of the commotion in the cellar, they both relish the quiet.

Early on Monday morning, before the workmen arrive at the site, Rangy leaves the cellar and goes to a nearby phone booth, calling into the radio station. He has memorized the number and written it down on a piece of paper, although he rarely forgets what his mind has taken a picture of. Worse luck, though, he's forgotten the woman's name who takes the cats, and he is counting on the talk show host to remember.

He explains to the woman who answers the phone that a number of homeless cats have been left inside the Moses Rocket building on State Street. He ignores the questions she puts to him. He says he's not fooling and is indignant when she asks if this is a prank. He appeals to her that the station needs to rescue the cats. "Call the cat lady in Windsor, the one who was on your show last Friday," he shouts. "She saves cats!"

He hangs up, believing that once the cats are discovered, the story of their rescue will be on TV.

He'd planned on going into *G. Fox,* a department store where he sometimes watches the news as if he's like any other customer who wants to buy a TV. But the call had shaken him—the questions the woman asked, and the doubt he could hear in her voice, made him change his mind. He forgoes the visit to *G. Fox* and returns to the Moses Rocket site, climbing up to the roof of his cottage.

The first person to arrive is the man with the yellow hat and then his workers. In no time, police cars pull up in front of Moses Rocket.

Rangy scrambles down to the cellar hatch, picks up Kitty, and climbs into the pipe. Later, he hears footsteps and talking nearby. Fortunately, whoever it is doesn't notice that the cellar hatch has been unsealed. How much longer will his luck hold out? *And what has happened to the cats?*

He must find out, and when he's pretty sure it's safe, he slides out of the pipe and goes outside, again climbing up to the roof. He crouches behind the chimney, watching as the cats are brought out of the building, put into vans, and taken away.

His eyes fill up with sadness and frustration, and he wipes them with the sleeve of his overcoat.

He's failed again. He so hoped that work on the building would stop, but later that day, the hammering started up as if nothing had happened.

That evening, he risks going into *G. Fox* at 6:00 to watch the local news. Before he reaches the electronics department, a security guard tells him to leave the store.

He has no idea where the cats were taken, and he hopes they are still alive. Maybe he should have gone to the cat lady himself. But after what happened, the trouble he's gotten himself into with the woman he's hurt, he's been afraid to speak to anyone.

He listens to the news on the transistor radio, but no one is talking about the rescue of cats.

Despondent and desperate, he thinks he might put a match to Moses Rocket and burn it to the ground! But he just can't do it. The building is his connection to the past, to Mom and Dad, and the home they'd shared for so many years—the life he'd once had before this terrible one he is living now.

The building provides memories that soothe him, and he cannot destroy them. He thinks sadly that what people are doing is ruining it, and it hurts him to see the latest change, the stones on the building as pink as the candy that Dad always said was bad for your teeth.

He thinks that maybe he should burn down the building next to Moses Rocket that was put up in the very spot where there had been lawns and flower gardens and where once he'd had his picture taken with other children at the company's yearly Fourth of July picnic.

He'd begged Dad to try and get a copy for him to keep, but Dad said all of the photos taken that day belonged to the company and were put in special files.

He'd readily burn that concrete building to the ground, but he's too worried the fire might spread. He just could not do it, could not risk that kind of damage to Moses Rocket.

23

Sy

Again, the bi-monthly walkthrough with Swanson is scheduled at Moses Rocket for 11:00. For the next few hours, Sy will work from home and then go directly to the site. He hears Julie come into the house after bringing Heather to school and goes downstairs. She smiles and says, "Coffee?"

"That would be nice."

When the coffee is made, he and Julie sit at the kitchen table and talk about Heather and weekend plans. Julie says softly, "You haven't been yourself lately. Is something wrong?"

A few nights earlier, he was in bed, tired, drained of energy, but unable to sleep. He heard her come out of the bathroom, sliding into bed quietly. "Are you awake?" she said. He didn't answer. She touched him lightly, hesitantly, as if seeking permission. He turned and looked at her, thinking *this lovely woman is my wife*, gathering her in his arms. Her body was warm and fragrant from the bath, arousing him. He hadn't wanted to think of Apple, but her image came to him unbidden.

"I'm pretty beat tonight," he said. Julie moved away without a word.

Now he tells her, "It's this project, Julie. I wish it was over."

Taking his hand, she says, "I understand, Sy. It's all right."

He doesn't deserve her forgiveness, her understanding. He's confused and needs help—how can he go on like this? How can they go on like this?

He's back in his office upstairs when a call comes in from Mike Raymo. He's shouting into the phone, sounding harried and upset. "Sorry to bother you at home, but we got a problem here. You need to put off the walkthrough."

"What happened?"

"You're not gonna believe this."

His stomach churns.

"Somebody dumped an army of cats into the building."

"What?"

"That's right. An army of cats inside Moses Rocket. They've been here all weekend, feeding and crapping."

"What do you mean?"

"What do I mean? I mean that whoever did this left an opened bag of cat food so they could get at it. The place smells like cat shit. We got to hose down the whole building."

"I'm leaving right now, Mike."

"I notified the police, the animal warden, and the SPCA. My men have been rounding up cats since they got here."

First, Sy calls Swanson. No answer, so he leaves a message the walkthrough is canceled, and for good measure, he alerts Tillie.

"He's not here yet," she says, "but I know how to reach him." She hesitates. "Is everything okay?"

"It will be. Just a glitch. No worries."

Back in his car, he wonders about Tillie. Lately, she seems to have some greater unspoken authority—he should keep that in mind.

He pulls up in front of Moses Rocket. The site is quiet, the heavy equipment idle, and he assumes most of the workers must be inside, cleaning up.

On this bright cloudless morning, the sandstone is so vividly pink it makes him uncomfortable. A terrible mistake.

He blames Mike. As the foreman, he should have had a small portion cleaned first and sought approval on how to proceed. Sy hadn't spelled that out in the specs (and is sorry he hadn't), but Mike is experienced enough to recognize a potential problem and then move ahead only after he has the project architect's approval. He wonders if anything can be done to darken the surface.

He puts on his hard hat and enters the building. It might be all in his head, but he thinks he can actually smell the odor of cat urine. Swanson is fastidious. If he had even a whiff of something unpleasant, he'd be incredulous, wanting an explanation.

Who could blame him for that?

Inside the building, workers are hosing down the floors. Water is drying in some places and pooling in others. One of the men shouts at him. "Watch where you're walking!"

The men are obviously pissed off, looking at him as if he's somehow responsible for them having to clean up the mess.

Equally pissed, Sy murmurs, *"Tough luck."*

The building reeks and it will probably take a few days of airing out to get rid of the smell. The whole episode disgusts him.

Mike approaches, annoyed and angry. There is no time this morning for pleasantries, a handshake, and banter. "I appreciate your getting this cleaned up," Sy says.

Mike answers curtly, "Unfortunately, that's my job."

Sy wants to tell him that securing the building is also his job, but this is not the time.

"Are all the cats out?"

"One of my guys is checking now."

"That's good," he says, hardly believing he's even having this conversation. "Have you checked the alarms?"

Mike seems aware that a search for blame has begun. "Like I told you on the phone, there's nothing wrong with the alarm system. All of the doors were locked. When we started on this site, you remember, I asked for more security at night."

"I recall that Swanson refused."

"Yeah, well, there's nothing more the guys and I can do. Everything that can be locked up is secured before we leave. I told the cops about the tramp I'd found in the building last winter when Katherine and I were on the third floor. The alarm never went off then either."

"You called the alarm company? Have someone look them over?"

A muscle in Mike's jaw twitches. He appraises Sy's well-groomed appearance, from the shiny hardhat down to polished leather shoes, barely hiding his contempt as if Sy is completely ignorant about the real world of construction and has no clue what Mike has to contend with all day, every day. "Like I told you on the phone—everything checks out."

"Who could have done it? And why? It must have taken time to collect so many cats—"

"Your guess is as good as mine. The cops think it might be the neighborhood kids, catching and holing them up in an abandoned building, bringing them here as a prank."

"I canceled the walkthrough with Swanson."

"That's your call. Right now, I'm off. I've gotta pick up some commercial disinfectant. My whole day's screwed."

Mike opens the door to his truck, puts one booted foot inside, and turns. "A patrol car will be stationed at the site for a while."

"Good, that's good," Sy says.

He's offended Mike, questioning him about the alarms. As the truck passes, he waves to him in a friendly manner, but Mike looks straight ahead. *Maybe he should send a couple of cases of beer to the site at quitting time?*

Feeling like an exhausted juggler, performing for Swanson, Mike Raymo, and all of the others involved, like herding cats, he thinks ruefully, "The hell with it!"

On his way to Cole & Siegel, he questions if it is wise to tell Swanson or Tillie the reason why the walkthrough was canceled. Neither one would come to the site alone, and he'll warn Mike ahead of time, not to mention it.

Early in the project, Swanson had been firm and even rude regarding his own responsibilities. "Don't expect me or my staff to go down there for every change—that's what we hire you people for."

For the most part, Swanson's been satisfied with updates and routine inspections like the one scheduled for today. Sy is aware that will change once construction begins on the housing units. Swanson will put all of his attention and interference into their renovation.

The Keeper

If Swanson or Tillie hear about this incident from another source, Sy is prepared to play it down as an inexplicable prank, bizarre but essentially harmless, assuring them there was no damage to the building and nothing to worry over. Swanson is unpredictable. He might laugh, or he might be quick to blame, outraged that an incident like this could occur on his watch. It'll depend on his mood.

Any day now, Sy should have Swanson's signature on the block floor plans. With Jed's backing, he was unusually firm during his discussion with Swanson, telling him the decision to bring offices into the center of each floor came from the top, hinting that Jed would not reverse the decision unless he spoke to Charter Oak's chairman. Swanson, wily as usual, gave him little response and said he would be back in touch. Since he hasn't heard from him, he can assume that the issue is settled.

Coming into Cole & Siegel's lobby, Sy passes Violet without looking at her. He is in no mood for one of her barbed remarks. She always seems to have some unspoken agenda, a trait he finds unnerving. Wearily, he enters his workstation. There is a large dark blotch on his drafting board. Switching on the lamp, he finds a black cat made out of construction paper. He grins and looks around, letting them know he can take a joke. "Cats? You got to be kidding me. Come on, give me a break here."

The interns laugh with him and go back to work. Yet something about it stirs him up, makes him feel foolish, victimized, that he has to put up with such nonsense.

He drops his briefcase and heads for the coffee room. On the wall, a similar cat figure leers out at him. He fills a cup with black coffee and returns to his workstation. As soon as he sits down, the intercom buzzes. He picks up, hearing a chorus of "meows" and almost hysterical laughter. He laughs it off and shrugs, wondering how anyone downstairs ever gets any work done.

For most of the day, he stays at his drawing board, working through lunch, eating the sandwich Julie had placed in his briefcase before he'd left home, catching up on paperwork and blueprint changes from Swanson that he has to review with painstaking attention to detail before passing them on to Lucy. At four-thirty, he decides he'll leave on time for a change—Apple is still in Springfield, helping out her family. Putting work into his briefcase that he'll do at home tonight, it hurts to think how much he misses her.

He has a millwork print he wants to drop off with Henry before leaving and walking through his department hears shouting from Archie Kendall's cubicle. "I can't find a damn decent swatch on that wall, Oscar! Where the hell did all of the red swatches disappear to?"

"I have no idea."

"This isn't a bit funny."

"Can't we at least try another color, Arch?"

"Clients like red."

"Can't we specify another color just to get a reaction?"

"Damn, Oscar, I want those red swatches!"

"I thought it was my job to pick fabrics."

"Of course it is. But I'll show you what my client wants, and then you can put anything you want on the goddamn board, as long as it's red and looks the same."

Oscar brushes past Sy. Apparently, he'd removed all the red swatches from the fabric wall. His scheme has backfired, and now Archie is ticked off. Sy thinks it would be a real shame if Oscar ever left the firm—he's young, talented, and highly creative.

Sy goes downstairs, and as he enters Design, he hears the sound of a cat's meowing. Pete, too, is laughing. Sy shakes his head, grins, and says, "You should have been there."

That's enough to quiet them. Of course, he sees the humor in it, but he's had enough, thinking they are all children. Finally, Pete calls out that they should get back to work. "The clock is ticking, my friends."

Sy hands Henry the millwork drawing and goes back upstairs to pick up his briefcase. The interns are preparing to leave, standing in a group, talking among themselves as they often do, and making plans for the evening.

Waiting for them to leave, Scott comes into his workstation. "You've had a day," he says. "Want to get a brew?"

"I'd like to, but Julie is expecting me."

He only mixes with the staff when it's required. He's aware Scott wants the whole story on the cats; in fact, he imagines they'd all like to know.

It's so grotesquely strange. In some way, he doesn't blame any of them, but they'll get nothing from him. He has a few facts, and those are too embarrassing to mention—the odor, the cat food, the cleaning up, and the men's resentment at having to do it. The situation itself reeks of failure.

"Have a good night, then," Scott says.

He wishes him the same and begins wondering again, as he has most of the day since getting the call. *Who would do it and why?*

He doesn't believe it was kids, so maybe it's someone who has an ax to grind with Charter Oak, wanting to stall the project or have it suspended altogether. Someone must have been planning this for a while, collecting the cats and having a place where they could stay temporarily. And it might well be more than one person. Thinking logically, it must have been. What is confusing is that any rational person would realize that it was not an effective enough act to stop the project but one that would only stall it for a few days at most.

He is left with the dilemma of why? Still perplexed, he leaves for home.

24

Katherine

She is back at work full-time. Her colleagues have been kind, greeting her pleasantly, a few words, some hugs, then leaving her alone, as if this is a morning like any other.

For the last twenty minutes, she has been sitting in her workstation, thinking it is almost impossible to get started in what seems like chaos. Her desk, part of the floor, and the top of the file cabinet are again covered with samples, blueprints, and phone messages. It will take her most of the morning to sort through it. Then, at noon, she's out for a "great to have you back lunch" with Jed and Sy.

Jed had called her over the weekend, inviting her. "We miss you around here," he said, sounding genuine.

She should have declined. She's in no shape physically to socialize, and her back could go out at any moment. But Jed sounded sincere, and despite her misgivings, she felt she couldn't refuse.

The intercom on her desk buzzes. She sees that it is her friend Holly calling. "I've been waiting for you, Kat," she says.

"Where are you?"

"I'm down the hall in my office—where else would I be? Listen, Sal and Jan are out on a site, and I have something I need to tell you before they get back, something I think you should know."

Katherine hasn't the time to engage in a long confidence, but Holly insists. "I promise you'll want to hear this."

She and Holly have talked a few times on the phone, but this is their first in-person meeting. Holly is wearing a long, flared skirt, peach-colored, and a white maternity top. She looks tired, her pregnancy more pronounced.

Katherine is aware of the sadness and concern in Holly's eyes and steels herself, afraid she might break down, and then she does, and she shakes her head as if what has happened is all a terrible mistake.

Holly hugs her, and Katherine feels the warmth of what Holly often refers to as "her wondrous bump."

"I'm all right," Katherine says, using a tissue to blot her eyes. "The better for seeing you," and she smiles.

For them both, that's enough, and no more need be said.

Holly is perspiring. Katherine takes a clean tissue out of her pocket. "It's too warm and stuffy down here for you."

Holly takes the tissue and wipes her forehead. "One more week, and I'm out of here." She laughs, her eyes glowing with anticipation, holding her stomach as if it is a bundle she can carry. "We feel tired today. We rolled around all last night."

Katherine feels the unsettling emotion of more change entering her life. "You know I'm going to miss you."

"I'm not moving out of the country."

"That is exactly what I feel you're doing."

"I'm counting on you to bring me all the delicious gossip when I'm drowning in diapers and who knows what else."

Holly signals for her to close the door. "What's going on?"

"Kat, has anyone mentioned to you that a new designer has been hired for your project?"

"Where did you hear that?"

"Sal told me. He got it from Jan. I don't think he was supposed to tell me."

Of course. Graphics is a small department—just the three of them—but Sal and Holly are close.

"Her name is Apple—Apple Messina. Sy met her at Genesis. Sal told me he thinks she came in as a Senior, but no one's been told."

Katherine shakes her head, rejecting what she thinks of as speculation. "I think he's got it wrong, Holly. We need more help, but not at the senior level, and Sy knows that. If he had Swanson's okay to hire another person, Pete would move Deborah up to the Senior spot until I returned. That's how it works. Also, Pete would have told me, let me know."

"It seems Deborah's been passed over. While you were out, Sy stopped taking her to meetings at Charter Oak. So, Pete hasn't mentioned this to you at all?"

"No, but we're meeting first thing tomorrow."

"Your whole department is upset."

"Of course, if this is true, they would be. Bringing in someone new on an established project at a higher level threatens everyone. Pete would never allow that."

"She's been assigned to the empty workstation next to Oscar. He overheard her asking Sy the difference between desk height and computer height. It's already become a joke. She seems very young and inexperienced, and I felt sorry for her."

"Oscar is never mean—I'm surprised."

"I must say—she is quite beautiful."

Katherine is irritated and answers crossly. "I can't wait to meet her."

"Well, you'll have to, Kat. Her uncle died, and she took personal leave."

Katherine doesn't want to upset Holly and contains her anger until she is back at her desk. While she was out, she often communicated with Pete, and he never mentioned that another designer had been hired. She trusts him. Maybe he didn't have the time to fill her in before he went away. She thinks that's the trouble with unfounded rumors. People get things wrong, and misunderstandings occur.

She quiets herself with the thought that there may be a new hire, but not at the senior level. While she was out, she also kept up with Tillie. If a new designer had been hired, surely Tillie would have told her.

On her drafting board, she finds a note from Sy. He must have left it there while she was with Holly. He wants to meet at five o'clock for a few minutes if it's convenient.

It's not "convenient." She'll be wiped out by then. And she'd rather meet with Pete first. But she can't think of a way to get out of it.

The thought of meeting with him is distracting, and it's difficult to concentrate, but she begins another attempt to sort out the mess in her workstation.

A short time later, she hears Deborah arriving, and she calls over the panel that divides their stations. "Deborah, hi. Do you have a few minutes?"

Another warm hug from one of the people she works with, and she has to take the time to assure Deborah that she's well.

"I looked for you when you came by last week."

"I was trying to catch up on work, but once I got here, I realized working at home made more sense."

"Henry said."

"Listen, Deborah. I want to thank you for all you've done—mountains of work."

"I was glad to do it, and I'm so happy you're back. We all missed you."

"I heard some gossip that we have a new designer on the project. Is it true?"

"Yes, but she's not here. Her uncle died, and there were some family complications. I don't know when she's expected back."

"What's her level—have you been told?"

"I don't know. When she came in, Pete introduced her to Henry and me and said she'd be working with us on Moses Rocket. He asked me to help set her up in the workstation next to Oscar and to take her around and introduce her to everyone."

"What is she working on?"

"I'm not sure. A few days after she started, Sy gave me a list of assignments, saying that he was taking her to Charter Oak for his meeting with Swanson."

"I don't understand."

"When you were first out, he brought me to meetings. But then, when Apple was hired, he stopped. I worried that he might have been disappointed with my performance."

"How could he be? You're doing a great job—and always have."

"It's not fair, is it?"

"I don't understand why Pete didn't explain her status to you and the rest of the team."

"I wonder if he was waiting for you to come back. He's been away, too."

"The people responsible at Charter Oak know you and depend on you, Deborah. What Sy is doing isn't good for the project. You have my word. I'll straighten this out when Pete gets back." She stops then, believing she's said enough.

At noon, Katherine meets Jed and Sy in the lobby. She's aware they are both disconcerted by her appearance. She is pale, looks exhausted, and is much thinner. She holds herself stiffly, seemingly with less confidence. It's an awkward few moments, and they all look relieved when Jed says, "Let's get going," and she and Sy follow him out to his vintage Mercedes.

Jed opens the car's back door, and Katherine slides in slowly onto a comfortable leather seat. Jed and Sy settle into the front. Katherine notes that the car's interior is pristine and really quite beautiful. Jed, or someone, has taken very good care of this car.

She's always been fascinated and challenged by "interiors" of all sorts, commercial building interiors especially, and thinks of the first time she went inside Moses Rocket. The machinery had only recently been moved out, enabling her to contemplate the structure's bare bones, the rows of long windows, the unbelievably wide chestnut floorboards, and the high ceilings, all looking somewhat bedraggled.

Yet it was a marvelous light and open space, and she began imagining how it might be repurposed. Energy-efficient windows with handsome frames modeled after the original ones. Refinished floors, black painted utility pipes hanging in plain sight at the ceiling, like modern mobiles, and walls of creamy white. She'd envisioned the space set up with 9' glass-fronted offices in the center and open workspaces for the staff at the windows. She imagined it spare, uncluttered, and clean.

In the past, she would have enjoyed a lunch out at this point with the architect assigned to the project and one of the firm's partners, taking the time to regroup and ease tensions, to voice recognition that the business of design and architecture is impersonal, and they are all in this together, recognizing that clients have their own agendas and what matters is that they can proceed together toward a successful completion, one that satisfies a client's needs while maintaining artistic integrity.

During her time with Jack Heft, this approach had usually produced a satisfactory outcome, but there is something "off" about Moses Rocket, that sense of working together as a team, and she no longer feels as challenged or excited.

Her leg is throbbing. She should have worn her back brace. She's grateful when Jed stops the car right in front of the restaurant, a remodeled eighteenth-century home at a crossroads where Route 4 narrows. She's anxious to get out of the car and stretch out her leg and have the lunch over with.

The Keeper

An earnest-looking boy of college age runs up and opens the car doors. She takes a few steps to the restaurant's entrance, concentrating hard on her manner of walking, hoping her awkwardness isn't too noticeable.

Inside, the hostess leads them to the table Violet has reserved, and they sit in front of a fireplace where a giant pottery urn filled with dried grass sits in the hearth. "Still too warm for a fire," Jed says dismissively as if he's offended by the attempt to dress up the hearth.

They sit in straight-backed uncomfortable wooden chairs, and almost immediately, a dull pain thumps along Katherine's left upper thigh. Adjusting her position, the ache travels to her spine. Aunt Ellen's pillow comes to mind, and how good it would feel at this moment against her lower back.

A large oil painting of a woman hangs over the fireplace, reminding Katherine of the paintings she discovered in the farmhouse attic while staying with Lucy. The woman is exquisite in her blue silk dress, an intricate piece of lace at her throat, a gorgeous gold and pearl bracelet on her wrist, and two ornate rings on her fingers. She appears self-contained and confident, and Katherine enjoys looking at her.

A basket of hot rolls is placed on the table and a glass pitcher with slices of lemon peel cut in the shape of fish swirl at the bottom. Clever, she thinks, but taking a sip, she's nervous one of them might get caught in her throat.

Sy passes the rolls, the pats of butter imprinted with rosebuds. The damask tablecloth and napkins, the heavy sterling silverware, smoothly worn, is beautiful. She thinks the lunch must be costing a fortune and that it is a nice thing for Jed to do.

"This is a lovely place," she says, "I've never been here before," for something to say that sounds pleasant and normal, letting them know she appreciates the gesture.

"Nan's favorite," Jed says. "Sy, have you ever brought Julie here?"

Glancing at the beamed sloped ceiling, the wallpaper purposely faded to look antique, the dulled green paint, knowing that Julie's preference is for sleek, modern furniture and walls that are painted, he says politely, "No, but I should."

One man stands at a polite distance from the table, and every so often, he nods, and a waiter appears and fills the water glasses. Classical music plays just at the right volume for conversation. Jed orders a bottle of chardonnay. "Make sure it's cold," he says.

"Yes, sir," the man says deferentially, and a look of what seems like satisfaction flashes across Jed's face.

The wine gets poured, and Jed toasts her. "Welcome back, Katherine. We all missed you."

Her leg begins trembling, and her back muscles spasm. She takes a long swallow of wine, shifts on the chair, and takes another. "Cheers and thank you," she manages to say.

A pleasantly superficial conversation follows, with Sy mentioning that he's seen the Stieglitz exhibit in New York. He's enthusiastic about the later photographs, the ones of clouds. Katherine is drawn to his earlier works, the series of Georgia O'Keefe's hands. "I haven't been to the city in a while," she says. "I love his work, and I'd like to see the exhibit."

"It just opened," he says. "There's plenty of time."

Sy is someone at the firm she's enjoyed conversing with when the subject isn't about work or the Moses Rocket project. He and Julie frequent the theater and museums, often accompanied by their daughter Heather, as young as she is. Lately, she hasn't heard much about their city outings. Julie sometimes comes into the firm, bringing him a lunch he's forgotten, some needed paperwork, a blueprint. She never lingers. She is an attractive woman with luminous skin any woman might envy. She wears understated clothing and seems both intelligent and supportive.

Jed talks about his wife Nan's extensive flower gardens, and Katherine experiences the sadness that always comes when she thinks of Luke and his beloved landscapes.

Katherine finishes her wine, and Jed refills her glass. The wine helps to quiet the muscle spasms, and she relaxes a bit. She looks at Sy eating his poached fish and thinks maybe she's been too hard, too hasty in her judgments. Why shouldn't they work together more harmoniously?

Jed orders a second bottle of wine. She scoops up the last scallop on her plate and drinks water hesitantly, but no need; the lemon fish school cooperatively at the bottom of the glass.

While they are having dessert, she is mystified that the subject of Moses Rocket has not come up. It would have been a perfect opportunity for them to fill her in and tell her that a new person has been hired, given her facts about Apple's background and work experience. It might also have enabled her to discuss Deborah's status and ask why Sy has stopped having her accompany him to meetings at Charter Oak. But not a word, even as they linger over coffee.

When it's time to leave, Jed excuses himself, leaving Katherine and Sy alone at the front entrance. Her ankle is swollen, and she leans against the doorframe, thinking of her mother's chair in the farmhouse sitting room and the pleasure of having nothing to do but sit and watch the flitting birds in complete silence.

"I left a new signed-off plan on your drafting board from my meeting with Swanson this morning," Sy says.

She faces him and finds something unsuspected in his expression, something hidden and suspicious. All of her good feelings fade. "I haven't seen it," she says.

"I put it there before our lunch."

"Oh, well, I'll look at it when we get back," she says with a smile. "We're still on for five o'clock, right?" thinking now that the meeting will give her an opportunity to ask about Apple Messina.

Jed's car is brought around, and the valet opens the doors. All of a sudden, her leg stiffens, and momentarily she's afraid she won't make it to the car. She moves slowly, a bit unsteadily, unaware of the glance of something like pity exchanged between Jed and Sy as she maneuvers her body into the car's back seat.

Back at the firm, she passes through the lobby, picking up her messages, grateful that Violet is on the phone, and she can't stop to chat. Her back muscles have tightened. She's in agony and needs some *Motrin.*

She takes the stairs slowly, gets to her workstation, and sits down at the desk, massaging the muscles in her calves and her spine, grateful for the privacy provided by the walls. She grudgingly admits she can half-understand why Swanson and the VPs do their utmost to hold on to the small privileges that come with experience and promotion.

There's a message from Pete reminding her about their eight-thirty meeting tomorrow.

With new awareness, she now understands that this has all been carefully planned. At the meeting, Pete will clarify what's happening.

She has second thoughts about asking Sy about the new hire. It might lead to an argument, a confrontation she's not ready for.

Heading toward the women's room, she pauses at the workstation assigned to Apple. It looks as if no one is using it. The in/out boxes are empty. There are no messages on the desk. No blueprints on the drafting board. She is truly perplexed and agitated. *What's going on?*

In the women's room, she pulls a small plastic cup out of the holder, fills it with water, and swallows the pills. She glances into the mirror above the sink and is upset at how worn she looks. She applies lipstick and blush and waits for the pills to do their work. She wishes she was at home and yearns for the ice packs that are so effective when her back spasms. When she feels the *Motrin* beginning to kick in, she returns to her desk, wishing there was time for a twenty-minute power nap.

She unrolls the set of blueprints Sy left, checking to make sure she has the most up-to-date copies, finding "meeting with Swanson," Sy's signature, and this morning's date. Briefly, it is somewhat soothing—the familiarity of settling into the complex function of design analysis.

A multitude of red pencil marks show minor changes on the first and second floors of Moses Rocket, and they seem reasonable. But changes to the cafeteria layout have been dramatic. The executive meeting room has been moved to a location with windows on three sides, nudging the employee's cafeteria into a somewhat angular and dimly lit space which undoubtedly will require more lighting than specified at present. The tile layout as she'd designed it will need revision and new drawings issued.

She can't quite believe what she is looking at and rolls up the blueprints, securing them with a rubber band. She cannot, will not allow these changes. She won't bring them up during her meeting with Sy. At home tonight, she'll go over the whole scheme and present her opposition to Pete at their meeting tomorrow. She feels certain that he'll agree with her that the changes are a bad idea.

At five o'clock, she goes upstairs. Sy stands up to greet her. "Katherine, I can't tell you how sorry I am over what happened. I didn't want to bring it up during lunch."

"Thanks. I appreciate that."

"And you're feeling well?"

"Better each day."

"That's good—that's good to hear."

He sits back down and picks up a piece of paper with some notes on it. "I want to bring you up to date—it shouldn't take long. You might already know some of what I'll be telling you."

"That's why I'm here," she says, opening a notebook, pen in hand.

He speaks considerately as if he's concerned, as if after what happened, it is what she deserves. "First of all, as I said in the note I sent while you were out, the committee approved the tiles you specified with only a few changes, and I've left the prints on your desk."

"Yes," she says."

"The working drawings can go out to bid. Lucy did a great job."

"Like always."

He looks up as if she meant more than what she said. She looks back at him, giving nothing away.

"Everyone is impressed with the tiles. You know, Katherine, I was wrong about how they should be displayed. I recall giving you a hard time over mounting them on boards, but you were absolutely right to present them that way."

She shrugs as if to show that the encounter has been forgotten.

"Your design showed to advantage. They could clearly picture how they would look once they were installed." He laughs. "There was none of the usual haggling."

He says nothing about the latest changes, and she doesn't bring them up. He goes on. "I am sorry. I know how hard you worked, but they rejected the modular carpet specs."

She wonders who the "they" are and asks. "Swanson and the committee members?"

"Swanson, yes. He outright rejected them. I don't really know if the committee felt the same."

"I talked this over with Pete a while back, and he suggested a compromise. A tasteful low pile carpet in the VP offices and the conference rooms. Modular tiles everywhere else. What do you think?"

"Swanson won't go for it."

"How do you know?"

"He told me flat out and refused to discuss it any further."

"We can't allow him to design the interiors. Isn't that what we were hired to do?"

"I understand how you feel, and I think you're absolutely right about modular carpet. I also don't want us to argue over this. It won't do us any good. They've rejected the idea, and Swanson warned me not to bring it up again. I talked it over with Tillie. She understands there's nothing more we can do.

"I've documented our concerns, so we're covered. You know as well as I that an issue like this has the potential to stall the entire project."

She feels terrible that she'll have to tell Sam Winston that modular carpeting will not be used in the Moses Rocket interiors. He's been patient, and it will be a blow. She was so certain she could convince Swanson why it should be specified. But because of what happened to her, she never had the opportunity to meet with him.

Sy glances at the time, looking relieved that as far as he's concerned, the meeting is over, that he's done the right thing bringing her up to date, and anything more should come from Pete. "I didn't realize it was this late, Katherine. I've got to get going—"

"Sure," she says, and as if it's an afterthought, thinks she'll mention that she's heard there is a new designer on the project. When she hesitates, he dismisses her. "So we're good, Katherine?"

"I guess we are."

25

Katherine

The next morning, she parks at the front of the building, armed with the blueprints she wants to show Pete. She has a great many questions and needs answers.

Disappointment and anger are driving her when she steps into the lobby. Violet is not at her station, but Pete is there, pacing back and forth.

His handsome face looks tired and drawn, but he smiles warmly and welcomes her back.

For just a moment, she forgets about her concerns and the offending blueprints in her briefcase. Seeing Pete reminds her, more than anyone else has, that she is different, changed, vulnerable, and not as confident. A brutal attack has left her fearing for her safety and with a back injury that might be long-lasting.

To her dismay, she tears up and has to turn away, asking him about Violet. He answers quietly. "She's gone downstairs, Kat," code words for Violet using the women's room. "She'll be right back."

It's always bothered Katherine that Violet isn't allowed to use the first-floor women's room, only a few feet from her switchboard. It's a small, bright, and lovely space with vintage black and white floor tiles, a white sink and toilet, light grey painted walls, and a pretty oval mirror that looks like an antique.

It is designated solely for the firm's female clients and visitors, although women on the first floor, like Felice and Lucy, use it all the time, and no one seems to care.

Katherine once urged Violet to do the same and was struck by her response. "Don't you know it's against the rules, Katherine? I could get fired."

Katherine wanted to laugh and tell her that would never happen, but she didn't. Violet looked too upset.

Pete asks if she has anything on her schedule before their eight-thirty meeting. Katherine only shakes her head, still thinking of Violet and the fact that she's not been offered the use of the women's room close to her desk.

"Great, we can get an early start. I've booked David's office for our meeting."

They sit at a round conference table, aware that this is going to be difficult, and that is why it's being conducted in David's rarely used office. No one will interrupt or overhear their conversation.

"How're you doing, Katherine?"

She sighs. "I'm doing all right, Pete. I'm catching up. I tried to come back earlier, but it was too soon, and, honestly, I was overwhelmed. If it wasn't for Henry's help, I'd be even further behind."

"I heard about that. It was a kind thing for him to do."

He glances down at the sheet of paper in front of him as if reminding himself why they're in this office together.

"There've been some changes downstairs that you may or may not be aware of." He pauses, and when she doesn't respond, he goes on. "I could have told you on the phone but thought it best to wait until we could talk in person. I've hired a new designer to work on your project."

"So it's true."

"The situation is complicated."

"How so?"

"I'll cut to the chase. Katherine, Will Swanson doesn't like you."

She's so relieved. She laughs—this meeting has nothing to do with the quality of her work. "Who says?"

Pete's startled by her cheery tone and sits up straighter in the chair as if reminding her that no matter how close they've been in the past, he is not just a friend but also her boss, the man in charge, and answers her with authority. "I think you know who, and there is no reason why he would fabricate something that could be so easily checked out."

"For heaven's sake, Pete, I don't care if Swanson likes me or not—that's his problem. My concern is what's happening to Moses Rocket."

"You should know that Jed does care and is also worried. He believes this project hasn't run smoothly because you and Sy have been at odds from the start. His exact words to me were, 'They were at each other's throats from the beginning.'"

"True enough," she says. "And I'm proud to say we've never been on the same page regarding some of the design decisions. I fought with him many times over the changes he allowed Swanson to make because I love the building and the concept, and that is the same reason why I put up with Sy all these months. He's difficult to work with because he really doesn't trust his staff."

With that, she reaches into her briefcase. "I want to show you something." She unrolls the set of prints and begins pointing out the changes that she feels are so inappropriate. Her vehemence heightens as she indicates the area encompassing the employees' cafeteria and the executive dining room. "The original design ruined—all ruined!" she says, believing he will understand. "This had already been signed off on!"

He hears her out but only glances at the blueprints.

Suddenly, it's clear to her that he's aware that the changes have already been approved and what she's come to think of as "her building" has been hijacked by Swanson, appeasing recalcitrant VPs, by Jed seeking favor with a client for a future project and by Sy, pandering to Swanson's every whim.

Maybe, somewhere in all this, she is at fault, too.

She's taken risks, kept secrets, and been disloyal to Pete by working with Tillie without his knowledge. She sits back in the chair, thinking that she should tell Pete and explain her reasons for having done so, although some instinct tells her he might already be aware of it. She decides not to bring it up at this meeting.

He slides the sheet of paper across the table. "Moving forward, I've outlined the project responsibilities as far as our department is concerned. Have a look."

Sy is the designated Project Architect. No change there. Directly below his name is the new hire, Apple Messina. That is as far as she gets. "What's going on, Pete? Am I being replaced as senior on this project?"

"Of course not."

She looks again, more carefully. "The new hire is reporting to Sy?"

"That's what Jed wants."

"What do you say?"

"I say Jed's the boss."

"I'm confused—what is her level?"

"She's under contract and has no level. Whether she gets hired permanently will be decided after this project."

"Where does this leave Deborah?"

"She'll be working on the project the same as she has been as Junior Designer."

During most of the exchange, Pete made eye contact with her. With this question, he shifts in the chair, hesitates, and looks elsewhere. "Deborah will go with Apple and Sy when she's needed, just like she went with you and Sy when it was necessary."

Katherine is shocked. "I don't understand why she was hired when Deborah could have taken over while I was out. That's how it usually works."

"Swanson. He got the approval to budget for another designer. He said he appreciated working with Apple because she listened to his ideas."

"From what I've heard so far, she's not that experienced."

Pete shrugs.

She takes a deep breath and starts again. "Let's be clear. You want me to continue on this project without design input?"

"Well, yes, that's right."

"You really don't expect me to agree?"

"Jed values your management and organizational skills, and so do I. For the firm's benefit, we need you to continue on this project.

Tillie and the committee at Charter Oak have a great deal of respect and trust, and I'd say appreciation, too, for your contribution. We think they'd be upset if you were no longer a part of the team."

She doesn't know what to say. Her future on this project has been decided. It's all there right on the sheet of paper. It takes her a moment.

"Pete, here is what you can tell Jed. I will continue on this project only in my present role as Senior Designer, with design input. Under no circumstance will I take responsibility for the work of a designer on my team that doesn't report to me. If that's not agreeable, I'll resign."

"Don't do that, Katherine."

She knows by the regret in his voice that the possibility of her leaving had been discussed, as well as the possible decision to let her go.

"I can't do what you're asking, Pete."

She leaves the blueprints, along with Pete's proposal, on the table and walks out of the room. She heads downstairs, spending a few surreal moments packing up her workstation, leaving behind all of the outdated and current information thus far on the project. Let Apple and Sy sort through it!

She will not be available for consultation. She shoves her few personal items into her briefcase, leaves by the building's side door, and walks to her car, eager to get away.

26

Sy

On the now increasingly rare nights when he is at home for dinner with Julie and Heather, he wants to be "present," feeling he owes it to both of them. He reverts to doing the fatherly tasks and rituals that Julie has always encouraged and in which he truly finds much pleasure.

During the meal, listening and responding to Heather's chatter, he is intrigued and delighted by how she answers his questions.

Since starting at her new school, she seems a little more grown up, more curious. She has a wonderful sense of humor and is bright and happy. Her insights into what she sees happening around her often amuse them. He feels a love for her that is deep and powerful, and he is grateful for all of Julie's maternal efforts.

For just an instant this night, he wishes that everything could go back to the time before his affair with Apple had started. Once he'd been as happy and contented as he expected he could be, his life ordered and predictable.

Heather has had her bath, and she's sitting up in bed waiting for him to come in and read her a story. She listens and doesn't interrupt with questions, seeming anxious for him to finish. He senses something is on her mind, and he is touched, seeing how she maneuvers to keep him there, telling him "secrets" that have mostly to do with her classmates.

She charms him, and he lingers, wholly aware that he is compensating for the time he spends with Apple.

"Mommy has something very important she wants to talk over with you," she says.

"Well, then, maybe I should go down and find out what it is."

"Oh, Daddy, can we go? Can we? Please say yes."

Downstairs, Julie looks young and fresh, curled up at one end of the sofa, wrapped in a shawl. "The nights are getting a bit cooler," she says.

She has poured them each a glass of wine, and he carries his to a leather chair, puts his feet on the hassock, and takes a sip.

"I've got something I want to talk over," she says.

"Heather warned me, but she didn't say what it was."

Julie grins. "She wasn't supposed to."

He looks closely at his wife's pale and lovely face, wondering if she has ever suspected he's been unfaithful. But he finds no accusation in her expression, no sign of hurt or disappointment. Just a young mother untiringly devoted to her family. "So, what is it?"

"My sister has invited us to California—the trip is a gift, all expenses paid."

"That's very generous."

"She can afford it."

"Is there a catch?"

"You could say so. She wants to take Heather to Disneyland."

"When?"

"That's up to you—your work. I wouldn't mind if Heather misses a few days of school—she's doing so well. We could leave on a Friday and return late Sunday night on the following weekend. That would give us almost eight full days."

He hears how much she would like to go. *When could he possibly get away? And could he leave just now when Apple is due back?*

"It's not a good time work-wise."

"When do you think it might be? I'm a bit upset with Leah. She told Heather before discussing it with me." Then she smiles. "Truthfully, I'd love to take her on a trip to someplace like England, doing castles and museums like The World of Beatrix Potter."

"We'll have plenty of time to do all that. She's still very young."

"I suppose."

He thinks of all the great things they might do together in the coming years, like the trip Julie just mentioned and hiking and camping out as a family, activities he'd been curious about as a boy but hadn't experienced because his parents were much older, and his father too preoccupied with his practice. His mother took him to plays, to local museums, and when he was older, to concerts and offbeat films, but as a family, they'd gone out infrequently, most often only to have dinner.

"Give me a day or two. Let's see what I can figure out," he says.

In the morning, on his way to work, he drives by Apple's apartment. There are no lights on—he hadn't expected there would be—and he knows she'll reach out to him when she returns. *Soon,* he can't help hoping.

What if she decided not to come back? Would he pursue her? They had one conversation regarding their relationship right before she left for her uncle's funeral. He cut it short, telling her this wasn't the right time, and she didn't argue.

He comes into the firm's lobby, and Violet stops him, saying almost sharply that Jed wants to see him at noon. "Put it on your calendar."

He nods silently and walks past. He doesn't like how Violet speaks to him and has no idea why she is so curt, and thinks the less he has to do with her, the better.

On his desk, he also finds a hastily scribbled note from Jed that he wants to meet with him in his office at noon. The meeting sounds urgent. *What's happened? A new crisis? Has Jed got wind of his relationship with Apple?*

He's been more than careful. He'd told Apple what she could expect from him at the firm, how he would have to behave in front of the others, and he's been meticulous about never being alone with her in the building after hours.

For the short time she was here before her uncle died, they drove almost every day from the firm to Charter Oak, something he would do with any designer assigned to one of his projects.

He'd overhead Oscar in a conversation with Deborah referring to Apple as an "airhead," and the remark both hurt and angered him. He began briefing her more fully on the project, wanting her to be able to participate knowledgeably with Henry and Deborah. He can't defend her, but he can provide her with information that other team members lack so that she is better informed. He urges her to speak up at meetings.

She listened to his advice, took notes, was eager to learn, and he thought they seemed like nothing more than two professionals working out a strategy before a meeting, just as he would if Deborah were accompanying him to Charter Oak.

There is nothing to hide, nothing personal in their public togetherness. Considering all this, he concludes that it is unlikely Jed is aware of the relationship.

In his briefcase, he has gifts for her.

After his father died and Sy closed up the office, sorting through boxes of files, he found the appointment book for the very day he'd first seen her when she came in with her mother. He'd taken the page out and kept it. While Apple's been away, he had the sheet preserved in a bar of Lucite.

Anyone noticing it would think it was a somewhat interesting paperweight (with nothing that might connect them in any way, just her name and the date). He'd drawn a golden apple in an appropriate spot. It is really quite nice, and he's eager to give it to her.

On that same afternoon, passing a boutique in West Hartford, he'd seen a necklace that brought her to mind, a chain of silver, each link delicately hand-wrought. It looked fragile, yet it was solid, enduring, and beautiful.

When it is almost time to meet with Jed, he wonders again what could be so pressing—maybe something to do with Katherine?

Jed was disappointed when she quit, but that was no fault of his. Jed told him in confidence that he thought she'd return once she got well. "After what happened, she was pushing herself too hard. She needs time, and the door is open. I always liked her."

The cat incident is history. Jed dismissed it as a kid's prank and warned him to keep on top of Mike.

In spite of these setbacks and Swanson's often obstinate behavior, he's gotten most of the approvals and sign-offs that he needs to keep the project moving to the next phase, the cottage renovations.

Without any warning, he starts to feel shaky and slightly nauseous. His heart pounds in his chest, and he breaks out in a cold sweat. He sits back in his chair for some time, feeling weak and tired.

The lightheadedness slowly fades, and it takes a few minutes before he feels well enough to stand up. He goes into the men's room, and fortunately, it is empty. He leans over the sink, splashing cold water on his face, and feels a little better. He always carries a comb in his back pocket and, taking it out, runs it through his hair.

Walking to Jed's office on the opposite side of the building, he hears a squeaking sound. When he pauses, the noise ceases. He takes two or three steps forward, and there it is again. Violet has been watching him. "What's wrong with you, Sy?"

His face darkens. "I thought I left something at my desk, but I see I've got it."

She shakes her head and returns to her lunch hour crossword puzzle.

He walks swiftly across the lobby until he's in the carpeted passageway to Jed's office, out of her sight. He slips off the tasseled loafer and begins flexing the shoe.

Just then, the door to Felice's office opens, and she steps out, looks at the shoe in his hand, and giggles. "Gonna beat on Jed's door with that shoe, Sy?"

He grins good-naturedly, but he's annoyed. "If that's what it takes," he says.

Felice is the kind of person he intuitively mistrusts. He's seen her hug and reassure employees. She's too familiar, too "touchy-feely," in his opinion.

He knocks lightly on Jed's door and hears him say, "Come on in and close the door."

He walks in nervously toward the chair in front of Jed's desk, hearing what seems to him like a loud squeak every other footstep.

But Jed doesn't seem to notice. "I need a favor," he begins and then, as if he's been too abrupt, says, "I imagine you'll be glad when this job is over. It's been tough this one. But they'll be other, better ones in the future."

"Thanks, Jed. I appreciate that." The anxiety he feels eases somewhat. "What's up? Why did you want to see me?"

"I got a call last night from Swanson's boss—he's a friend of mine. He told me Swanson is getting 'the golden handshake' after this project. In his case, it won't be voluntary; he won't have a choice. Someone here has to interview Swanson as if he's going over with the rest of the VPs. I'm asking you to do it."

"I don't understand."

"All Swanson's been told is that he's moving to Moses Rocket with the others—he wasn't too happy."

"Is that why he's being let go?"

"No, course not, or they'd all be canned—none of the VPs want to move out of the home office. Swanson's been around for a long time—apparently, some people think too long."

Jed swivels his chair toward the forest preserve and pauses.

Sy recalls the day early on when he and Katherine had argued over how to deal with Swanson. She claimed he was "dead weight" and that Charter Oak didn't know what to do with him, and that's why he'd been given the assignment. He'd hardly listened, already tired of hearing from her how she'd worked in an insurance company and knew how they operated.

"Let me get this straight, Jed. Charter Oak wants Swanson interviewed about the furnishings in his new office as if he's going to Moses Rocket, but we shouldn't include those in our furniture bid?"

Jed swivels his chair back to face Sy. "That's correct. This has been coming for quite a while. The company is disappointed with his performance on this project, but they'll let him ride it out. In reality, Tillie has taken over his responsibilities—for a while now—and I hear she's in line for a promotion. There's some talk that she might be sitting in the office meant for Swanson." He laughs lightly. "It'll be a first—a female VP—a black woman at that. Shows how things are changing, and I say, 'It's about time.' You'll be working with Swanson until project completion. After that, he'll be gone."

"Rough," Sy says and means it.

"Not a word to anyone. Swanson's name should be on the block floor plans as if he's moving with the other VPs. When you interview him, he might be testy."

"He's always testy—"

"He fought hard not to get transferred—" Jed shrugs. "Give him anything he wants."

"With pleasure—but won't he wonder why I'm interviewing him and not Deborah?"

Jed pauses. "Why don't you sit in on all the interviews with the VPs moving over? Or wait, better yet, take Apple with you when you interview him. From what you've told me, she'll distract him."

Sy leaves Jed's office and walks back to his cubicle, no longer heeding the squeaking shoe. In one sense, he feels relief over this change in his relationship with Swanson. He no longer has to worry about constantly appeasing him.

Yet the task Jed's given him is an unpleasant one, and he's perplexed why Charter Oak isn't telling Swanson upfront that he will have to retire. It's a heartless and underhanded way to treat a longtime employee.

He wishes Katherine hadn't quit—he'd give her this assignment in a heartbeat. As Jed suggested, he'll have Apple interview Swanson—she will keep him distracted.

He won't tell her that Swanson is being let go and will never use the furnishings he's chosen. It might make her too nervous, too hard a thing for her to pull off.

27

Rangy Barstow

He won't give up! His latest scheme to halt progress on the Moses Rocket renovation requires him to spend a great deal of time inside the building at night.

He begins at the top floor, carefully going to every third newly installed window. Using a sharp utility knife, a sturdy screwdriver he found in Dad's toolbox, and a flashlight of his own, he scrapes and picks, removing the sealant from the new windows.

Every night, a security car is parked out front. Rangy has to stop what he's doing when the officer gets out of the car to walk around, inspecting the building for intruders, and shining his big flashlight into the building. Rangy is always relieved when the man returns to the car and slumps against the seat, most likely falling back to sleep.

Each time he starts again diligently and steadily with the dedication of someone who must finish what he's started no matter how long it takes, no matter how difficult the job. By this time, his fingers are bruised and sore, but he believes the final results will be worth his discomfort.

When he gets down to the first floor, he has no choice but to work without the flashlight, and it takes longer to finish. Every day he checks the weather forecast on his radio and soon hears that the first storm of the hurricane season is on its way. "It's gonna be a doozy!" he tells Kitty.

One day later, a sudden downpour prior to what is expected to be a full-scale hurricane swells the Connecticut River, flooding homes and restaurants along the banks. Joyfully, Rangy climbs up to the roof of the cottage and watches the rain falling on Moses Rocket.

The red clay at the building's base now has the texture of swamp mud. The wheels on the bulldozers and cement mixers begin sinking into the muck, and, as a precaution, Rangy assumes, they are removed to the street.

At the hurricane's approach, the wind and the rain are so violent Rangy comes down from the roof. He can hardly see in front of him and thinks he should make his way into the cellar. But something stops him.

Standing in the yard in a small space that used to be the garden, he removes all of his clothing. He is as still as a statue while the rain pours down on him, washing him clean. When he's had enough, he picks up his clothes and goes down into the cellar. He pats himself dry with a rag and puts on the only halfway decent clothing he has left.

Safe for now with Kitty, he worries that the cellar could flood, although that has never happened in his lifetime as far as he can remember. Hearing the rain, the hailstones pelting against the walls, and the wind that might take off the roof of the cottage, he fears he and Kitty might be discovered.

When Dad was alive, he turned the threat of a hurricane into an adventure. He soothed Rangy when power was lost, and the house darkened. He lit the downstairs fireplace, and they would sit in front of it, toasting marshmallows, Dad telling him stories. He remembers all this while holding Kitty and worrying, thinking, if they have to leave here, where can they go?

28

Violet

"Excuse me, Violet."

"Hold on, Felice, hold on. I need to transfer a call to Archie." When that is done, she smiles. "What can I do for you?"

"Companies in Hartford are stopping work at three and sending employees home."

"I hear they're predicting a bone-fide hurricane," Violet says, sounding awed by the prospect.

"Jed said we'll close, too. Fortunately, it's a Friday."

"You want me to notify everyone?"

"Please. Alert the department heads. Tell them people can leave around three."

"That should give everyone enough time to get home," Violet says. "It's not supposed to hit hard until after four."

"I hope the power doesn't go out."

"Have you got flashlights and candles?"

"Yes, but I live alone."

Violet wonders if she should invite Felice to stay with her, even though she thinks Felice has gotten on the wrong track here, being much too chummy with the top brass when she's supposed to be neutral.

"I think I'll go to my sister's," Felice says.

Violet is relieved. "Good idea."

Around two o'clock, Pete walks out to the parking lot at the back of the building. He looks up at the sky that has turned from gray to a dull yellow color and then lowers his eyes, searching for even a breath of wind, but the woods now are eerily still.

He goes back inside and tells his staff to leave. "You all better head for home," he says. "The wind's going to pick up any minute. This is gonna be one wicked storm, and you don't want to get caught in it."

Oscar whispers to Henry, "Did I hear that right? Did he say 'head for home?' What is that?"

Henry laughs and starts packing up.

"What about you, Pete?" Oscar says. "When will you head for home?"

Pete catches on and gives him a look. "I won't go until you all clear out."

Oscar slips into his sport coat. "You don't have to tell me twice."

Pete is the last to go, shaking his head as if it is a shame to lose all these hours to a storm. He shuts off all the lights but one in case someone comes back into the building unexpectedly. He thinks they'll probably lose power if it is as bad a storm as they're predicting but leaves it on anyway.

It's almost three o'clock.

Scott knocks on Sy's partition. "Hey, you gonna ride out the storm?"

"I'll be leaving in a few minutes," he says.

Apple returned earlier in the week, and he wants to see her before he goes. He picks up a blueprint and heads downstairs as if a question has come up, something he needs to check up on with her, but she's not at her desk. He looks for her in the print room, but the machines have been shut down, and Neil has already left.

He hurries back up the stairs, thinking she must have gone with the others, and goes out to the parking lot. A strong wind blows a part in his hair straight down the center, and he looks like a man gone mad, searching the parking lot as if his car has been stolen.

He goes back inside, trying to remember if Apple drove to work—some days, she takes the bus. He's almost desperate enough to ask Violet, but as he approaches, she looks up at him without a word, and he decides he won't.

He calls Julie and asks if she needs anything. She wants him home. "I picked up Heather earlier," she says, sounding upset. He goes downstairs one last time. The room is empty. Apple is probably safe at Harte Lane by now. He'll call her from his car.

Violet picks up her crossword puzzle book, stands, and looks outside. The wind is blowing violently. A roar comes through the glass, beckoning her home where chimes and bells from her collection on the sunporch peal so delightfully. But can they withstand a hurricane?

Several trees are bent almost to the ground, and the wind is tearing leaves off the branches, so they look like a flock of tiny birds in flight. She can't wait to get outside! Something new for her, walking home in a hurricane, and she's not frightened at all. It's after three. The sky is turning darker. She'll miss out if she doesn't get out of here now, but what a nuisance she has to stop downstairs. She's tempted to use the one up here but thinks better of it.

One light has been left on, and she's thankful that at least she can see where she's going. She slows down a little, walking through her favorite department at the firm. What happens here intrigues her. She grew up in an atmosphere of uniformity.

Everything she and the other girls at the orphanage used—clothing, sheets, blankets, and towels—were the same bland, dreary colors. She supposes that it made life easier, but it left her hungry for things she'd never had, like bright-colored clothing, bedding, and housewares, especially painted dishes. The cabinets in her kitchen are bursting with them.

Making her way through the chaos of sample books scattered on the floor, the patchwork quilt effect of the hundreds of swatches on the fabric wall, and the shelves of carpet samples and furniture catalogs, she laughs softly, thinking that the cleaning service sure has their job cut out for them down here.

She opens the door of the women's room and presses the light switch. She freezes, not believing what she is looking at. Apple, the new designer, is slumped in one of the chairs, her head against the seat back, her eyes closed. The chair is stained, and blood is dripping on the floor. "My god, sweetie! What's happened to you?"

Apple's lashes flicker, and she grabs hold of the front of Violet's dress.

Violet removes Apple's hands gently and pulls the second chair over so that she can lift up Apple's legs to the seat. "You're white as a ghost," Violet whispers, wasting no time taking a cell phone out of her purse to call 911.

"Hurry," she cries. "She's lost a lot of blood." She instructs the ambulance to come around to the side door.

"There's a bell there. Lean on it!"

She pulls paper towels out of the holder and turns on the water, but only a few drops come, and then nothing. The light is on in the room, but she wonders if power has been lost somewhere in the building. She won't leave Apple to search for the circuit breakers and kneels next to the chair, folding Apple's icy hands into hers, marveling at the young woman's long, beautifully shaped fingers, which are cold and stiff.

A plain woman herself, Violet wonders how it is possible that someone could be born this perfect, this lovely. There isn't a wrinkle or a mark of any kind on her. She notices a pretty silver necklace that seems as if it's pinching the skin at Apple's throat. "Is this hurting you?"

Apple is silent, and taking matters into her own hands, Violet gently unclasps the necklace and, not quite knowing what to do with it, slips it into her purse for safekeeping.

A cell phone buzzes, and it is not hers. She looks around and finds one lying on the corner of Apple's chair. Violet picks it up, sees that Sy is the caller, and doesn't answer.

Violet is frightened when Apple begins speaking in a disoriented fashion, hearing the name of someone who is no surprise to Violet. "You want me to get hold of Sy?"

Her question causes so much agitation that Violet quickly soothes her. Then Apple goes silent again as if she's slipping into unconsciousness. "Talk to me, Apple. Talk to me. You must hold on!"

She strokes her hair and her face, talking to her to keep her awake. "Why darling, why Sy, a married man?"

Violet gets caught up with her own feelings and says aloud, "Of course, I've known for a while. And I didn't like it one bit, especially when Julie would run in here with something he forgot at home. It didn't seem right or fair— not to either of you."

"He was Dr. Greene's son—"

"What—"

"Different, he was different from anyone I knew—" Apple's fine lashes are wet. Tears trickle down her face.

Violet dabs them with the paper towel and speaks to her soothingly, reassuring her that everything will be all right.

Violet lowers her eyes to the purplish clots of blood on the floor, on Apple's clothing, and on the chair. She wishes with all her heart she could clean up and conceal the evidence of Apple's miscarriage.

The ambulance crew arrives, and they tell Violet it will take a few minutes to check out the patient and get her on the stretcher.

She has enough time, she thinks.

She races up the stairs into Sy's cubicle. His desk is locked. She sees a childishly decorated glass jar filled with pencils and pens and slides the necklace inside.

It is pitch dark with the hurricane's imminent approach when the ambulance crew leaves Cole & Siegel, taking Apple and Violet with them. At the hospital, Violet calls her friend, Nan Cole. Nan puts her husband, Jed, on the phone to speak with Violet.

"What is it, Violet? What's happened?"

"Mr. Cole, the women's room—"

"Yes?"

"No one can go in there," she sobs. "It's just terrible."

29

Lucy

After the house loses power, Lucy spends the whole night awake.

In the flickering light of a lone glass-covered candle beside her bed, the lines of the gloomy room with its heavy antiquated furniture and blotted mirrors seem strangely softened.

There is no reason for her to be in the dark. She has a generator, but she'd never asked Luke how it worked. She has no idea how to start it. She'd better take an interest in such things if she plans to stay here. She doesn't want to spend another night huddled in bed, afraid the roof might fly off with the next gust of wind or the house itself, lifted forever off its foundation, and she along with it! It's an old house—anything could happen.

Early last night, Silvano called, asking if she needed help. He said he might drop by this morning. She should get up and get dressed but stays where she is, not wanting to face the damage outside. *Oh, it's all too much!* Without Silvano or some other landscape contractor, she wouldn't be able to manage here at all.

In a recent conversation, Silvano told her that he rents a condo in downtown Hartford. "It is all I need," he said. "I am much too busy to take care of another property."

He has a home, a "modest villa" in Tuscany that he'd inherited from his parents. It's been in his family for generations. "Over there, I have the kind of beauty you have here—it is a lot to manage, but I love it."

She was curious and asked, "How much time do you spend in Italy?"

"I go back and forth quite often. I leave my nephews, my sister's boys, in charge of the nursery—they do excellent work—you'll have to meet them sometime. Eventually, they'll take over."

She wondered, later, if a condo was all she needed.

She puts off going outside, has a piece of toast, and then a second cup of coffee, thinking of the benefits of condo living as well as the drawbacks. From what she already knows, in most cases, a management company takes care of the property. At this stage of her life, it seems like a very good idea.

In that mood, she takes a jacket off the hook by the door and steps outside. It is a clear, bright morning as if the hurricane has cleansed the entire earth. The sky is cloudless and so deep a blue she can't help thinking that having such a day might be worth a storm.

Starting down the long drive, she turns into a small field that Luke called "the orchard." One of the pear trees is cleanly split in half, branches and withering leaves scattered across the still-wet lawn. What a shame, she thinks. Luke had planted it when he was a young man, still intending to spend his life as a botanist. She has never understood why he couldn't have found some way to do what he wanted without his father's help. She asked once, but he didn't want to talk about it.

Perhaps his mother and her illness kept him here, or maybe Katherine? She was young when her mother passed. He must have felt an obligation to help raise her.

She drags one of the large branches away from the driveway's edge, feeling a deep sadness again for the lost tree. Several bushes look terrorized, most of their leaves blown off. Two more trees have been uprooted. With each new discovery from the storm's violence, she feels more overwhelmed.

Just then, Silvano pulls in, leaving his truck at the bottom of the drive, and she watches him walk up to where she is standing. A pleasant feeling stirs inside her.

He smiles and calls out, asking if she is all right.

"I'm fine," she says, "but the property has taken quite a beating."

"No worries, Lucy. I'll send the guys over in a day or so to clean it all up."

She shows him the uprooted trees.

"We might be able to save them, but I'm not sure. I'll get my nephew to stop by late this afternoon. He'll take a look at them. He knows all about trees."

She thanks him and invites him in for coffee.

"I would like to, Lucy, but I've got a lot of properties to check on. This was a bad storm. But I'll see you in a few days, okay?"

She assures him she'll be fine and goes back to the house, thinking how much she appreciates his help, when her phone starts beeping. "Lucy, it's Jed. Are you all right out there?"

"I'm fine, Jed. I lost one special tree, and two are down. My landscaper was just here, and he thinks they can be replanted. But, oh, the grounds are a sorry sight."

"That's too bad."

He's never called here before, concerned for her welfare. "You and Nan? Everything all right?"

"We're fine, too, Lucy, but I called because I need your help."

"What is it?"

"I need you to take over the Moses Rocket project."

She's shocked into silence.

He tells her everything he knows, all that Violet told him about what had taken place in the women's room. "It seems Violet has known about Sy and Apple's relationship for a while. She never told anyone—not even Nan, and they are good friends, working together at the soup kitchen."

"Will Apple recover? Will she be all right?"

"I don't know—if it hadn't been for Violet—I think she might have saved that woman's life. I met with Sy this morning. He's pretty shaken. I need a little time to think this through."

"How awful… how sad."

"It is too bad. I hardly knew her, but she seemed like a nice young girl and pretty, too."

He pauses for a moment. "You know, Lucy, I wish I'd fought harder in the beginning, to have you as the Project Architect on Moses Rocket."

"Why is that?" she says, feeling she deserves to hear him say that she would have done a better job.

"You had the experience, the personality to deal with a character like Swanson. Now let me be clear. If you agree to take over, you'll have full authority. I'll put what I'm offering in writing and get Felice right on it. In the meantime, we need to meet so that I can fill you in on some issues you should be aware of having to do with the main building. There's been a lot of water damage, and we have to get to the bottom of it."

"Full authority, you said."

"Yes, that's what I said."

The buildings are almost completed, but the cottages have not even been started on, and they would be all hers. She thinks of her father, the day he drove her through the site, relating the history of

Moses Rocket. Her interest in the complex had started back then, with him.

It had occurred to her while she was listening to Jed to give him a hard time, to tell him she wanted to think over his offer. But spite is just not in her nature. He was genuinely upset, and she thought better of it and simply said, "Yes, I will do it."

After her meeting with Jed, her first call is to Katherine. She explains briefly what happened and asks her to return to Cole & Siegel to work with her on the project. "If you don't want to come back permanently, I can hire you on a contract basis. I have that authority."

"What happened to Sy?"

Lucy hesitates and wonders if she should tell what she knows. "It's a sad story, Kat. Next time we meet, I'll explain. For now, he's going to be in Boston on a special project for a good friend of Jed's."

"So he's finished with Moses Rocket?"

"Yes, he is."

"And Apple?"

"She's gone back to Springfield—that's where she's from."

"I'm so happy for you, Lucy. You can salvage some of the interior spaces and then put your signature on the cottages—you must be excited."

"I guess I am. But will you come back so that we can work together to complete this project as we'd once envisioned?"

"I appreciate your offer, and it would have been nice to work together, but no, Lucy, I won't come back. Would you think about giving Deborah a chance at the senior slot? She deserves it. You'll find that she's smart, dependable, and trustworthy."

30

Rangy Barstow

In the morning, he's grateful that he and Kitty have come safely through the storm, and the first thing he does is go outside.

After so many hours in the damp cellar, the air is fresh-smelling and still. The sun is strong, even this early, and the sky is a pretty blue color. He takes care of his personal needs, and he's grateful to see that his wash pail is full to the top.

He walks around the cottage, inspecting it for damage, but the sturdy little building has come through the storm just fine, like always. He climbs up to the roof and sees that it has lost a few shingles, but he thinks it's probably going to get a new roof anyway when the cottages are renovated. With fear and anticipation, he looks across to Moses Rocket. It has survived the hurricane just as he expected it would, for it, too, is a solid building, yet he hopes he's done enough damage to stop the work inside.

He sees the man who drives the pick-up, the one who checks the alarms, coming out of Moses Rocket just as a car pulls up as if he is expecting someone. He is holding the yellow hat in his hands. Two men climb out of the car, say a few words, and then all three put on yellow hats and enter the building. Minutes later, Rangy sees them inspecting the top-floor windows.

After a while, they can be seen on the second floor and then at the bottom. They have been in the building for quite some time.

That day, the hammering and sawing never start, nor does the unsettling music that blares from morning till quitting time. It's almost too good to be true. Rangy thinks he may have accomplished what he's struggled so hard for, and this time he didn't hurt anyone.

Rangy has two treasures that he will never give up, no matter what, Kitty and the transistor radio. In the morning and at noontime, he listens to the news, hoping to hear how Moses Rocket has been damaged. It must be bad because work has not yet resumed.

At night, talk shows are his favorites, and he often speaks aloud to the guests and to Kitty. Finally, he hears on a local news station what he has waited for. "Serious water damage has occurred at one of the buildings at the Moses Rocket site."

It seems the installers are blaming the manufacturer; in turn, they are blaming the installers for careless work. Rangy is delighted and also relieved that no one suspects he might be the culprit, and for several days he is happy.

Then the worst happens. Equipment is moved across the road to the front of the cottages. He fears work on them is about to start. *Where can he go? Where to bring Kitty? What do people do with their animals when they have no place to live?*

That night when it is still light out, he takes Kitty up to the roof and settles next to the chimney stack. He watches as the sunlight departs, leaving rose-colored streaks across the sky and one pure white one as if drawn by chalk.

The colors meld, become more vivid, and deepen. He feels a sense of wonder at what he is looking at, but his thoughts remain troubled.

Where can he go?

He snuggles against the chimney stack, needing the day's leftover warmth from within the bricks. Now Kitty is trying to climb out of his shirt pocket. Her claws have sharpened, but she's remained tiny and could get hurt up here.

He puts her in the pocket of his overcoat so she can't escape and thinks he should go back to the cellar, but it's still light out, and he stays on the roof, listening to some nice, soft music coming from his transistor radio and shuts his eyes. When the brief concert is over, he opens them.

The city has turned to gold—gold glinting everywhere. He is overwhelmed and gets up and looks all around, and for anyone on the street looking up, he appears as an object of interest that someone had brought up to the roof and forgotten about.

In all that glitter, Rangy finds his answer.

"Cook," a thin man with oily hair, fierce eyes, and a bulbous nose used to terrify Rangy when he'd eaten at the shelter's soup kitchen.

But he can't let that stop him.

He has run out of options and has no other choice but to seek him out. Living at the shelter is a last resort, and he thinks, from what he's seen there, that they might let him in since he's homeless, but he'll need Cook's permission to bring Kitty with him.

The heart of the shelter, once a large rambling late-nineteenth-century mansion, is the soup kitchen, the scullery, still called by its old-fashioned name where dishes and pots get scoured, and the dining room with row upon row of metal tables and chairs.

Cook serves two meals a day and supervises the permanent kitchen staff and all of the volunteers. Everyone says the food he serves is better than what you pay money for in many of Hartford's restaurants. His real name is long forgotten. It's rumored that he spent his whole life before he came here in the Navy as a mess sergeant, but no one knows for sure nor dares to ask. He seems unapproachable.

Near the rows of metal tables, hungry people wait for as long as it takes for the signal to come up to the serving line at the head of the room, where bowls, plates, utensils, and napkins have been placed alongside large pots of soup, casseroles, stews, such as the beef and basil, one of Cook's specialties, all ladled out by volunteers.

On some days, Cook's shouts and threats stream from the kitchen, where he's usually alone except for one staff member, a shy, quiet man named Everet, who is often called on to calm Cook down. Other times, in a quieter mood, Cook marches along the back of the serving table, inspecting the food and its presentation, like a drill instructor.

The late afternoon air outside the back door of the shelter is soft now. A few undamaged trees keep the yard nicely shaded. Rangy approves of the high wooden fence enclosing the yard, and that trash is kept on the other side of a gate, in the wide alley, inside closed bins.

The grass has been cut, and the yard is impeccably clean, although there is no sign that anyone uses it. Rangy thinks that is too bad.

Two hours before the main meal of the day, with great trepidation, he approaches the back door, the one that leads to a small hall into the kitchen. He smells the aroma of food cooking, moistens his lips (as always, he is hungry), hears the sound of pots clanging, and then he hears profanity, exasperation, and frustration and almost turns away. But he is desperate.

Mustering all of his courage, he knocks timidly on the door. When there is no answer, he knocks louder. Cook flings the door open. "What do you want?" he barks.

Frightened, Rangy steps back and stutters his plea that Kitty is allowed to stay with him.

"Come in the front door if you want to eat!"

"But—"

"Go away! I've got enough problems—my freezer shut down!"

Quicker than he's used to speaking, Rangy says, "I can fix it. I can. If you take Kitty, I can fix it for you." His heart thumps fiercely so that when all of the words come out of him, he is breathless.

"You?" Cook roars.

With a desire to protect the small creature he has come to love and is unable to abandon, he speaks more confidently than he imagines. "I can. I'll show you."

Cook takes a second look at Rangy, aware that many of those who come to the shelter once had decent and productive lives. He scowls at the hands of the wall clock behind him, thinking of the frozen meats that might spoil, and, desperate himself, says, "You better not be wasting my time!" He brings Rangy into the kitchen, stepping back from Rangy's unpleasant odor.

Rangy tells Cook they must slide the freezer out away from the wall and remove the plate across the back so he can look inside.

Together they move it. Rangy's strength (for the size of him) surprises Cook.

Rangy asks for a Phillips-head screwdriver. Cook provides it and stands to one side while Rangy deftly unscrews the plate. After a minute or so of careful study, Rangy discovers the reason for the freezer's malfunctioning. He asks Cook for pliers and some tape.

Soon, the freezer is humming, and together they jostle it back against the wall.

Cook's heart softens, albeit with a warning. "If I ever find that cat in my kitchen, I'll throw it out the back door and you with it."

"Yes, sir!"

"And you need to clean yourself up—you don't smell so good."

"Yes, I will," Rangy says with tears in his eyes.

"Go wait back in the hall," says Cook.

A number of students from the nearby college volunteer at the shelter. The young man that approaches Rangy looks like a college boy, neat all over and nicely spoken. "Hi," he says, "I'm Matt."

"I'm Rangy Barstow."

"Let's go downstairs."

Rangy hesitates, thinks they may keep him down there, and he doesn't move.

"Hey, it's okay," Matt says. "Downstairs is where we'll get you fixed up."

So Rangy follows him. The cellar is clean and well-lighted. Matt stops in front of a large closet. He looks Rangy over and then takes out a clean pair of pants, a shirt, underwear, socks, a pair of sneakers, towels, and a washcloth. "This is a special soap," Matt tells him. "You must use it over your entire body, your hair as well."

"Yes, I will," Rangy says.

Matt gives him a toothbrush, toothpaste, a razor, and a comb. "You take a shower first and then get dressed. I'll show you where you'll be sleeping."

For Rangy, it all seems like a happy dream. He listens carefully and follows instructions.

"Let me have your coat," Matt says.

"Is it all right if I keep my watch cap? It was my Dad's."

"Sure, but you'll have to give it a wash."

"I'll do that."

"You can undress in the shower stall and put the clothes you are wearing in this black plastic bag."

Rangy doesn't know what to do. Kitty is asleep in his coat pocket. He slowly brings her out and says, "I fixed the freezer upstairs, and Cook said I could keep her."

Matt smiles. "If Cook said it was okay, it's fine with me. But we have to lock her up while you're in the shower. Follow me. I know the perfect place."

Rangy follows Matt to a small empty room.

"Leave her here. She'll be fine."

Rangy steps tentatively into the shower—it's been so long that he feels nervous. The water is steaming hot, and he adjusts it. As water pours down on him, it feels so good, he can hardly describe it, and he stays in for a long while, washing his hair, and his body, with the special soap, and he even brushes his teeth.

He towels himself dry and puts on the clean clothes he's been given.

Matt takes the bag of Rangy's soiled clothing. "I'm sorry, Rangy, but I don't think it's a good idea to keep these any longer."

Rangy nods and says he understands. "Can I take Kitty now?"

"Kitty has fleas," Matt says, handing Rangy a bottle and an old towel. "Wash her with this, and we'll get you a flea collar. There's an old sink down here we use for jobs like this. Toss the towel into the black bag when you're finished, okay? You may as well wash your hat, too, while you're at it."

"That's a good idea," Rangy says. "Thank you."

"There's a sign that says once you're finished, you need to rinse out the sink with bleach and hot water."

"I'll take care of it," Rangy says.

"What a nice fellow," he says to Kitty while giving her a good scrub. Kitty squirms and meows, and Rangy tells her it will soon be over.

When he's finished, Matt takes him up to the room he's been assigned to on the first floor, a small alcove-like space with a bed and clean linens, a lamp, and a wall shelf. Not quite believing all that is happening, Rangy sets Kitty down to stretch out in the sun on the cushioned top of a hinged window seat where he'll be able to store his few belongings.

"There's a hook behind the door. You can put your hat there to dry," Matt says.

"Thank you," Rangy says.

"When you go in and out, you need to lock the door with this key so no one can open it by mistake and let Kitty out. Okay?"

"Yes, I will."

"You don't want to get into trouble with Cook."

"No, no, I sure don't!"

"It's a nice space, Rangy. A little small, but you'll have some privacy."

"Yes, thank you."

"Cook wants me to take you for a haircut. Is that okay with you?"

"Oh, I haven't had a real haircut in a long time."

"Afterwards, we'll get the flea collar and a litter box for Kitty."

Matt is smiling for all he's worth, looking Rangy over, thinking how different he seems from the man that walked into the shelter a few hours ago.

In his new life at the shelter with Kitty and Cook and all of the others who have no place to live, Rangy follows the rules that Cook had shouted at him as if Rangy had no understanding of language and needs every word emphasized. Eating regularly, in no time, he begins to put on weight. He feels more like his old self when Dad and Mom were alive.

Quickly and unexpectedly, he becomes an important addition to the shelter. He fixes the fickle furnace, sticking doors, the TVs, children's toys, and almost anything needing repair. Again, he hears his name called. "Rangy! Where's Rangy Barstow?"

Mostly, though, he keeps to himself, more out of habit and fear that he might say or do something that could get him into trouble, and he'd have to leave.

Evenings, sitting on the window seat, stroking Kitty, looking out to the street at the people who pass by, he feels safe. He's made peace with himself, with his mistakes, and rarely thinks of them.

When memories of the life he once had at the cottage with Dad and Mom arise, when sadness boils up, he reminds himself of what Dad told him after they had lost Mom. "We can't bring her back. We got to look forward, Rangy. It's all we can do."

31

Lucy

By early February, the project is running smoothly.

The buildings are in their final stages of completion, and work on the cottages is in full swing. Swanson hasn't been difficult. In fact, Lucy hardly interacts with him, working mostly with Tillie, and that's been a pleasure. Tillie is reasonable and straightforward and has taken a firm stance with the VPs moving to the site.

Lucy took Katherine's advice and requested that Deborah be appointed the Senior on Moses Rocket. They work well together and have become good friends.

It's a quiet Saturday, and Lucy wakes up feeling energized. *What should she do today?* She's given up matching sweats and slips into a new pair of jeans (that were made to look old) and a gray pullover shirt with a zipper down the front. Modern casual clothing that makes her feel good again about herself now that she's lost some weight.

She goes downstairs and comes face to face with the sorely neglected farmhouse. It needs a good cleaning. She's been meaning to hire a service, but she thinks she'll do it herself.

After breakfast, she starts in the kitchen, scrubbing the woodwork and the paneling with Murphy's, reassured by the grime she wrings out of the cloth that this is long overdue. Her efforts have restored the lovely grain in the wood, and she is so pleased she decides she'll get a bid on painting the walls. She's never liked their dull, dried mustard color. The sun-bleached window shades, too, are an eyesore.

She backs away and appraises the whole kitchen.

It's difficult to update a house that has such old bones. Changes have to be carefully assessed. She thinks of it as "harmony." *What color would she paint the walls? And would she replace the shades with anything?*

Interior shutters? Blinds? What of the strong light that comes through those windows?

Full of this newfound energy and interest in the house, she'd like nothing better than to strip it bare and start over. Pile all this dated furniture on the lawn and call someone to take it away. She laughs at the thought and admits it would be heartless. But something has to be done if she's going to stay here, thinking that is what Luke would probably have wanted her to do.

She recalls the time years ago when they'd only just moved in. She was feeling downhearted, even angry and resentful. She'd only agreed to this move after the months of discussion that had begun with good intentions to reach some sort of compromise, but each time concluded with tears and Luke folding her in his arms.

That day, Luke was in high spirits, coming down from the attic with items he recalled as a child that his mother had kept up there. "Family portraits," he said with reverence, holding them up for her. "There's more up there, but we can start with these two!"

"Start what?"

"Hanging them up—what did you think I meant?"

She'd looked at those somber, patrician faces with distaste. She couldn't bear to have them on the walls. She put up with relics like the stove, the heavy furniture, the threadbare rugs, and the yellowing dishes they ate off of, but she was not going to have those righteous faces observing her every movement. "No," she said with a firmness that startled him. "Please put them back."

He was stunned. "This isn't like you. Are you feeling all right, Lucy?"

"I'm perfectly fine."

"Be reasonable," he said.

"Considering everything Luke, like the move to this house, leaving a home I'd renovated and loved, and the studio I'd designed and never used, I might ask you to do the same."

He didn't argue but must have wondered why she so disliked the portraits. He never asked. She wonders if he'd ever forgiven her.

She is aware that the furnishings, the carpets, and pictures, the tattered shades, all look in some way agreeably entrenched.

She should have stripped this house of the past while Luke was alive instead of walking through the rooms as if she hadn't the right to change a thing as if she should be careful handling the vase a Wicks sea captain brought back from China during his 19th-century travels. She takes it off the shelf where it has always perched, turning it in her hands, admiring the beautiful enamelwork. It doesn't belong in the kitchen. She looks around for a place to put it, but nothing suits, so she puts it back where it was.

Rite. Right.

Those words. The rite performed, coming into this family, this house. All along, even while Luke was alive, didn't she have the right to change the house, to take charge, to take hold?

Just look at this place! A house has no business becoming a museum.

The young designers at Cole & Siegel had been wide-eyed, touring the house during a gathering Lucy hosted months after Luke was gone. They'd admired the architecture and the furnishings and were curious about Katherine and Luke's ancestors.

Lucy recalls how painful it was for Katherine to even be there. She'd only come to support Lucy's efforts to start building a life without Luke. When Katherine hadn't much to contribute, Lucy stepped in and told what she knew. In the midst of it, she became impatient with their reverential expressions and asked how they would change the house. "You're all designers. You must have some ideas."

They looked astonished, as if she were out of her mind. Oscar spoke up, saying the house was perfect, and the others agreed.

She thought they were just being polite.

"Nostalgia, a yearning for a way of life that's passed," Oscar explained. "Latchkey kids, Lucy. All of us. Our parents moved around, and most of us went to three or four different schools. We long for houses with a past, like this one, sloping floors and all. A great, great house," he concluded almost sadly, and the others nodded in solemn agreement. "We wouldn't change a thing."

At times, life can be so out of balance, Lucy thinks. People who've moved around often want to settle in one place, and she wishes she'd moved around and traveled more, like her friend Eileen. They keep in touch but have not yet found the time to meet or, to put it another way. Lucy hasn't worked up the courage to face her.

She knows her best friend will be hugely disappointed to learn that she's not set her brush to canvas for years. How could she explain to Eileen so that she might understand?

Lucy moves to the dining room, where Luke's ashes are kept in one of the high cupboards.

She's only used this room once since Luke was no longer with her—the night of the party. She actually despises dusting all the furniture.

"Waste of time," she says to Luke's picture, a framed pastel of him at age nine. Flipping the dust cloth over the frame, she says aloud, "I've got the rest of my life to do what I want. I'm young, like Aunt Ellen says!"

Someone is knocking on the door, and she tosses the dust cloth onto the dining room table and goes to answer. "Margaret!" she cries. "Come on in."

"I only stopped by. I'm going shopping—want to come along? We can have lunch out. It's been a while."

"I know, but I'm stuck housecleaning. Where are the boys?"

"With their father."

She thinks lunch out would be nice. She's been so busy, and it's ages since she's spent time with her friend.

"Wish you'd called earlier. I just feel like I can't stop in the middle."

Margaret makes a face but smiles and says she'll call in a day or two.

Luke had been ridiculously angry with her the first time she visited Margaret. "Lucy, how can you step one foot into that place!"

"Margaret is my friend."

"Why can't she come here?"

"She does when the boys are in school."

He was special, a decent man, infinitely kind to everyone, and he liked and admired Margaret, a single woman raising two kids on a teacher's salary. He loaded her up with vegetables out of his gardens and played catch with her sons, Morgan and Tate, at the farm, allowing them to freely roam the property. But he was completely irrational about anything to do with the development— he couldn't let it go. Lucy believes his rage is what killed him.

She recalls visiting Margaret, sitting outside near the pool that her boys swam in all summer long, floating on the water in their pink and green swim trunks like fluorescent frogs. Some days Lucy counted half-a-dozen boys in the water, shouting, pushing, splashing roughly, dunking each other's heads almost viciously into the water with great happiness, and Margaret apologizing for the chaos. "At least I know where my boys are, Lucy."

Margaret had no idea that Lucy felt somewhat disconnected from life at Pilgrims Corner. Yet, at the same time, when Margaret shouted "hello" or gave a friendly wave to her neighbors, Lucy experienced a sense of inclusion in the development's small community.

Lucy returns to the dining room. She's about to pick up the duster when she looks around.

Something is wrong. Something is out of place. The wall with Luke's portrait is bare. She goes around the table and finds it lying on the floor. "Oh no!" she cries, afraid the glass has shattered. When she picks it up, all she sees is Luke, a young boy, smiling up at her, the glass unbroken. She smiles back and says, "No worries, Luke. I'll get this back on the wall where it belongs."

There is a narrow straight-backed sofa in the room, and she sits down on it and turns the picture over. On the back of the frame, she finds faded ink notations, measurements of how high from the floor the picture should hang, and how far from the corner of the room. The handwriting is not Luke's. Harry's or Eleanor's? Which one? It wouldn't have been Harry, she decides. He wouldn't have had the time or the inclination. But Eleanor?

Probably. How could it matter to anyone if a picture was moved to a different spot? Why would anyone need this compulsive order in her life, making sure nothing ever changes?

She supposes Luke's mother may not have had much else to do out here, and yet, she could very well be wrong about that. From what she's been told, Eleanor loved it in just the way that Luke had.

Lucy recalls a book she read during her single literature course in college. The title was the name of a family home. Howards End! The mother was sickly too, and she had a great love for the property. Funny, the pieces of life experience that you relate to for one reason or another.

She shakes her head, reattaches the wire, puts the portrait back on its hook, steps away to see if it's hanging straight, and then turns, surveying each object in the room.

There is nothing of hers, or more accurately, of herself, to be seen. Not a new thought, but today the realization somehow hits home. Not only that, but the room (in her opinion) is quite unattractive and lacks that sense of harmony she craves. The furniture is awkwardly placed, not at all how she'd lay out a room if it were her choice.

She's given what the minister at Luke's church called an obligatory "widow's year." Suddenly, she thinks Ellen is right! There is no longer any reason to live out here alone without Luke, and she says aloud, "Luke, I can't do this! I just can't!"

She picks up her smartphone, searching for the name of the real estate agent that advertises in front of the houses at Pilgrims Corner. She calls, hears the ring, feels some regret, and almost hangs up. A recorded message tells her to leave her name, and the reason for her call, and someone will get back to her. Lucy complies with a mix of reluctance and hope.

An hour later, she is on her hands and knees scrubbing the slate tiles in the back hall when a man calls, introducing himself as Buck Eaton.

"I thought I called Vivian Carter's agency," Lucy says.

Buck tells her that Vivian is his boss. "How can I help you?"

Lucy explains that she is interested in purchasing a large condo in a safe and convenient location in the city.

"You've called at an opportune time," Buck says.

Lucy thinks, of course, he would say that any realtor would. After he gives her the particulars of the unit he has in mind, she agrees to meet him at the real estate office the following morning.

Buck is a nice-looking young man—clean-cut and earnest. He exudes a pleasantly scented, masculine aftershave. He's wearing baggy pants, a navy blue shirt, and a wide tie with flying gold and burnt orange birds in the pattern. His hair is cut almost to the scalp, reminding her of the boys she'd grown up with. "Are crew cuts back in style?" she says.

"Crew cuts? I don't know," Buck says. "I just got out of the Marines. It's a habit I guess—the short hair."

"It looks good on you."

"Thank you, Mrs. Gaston. Now we're all set to look at the condo I told you about on the phone yesterday. Would you like to drive over with me, or do you want to take your car and follow?"

They walk out to the parking lot. "Which one is yours?" Lucy says.

"The black Range Rover."

"That'll do fine. I've never ridden in one before."

"It's a good, safe car with a smooth ride."

She thinks Buck must be doing all right. "Nice car," she says.

"It's leased," he says as if he's doing all he can to be successful.

She likes his honesty, likes hearing him tell her about the condo.

"The five-story building was built in the 1920s in the middle of a space adjacent to the river," Buck says. "Earlier in the century, that area had been a park."

He pulls the car into a wide circular driveway, passing a large sign with Vivian Carter's name but no photo. She wants to ask Buck a little about Vivian, but he's focused and efficient, and there is no time. He stops the car at the front entrance, and they get out.

"No one off the street can walk in," he says. "This building is always locked."

The entrance door is solid wood and heavy to open. Buck unlocks the door and manages it nicely. "Right this way, Mrs. Gaston."

"Please, call me Lucy," she says, stepping into a spacious lobby with high ceilings and layered moldings that were routinely used in the nineteen twenties. The floor and the staircase are marble. "Lovely," she says.

"Want to take the elevator?"

"What floor is the unit on?"

"One flight up."

"Let's walk!"

He leads the way up a wide, curving staircase to the second floor while she takes her time, marveling at the details—the moldings, the intricate leaf patterns of wrought iron, the wide, pleasingly worn yet glistening mahogany railing. At the top, she admires an oversized window that naturally brightens the expansive hallway.

"There was a time that builders were true craftsmen and used to think of everything," Lucy murmurs.

Buck stops in front of a door with a bold numeral 8 in brass. "You first, Lucy," he says.

The entrance hall is a bit dark and narrow for the first six feet and then widens into a bright foyer. On the right, an opening in the wall leads to the living room, with high ceilings and, again, beautiful moldings. A fireplace is flanked by windows. "Charming," she says.

"The people who first lived here used to have—" Buck hesitates.

"What?"

"Servants," he says.

"The help, I think they used to call people who lived in," Lucy says.

They go into a room that is more spacious than any at the farmhouse, so bright and airy that it almost takes her breath away. "All this wonderful open space!" she cries.

"This is the dining room, but you can use it as a family room or a great room." He pauses, "I really like this unit, Lucy. Most all the rooms have views of the Connecticut River."

"I'm surprised it's still available?"

Buck shrugs. "It's one of the most expensive."

Still, she's enchanted and lags behind, thinking about the possibilities of such a place, while Buck opens doors and drawers.

"Lots of closet space, lots of storage," he says.

"I can see that."

"And how many condos can you go into nowadays where there are built-in bookcases?"

"I don't know, but they are wonderful."

"Small kitchen, eat-in if you want. Two bedrooms and two and a half baths." He suddenly halts his pitch. "Is that a drawback?"

"What do you mean?"

"A person usually has no need for so many baths, but that's how these places were built. That pantry in the back of the kitchen used to be a bedroom for serv—the help. That's why the shower bath is next to it—the half-bath was for guests."

"No, not a problem at all."

"This is the last two-bedroom. These units are going fast, Lucy. I don't mean to pressure you, but I don't want you to miss out. And if you do make an offer, you'll still have time to change your mind."

They are standing in the second bedroom, a square room with long, high windows. "Buck, can you tell what direction the light is coming from in this room?"

"North, I believe."

"Are you certain?"

He walks to the window and looks out. "If the sun still rises in the east, then this is north," he says cheerfully.

The north light and a view of the river!

Tall, drooping willows. A half-dozen or so of waddling ducks. A nattily dressed old man sitting on one of the benches close to the riverbank. She pictures herself sitting in that spot twenty years from now and, for a few moments, even wonders if anyone will be sitting beside her. The image appeals.

The river, too, winds through Hartford until it reaches the Hartford Bridge, past her old neighborhood and Johnny Crane's house, her father's close friend. His shredded nails moved across the pages of the rose catalog while she, a girl of nine, warmed her hands around a cup of cocoa that Kathleen, Johnny's wife, had made for her, and Johnny, with his brogue saying, "See Lucy, there's Razzle Dazzle Reds, Tiffany Pinks, Sunbrite Yellow—they're all here, all those roses thriving in my garden as you see here, aren't they something, girl?"

"Yes, they're beautiful, Mr. Crane."

Johnny called himself a "rosarian" after he won a prestigious prize for a rose he'd cultivated, a flower that had brought Luke one day, years later, to Johnny's house and to her. That's where they'd first met.

Is this what I want? She asks herself and, in the next breath, answers, *"This is what I need."*

"Buck, I'm going to take it," she says. "It's perfect."

On her ride back, she thinks of the farmhouse and Luke's gardens. What should she do? When Luke died, Lucy offered the property to Katherine. She had refused it. With all that's happened, might she take it now?

Lucy begins to feel the possibilities of a new life!

Late that same afternoon, she goes out to the barn, slides open the door and climbs up into the loft. Only once has she ever gone into the studio, and that was on the day Luke had completed the work, and then only because he insisted.

If they'd really decided together to move here, she might have adjusted better. The construction on their home in West Hartford had only just been completed.

She'd worked on the plans for a whole year, opening up all of the narrow dark rooms, adding long windows, peaked ceilings, and a large studio on the north side of the house. For a long while after moving here, she used to drive past the house, regretting that she'd given in to Luke, although she knew it was not his fault that Harry had passed at the same time the renovation of the West Hartford house was underway.

That first time Luke had been waiting at the bottom of the stairs, anxious for her response. He saw the look on her face as she came down and realized his efforts had been in vain. They were both frightened by the thought of another argument over moving here.

He led her into the house, upstairs to his childhood bedroom, the one they now shared. His love was insistent. Could she understand that he needed to be here and needed her as well?

For the most part, they'd had a wonderful life together, but she sees now that some part of her had been broken by the move.

The studio Luke built for her would go unused, and almost unbelievably, neither one had ever mentioned it again.

Entering the loft, she sees Luke's museum of farm tools displayed across the wall, hung with identifying tags and some information on when the Wicks had used them. To her right is the high-ceilinged studio. She hesitates before entering, so unlike the day she'd charged up here, her mind already made up that it wasn't what she wanted.

She looks at the room with a colder eye, admitting that most painters would indeed be happy to have a space such as this in which to work. Open, with good light and the wood trim that had aged so beautifully. It could be an inspiration in itself.

A large and sturdy easel stands in the center of the loft. Wheels have been attached to the legs. Only her paints, rolls of canvas—no other distractions in the room but a sofa, table, and lamp. Through the large windows, the farmhouse and the Pilgrims Corner development cannot be seen, only the landscape Luke had created.

With her arms full of dried paints and brittle canvases, she makes the first of several trips to clear out the space.

The Keeper

She'll sort it all out downstairs, or outside, anyplace but up here,

a room that reminds her of her own failures, this one in particular

that she must move on from.

32

Katherine

She is walking side-by-side with her brother Luke beneath branches that glitter with ice. His boots tread heavily on the pavement that's been plowed and sanded, and he watches protectively for oncoming vehicles that might skid toward the bank.

She is happy and laughing merrily, picking up a chunk of snow and packing it into a silvery white ball that she intends to throw at him, but when she turns around, he's no longer there. Almost instantly, she falls, feeling as if someone or something is pulling her down through the icy slush into a bottomless pit where it is cold and smothering. She cries out, stuttering and sobbing, and wakes from her dream.

It is mid-afternoon, and a warm light blankets the room, but she is trembling, her face wet with tears. Luke had been so near. His sad eyes, his cheeks drawn in from the cold, his steaming breath—it was all so vivid.

She doesn't think she'll ever get over missing him, but she is learning, in therapy, to finally allow herself to accept that he is gone and to grieve for him.

In the kitchen, she puts half a dozen eggs into a pot, covers them with water, and turns on the burner. She usually orders take-out, pizza, or Indian from the restaurant across the street, or perhaps something from Abi's Gourmet when she has a taste for what she thinks of as "real food." She is not in the habit of planning her meals. At times, she's at a loss as to what to have that's simple and easy.

While the eggs are simmering, she paces back and forth from the stove to the window overlooking the street that is mostly quiet before the five o'clock rush and sees from this vantage point what to her looks like an old man wearing a watch cap. She thinks she might have seen him before, one of the homeless that prowl Hartford, often appearing during the busiest hours to beg for change. She feels some compassion for him and watches until he turns into a side street at the end of the block.

It's settled now that she'll move out of the apartment and into the farmhouse. At times, she can hardly believe she's agreed to Lucy's offer. After talking it over with her and Mac, though, it seemed like a sensible idea.

In a state of both euphoria and sadness, Lucy said she felt the property belonged to Katherine and that she should be the one who ultimately decided whether or not it ever is sold. Lucy had already purchased her condo and was moving on.

If Katherine didn't take the farmhouse, it would have to be sold now—neither of them wanted to leave the house vacant.

Katherine made her decision after a session with Dr. Rablen. Discussing the idea, she'd unexpectedly broken down, admitting to him that the property meant so much more to her than she'd ever realized.

Now she's eager to have the move over with. She doesn't like feeling unsettled, although it will be a fairly easy transition. Lucy is taking practically nothing from the house, so anything Katherine will need is already there. She's sold most of her furnishings to the man who's moving into her apartment at the end of the month. What is left, like the plain white dishes she'd used, some cutlery, and a box of linens, will go to *Goodwill*.

Her clothes she'll take in her car, along with the framed prints she bought when she worked in New York. She'll also take the ficus and the pendulum clock that came from the sitting room at the farm. It seems a long time ago that Luke asked if there was anything she wanted from the farmhouse. "The clock in the sitting room," she'd said. "It reminds me so much of Mother."

Luke had carefully packed it up and brought it here, and now, she'll have to do the same, bringing it back—she still has the box.

In the kitchen, she pours cold water over the eggs, drains the pot, and puts five of them in a bowl—almost a week of lunches.

She won't bother making a sandwich and cracks the single egg into a napkin, peels off the shell, slices the egg in half, and shakes salt and pepper across the yokes. She takes an apple from a basket on the counter and goes into the living room.

She thinks she really should do something about finding a job. Initially panic-stricken without her work, the very next day after she walked out of Cole & Siegel, she'd called Jack Heft. He was out of town, out of touch, and he hadn't yet called her back. She hasn't looked for work since. It seems like too big a step.

Dr. Rablen is not concerned. "When you're ready to seek work, to take up challenges, you will know it." He's helped her to understand that surviving an attack of the sort she had endured often takes much longer than anyone might expect. He cautions her with phrases like "Baby steps, Katherine, baby steps. It's still early days." He suggests that something like updating her resume might be a good way to start thinking about the kind of work that might interest her.

Her favorite part of the day is nine at night when Mac calls. Soon he will tell her when he and the children are coming. That she'll see him again and finally meet Luke and Caroline is something she's looking forward to. She hasn't had much experience with children, but she'll rely on Mac to lead the way.

She often thinks about Moses Rocket and those last months on the project, even the time before what happened to her in the underground garage. From the start, she'd acted unprofessionally, quarreling with Sy, not being upfront with Pete, working secretly with Tillie, and worse, thinking that somehow this building was hers alone to renovate. She didn't work as a team, and her job demanded that. She can truthfully say she'd never behaved like that before and is uncertain what caused her to think that only she could bring about a successful outcome.

She needs to make amends and takes one of those "baby steps" and calls Pete. They've spoken a few times since she left when questions on the Moses Rocket project come up. "Can we meet in the coffee shop near the college?" she asks.

"Are you all right?"

"I'm getting there."

"Of course, we can meet—I'd love to see you—it's been too long."

They agree on a time the next day before hanging up.

Arriving early to ensure she has a booth that would afford them some privacy, she waves to Pete when he comes in a few minutes late. "I've ordered for us," she says.

He's the same, seeming harried and slightly disheveled, yet clearly glad to see her. "You look well, Katherine."

"Thanks—all I do is exercise and rest."

"Good, that's good," he says.

The waiter brings coffee and a plate of mini-pastries. They each pick one and settle in.

"Pete, the reason I asked you to meet—I wanted to explain, to apologize in person. You didn't deserve something I did, meeting with Tillie without your okay. I know I let you down."

He doesn't interrupt.

"My only excuse is that I got so caught up in that project in some negative way, wanting to control everything that happened inside the building and maybe out of it, too." (She is determined she won't mention Sy or Swanson. This is about her behavior, and she's not going to make excuses.) "I was unprofessional, and even worse, I was dishonest. I hope you can forgive me."

He reaches for her hand and encloses it in both of his. "We'll talk about this only once, and then I don't want it mentioned again. If forgiveness is what you need from me, of course, I forgive you. I also think you should know that I understand why you did it, the pressure you felt, and the lack of cooperation on the part of a PA that had his own less-than-scrupulous agenda almost from the outset. But Kat, I know what kind of person you are—we'd worked together for a long time—and when I found out what had been going on between you and Tillie, sure, I was hurt and maybe a little disappointed, but call me a fool if you want, it never changed the admiration I have for you and the dedication you've always shown, giving the projects you've worked on the best you had. Now that's the end of it. Can you accept that?"

Her eyes fill up. "I don't deserve it."

"Oh, dear Katherine, you do, you certainly do."

A few days later, she receives an email from Pete.

"They want you back, Katherine. They're after me to try and persuade you. Though I'd like it very much if you did return, I won't engage in any pressure tactics. You decide. It was lovely to see you. Keep in touch, Pete." And a P.S. "I could have called, but I thought I had a better chance (selfish on my part) of you returning if I gave you some space to think it over."

She won't return to Cole & Siegel. It's not a hard decision, and she emails him the following day. She needs to move ahead. He understands.

Then, seemingly out of the blue, like always, Jack Heft returns her call. He sounds flustered. "I called Cole & Siegel this morning, and some woman—"

"Violet."

"She told me you no longer work there."

"I left several months ago."

"She refused to tell me where you'd gone."

"She's not supposed to."

"She asked so many questions. I told her she should get a job with the CIA. I lost your number, and she wouldn't give it to me even when I explained our connection. I tried to get Lucy, but she was out."

"She's a busy woman these days."

"So I hear."

"So, how did you get it—my number?"

"I rummaged through some old files—why in hell is it unlisted anyway?"

"It seemed a good idea at the time, and I've never changed it."

"So, are you ready to come back to work?"

"I'm not sure, Jack. The very next day after I quit, I called you. I was afraid of being unemployed. But it's not so terrible. Not as bad as I thought it would be."

"Someone like you—how're you keeping busy?"

"Oh, I'm not busy at all. Well, I am moving back to the farmhouse if you call that busy."

He says nothing specific about what had happened, only that she was smart to take time off and care for herself.

"Truthfully, Jack, the attack, quitting my job, it's not been easy, but I'm feeling pretty good right now."

"Listen, Katherine. Remember last year I told you about the Georgian mansion off Pratt that used to be that stodgy men's club?"

"It's been empty for years—no one knows what to do with it," she says.

"A group of investors bought it. They want me to turn the whole place into assisted living units for Seniors."

"That's a great idea. The library's next door, two churches down the street, I think there's a new market—"

"I know, but I've convinced the investors the complex should have a heterogeneous population."

"Did they know what you meant?"

He laughs. "'A community within a community', I told them. Why should the elderly be isolated? Seniors like to see kids and younger people around them. And young people can learn so much from those who've aged."

While Jack is talking, she thinks of her Aunt Ellen. They have supper together once a week now. Ellen starts out okay and tries to be companionable, but she's unable to keep her opinions to herself or refrain from telling Katherine what she should do.

She can be cranky at times and somewhat demanding. She's a good person and, in her own way, very kind yet a little overbearing. "You're sure it can work, Jack—the generational mix?"

"I know it will if it's done properly. I've got a lot of good ideas."

"I'm sure you do."

"I've designed a large glass, brick, and wood addition that fits with the original building that structurally is in pretty good shape. But the interiors have gone to ruin, and I need you for them. You know the way I work. We'll save everything that can be saved if it fits with what we want."

"I'm not sure, Jack. I don't know if I'm ready."

"Don't let me down, Katherine. I've hired one other person, an architect just out of school. His name is Todd. He's a techie and knows all about computers. I've rented a space for an office downtown and have someone to answer the phone and do a little clerical work. You can begin tomorrow. You can begin today. Right now. I'm here 'til ten tonight." He laughs and says, "I want to get moving!"

She thinks about Jack's offer, wondering if she's lost the drive that's needed for such a project. Does she have the energy it will take? One way or another, she needs to make decisions about her working life and her career. The luxury of doing as she pleases, even if it is doing nothing, still seems hard to forego.

She owes Jack an answer. He is offering her a fantastic opportunity, and she'd be foolish not to accept. But is she ready?

She calls Dr. Rablen's office for an unscheduled appointment. He hears her out, as usual, asking pointed questions and listening at length before offering solutions. Finally, he says, "If you want to know what I think, I can tell you I believe you are ready for such a challenge. Before you accept, I think it might be a good idea to meet with your future employer in person. What are his expectations? Think over carefully what he says and set some guidelines. This way, neither of you will be frustrated or, worse, disappointed."

So that is what she decides to do and puts in the call to Jack as soon as she is back in her apartment.

That night, the pendulum of the clock seems louder than ever, as if it is longing to be back in the farmhouse sitting room where it had resided for so many years.

33

Sy

He is sitting in his home office at the top of the three-story house they have rented for one year in Cambridge. In the room below, he hears Heather's wise, small-girl chatter.

The three of them—he, Julie, and Heather—have finished unpacking boxes that had been in storage, arranging the assortment of stuffed animals and dolls from Heather's room in West Hartford.

Heather is soothing and consoling, assuring these real-to-her creatures that their new surroundings are safe.

He's spent a great deal of time with his daughter since the move. When it is too painful for him and Julie to be in the same room together, or when he can't bear to look at her as she is now, suffering and withdrawn, Heather, who needs and wants both of them, is there.

Evenings after supper, when the house is silent and stifling with all that's not being said, the three of them sometimes walk around Cambridge—Heather a bridge between. She asks why they're not "cuddling" in bed and why they go to sleep in different rooms. Julie answers firmly, "Because that is what we do." Heather asks again, at another time. It upsets him that Julie only repeats what she has said before to Heather, sounding a bit harsh.

The architectural firm across the Charles River where he now works is much larger than Cole & Siegel. It intrigues him that he now finds himself at a firm he once interviewed with years ago. They'd offered him a position then, but on Joel's advice, he'd opted for a smaller group.

He's revisiting that idea. After all that's happened, the near anonymity of being one among a dozen or so ambitious, well-educated, and experienced architects appeals to him.

Presently he's immersed in a new assignment, a proposed construction site, a small non-conforming lot that is both narrow and shallow. Along with other team members, he's worked hard to arrive at an imaginative yet functional design solution. He's valued here, and the firm's partners have already offered him a permanent position.

Jed expects him to return, and Sy is grateful for all that he has done for him.

In the hours he's spent thinking over the manner in which he's conducted himself, he's no longer so certain about his future or where he'll be living a year from now.

The house in West Hartford is vacant. Julie didn't want anyone living in it, and her parents stepped in to pay for its maintenance. There are distractions here for both of them—Julie has made friends, and Heather likes her new kindergarten. Julie is thinking of returning to school for her doctorate.

She hadn't discussed this with him, and he only found out when he overheard a conversation she'd had with her father.

She has told him that she is not able to commit to any decision on how or if they might go forward—she's not ready, and reiterated that she only came with him for Heather's sake and on the condition that he never see Apple again. He is fully aware that Julie is not only devastated but confused. What she decides regarding their future together or apart will be final.

He realizes now that he's never been capable of what he'd call "an honest relationship" with Julie. The hurt and misery he's caused her and Heather (she was brokenhearted that the trip to Disneyland was put off) and Julie's parents, who've always been generous and kind, appall him.

He'd never really seen himself as the kind of man that cheated on his wife and has been unfaithful, yet that is exactly who he is. Full of remorse, he admits wrongdoing. He admits he's behaved like an adolescent. He admits he's been disloyal, deceitful, and untrustworthy. He fears it is all unforgivable.

What he felt, what he ashamedly still feels regarding Apple, he could tell anyone simply and truthfully, is that he had no choice. It would be too easy to explain her as seductive. Childish to reveal that he belonged to her from the first moment he saw her when he was only a boy in Springfield, that, unwittingly (like his daughter Heather), Apple had found a way into that emotionally vulnerable place inside him where he'd never allowed anyone before.

He is devastated that Apple was pregnant with his child and miscarried. He can't get his head around the idea that she never told him. In the hours he spends up here in this room alone, he often wonders what he would have done if he had known or if she'd come to him for help.

He thinks he can never be certain.

He spoke to Apple once after she was back in Springfield. She was sweet, as always, telling him in a soft voice that she was fine. Before he could say anything more, she said it was best if he didn't call again and hung up.

"Daddy! Daddy!" Heather cries, sounding upset. He hears her climbing the stairs, and he turns his chair to face her. She holds out a furry toy that's been flattened in the move. He soothes his daughter. Wipes her face dry. He promises he'll fix it, fix everything, always. Julie calls up, wanting Heather to come down for her bath.

Outside the window, the moon is almost full. He feels Apple's presence and what it was like in her small apartment, the two of them sitting almost in tree tops on the small back porch. With his daughter's tears on his fingertips, he forces himself to pick up his triangle and his drafting pencil and continue work on the blueprint taped to his drafting board.

34

Lucy

Lucy and Silvano are at the kitchen table in front of three floor-to-ceiling windows, one of the few modifications to the farmhouse that Luke had allowed after they'd moved in.

"Sitting here gave my husband great pleasure," she says. "He loved watching the birds swooping into the many feeders he'd put up."

"This Luke of yours—he is a man after my own heart. Sitting here, everywhere I look, it is beautiful."

"Yes," she says softly, "it is all beautiful, and he'd worked hard at making it so."

And now, because of what she's asked Silvano to do, there is a hole in the lawn, a scar on all this perfection from equipment that is idling while he's inside with her having coffee. Earlier, the backhoe had scooped out a sizeable rock that she wanted to be moved to the cemetery across the road.

"You must think I'm foolish."

"I don't think that at all."

"It was thoughtful of you to come—yourself."

"You don't want a lot of people around when you are doing something important like this."

Silvano is so completely accepting, and she finds that characteristic both somewhat pleasing and reassuring.

"I've been talking to Luke since he died as if he can hear me. I've been angry with him and myself. I wish—I wish we'd had a little more time—"

"Yes, I know," Silvano says.

"But you've never been married—" and she wants to say, how would you know what I mean if you never made that long-term commitment?

As if he knew what she was thinking, he says, "I have been deeply in love, Lucy, with a wonderful woman. I have been a faithful partner in a relationship that meant everything. After it was over, there are things we'd both wished we'd done differently."

She's curious and waits, but he says nothing more, and she leaves it there.

She looks down at his hands. They are strong-looking like Luke's—two men who have spent much time out-of-doors—but

Silvano's fingers are longer, the skin much smoother. Luke's hands were often chapped, the skin roughened as if he were a farmer, not a lawyer. He was truly a man not meant to spend his life behind a desk.

"I was noticing your hands, Silvano. It doesn't look like you do such hard work."

"Mostly now, I supervise, and I only help when I'm needed. I have always worn gloves," he adds. "Always."

She recalls that Luke did not, and she used to remind him to, but he felt they were a nuisance.

"I've played the piano since I was a boy, and I've always made sure to take good care of my hands."

"I had piano lessons, too, but I never kept up. There's a piano in one of the front rooms here, and after Luke was gone, I thought I might try again, but there were too many other things on my mind."

"I play almost every day." Suddenly, he stands up. "Lucy, let me play for you!"

"Now?"

"When better? Is there anything special you'd like to hear?"

She recalls a time early in her marriage when she and Luke spent a weekend in Cambridge. After lunch, they'd browsed through Harvard Square, and passing a record shop, they heard music from an outside speaker and stopped to listen. "Albinoni's Adagio," she'd said to Luke. "It's so beautiful." He went into the shop and came out with the record, holding it up as if it was something he'd won.

"For us," he said happily. Her eyes fill up with the memory. "What kind of music do you play?" she asks Silvano.

"All kinds."

"Classical?"

"That was how I was trained."

"Might you know 'Albinoni's Adagio?' I have the sheet music."

"Would you like me to play it for you?"

"Yes, I would. Very much," not quite believing that she is delaying what has been planned, the reason why Silvano is here. "The piano is this way."

She retrieves the music from inside the piano bench and hands it to him. He looks it over, sits down on the bench, and lifts the cover of the piano. He starts, his fingers seeming to fly up and down the keys. "To warm up," he says cheerfully.

"It might need tuning," she says, settling in a chair.

He begins playing, and she relives the pleasure of that day when she and Luke were so young and the excitement they felt bringing the record home, playing it over and over through the years at special moments.

When Silvano finishes, they are both briefly silent, and then she says, "That was lovely, thank you." She can't hold back—her tears spill over, and she turns away.

He stands up and goes over to her chair.

"Lucy." He reaches out for her, and she takes his hand and gets up, feeling awkward, the tears still flowing. "I'm so sorry," she says.

"No, Lucy, don't be sorry. It is all right," and he takes her in his arms. When she recovers, he says, "I think it is time. When you are ready, I will meet you outside, yes?"

She goes into the dining room, opens the cupboard, and takes out the canister holding Luke's ashes, and then she remembers...

That night, like so many others, Luke had gone outside after supper. She'd given him one of her aggrieved looks, and he promised he'd be back in five minutes or so. As usual, five turned into forty-five. Feeling lonely and impatient, she decided to read in bed, drifting off at some point with the book in her hands, and woke up chilled. The light was still on, and Luke wasn't next to her. She called out but got no answer and thought he hadn't yet returned to the house. She got up, put on slippers, and went downstairs.

There was only one light on.

"Luke?"

No answer.

So you are still outside, she thought, slinging a jacket over her shoulders, going out to look for him.

The air smelled of cedar and pine. The half-heard noises from the housing development were mostly silent, and only a few lights were on. She stopped on the bluestone path, listening to the tree frogs' mating calls, wondering how anything so small could make such a racket. Suddenly, she felt uneasy, and then came the feeling of warmth she dreaded, spreading through her chest, up to her neck, and then her face.

She started to perspire and thought she'd better go back inside but felt herself lifted, as if she were flying through the air, her solid body turning, turning above the trees, twisting lightly through the branches, the leaves softly brushing her skin, and she wondered, *What's happening? Am I losing my mind?*

She stayed where she was while her body cooled. Then, remembering why she'd come out at a time of night when any sane person might well have such illusions, she cried out, "Luke! Where are you?"

All she heard was some creature scuttling in the undergrowth. She had a notion of ringing the cowbell that she'd had him put up to be rung when he was wanted inside, but it was much too late for that.

Calling out his name, she walked past the honeysuckle, past the phoebe's nest, past all of the things she'd never have noticed if it weren't for Luke. Then she found him. He was lying on his side next to the roses he'd planted earlier that day. She thought he was asleep. His body felt warm when she put her face down next to his.

When the ambulance arrived, the medics tried their best to revive him, but it was too late. She asked how many minutes made the difference and was told that each circumstance differed. *Had she come out earlier, might she have found him in time?* A question that has haunted her ever since.

Holding the canister, she crosses the road in front of the backhoe, lifts the latch off of the iron gate, and steps into the cemetery. She's worn boots with rugged soles that could manage the slippery places of still-wet leaves and grass.

The backhoe, carrying the rock, edges across the pavement. She walks further ahead into the cemetery, avoiding the sunken mounds that define where some of the Wicks are buried. A flight of dusky goldfinches swoops into the hedge, crying, "Clee-ip! Clee-ip!" as if wondering what the commotion is all about.

Lucy finds herself at Luke's great-grandfather's dignified monument, a tall gray granite stone, chosen perhaps to assure him a hierarchical place in the hereafter (she thinks), and has a lingering moment of doubt over what she is doing. But she chose the rock because it was an enigma to Luke, and he'd become fond of it in a perverse sort of way because it had irritated him every time he had to mow around it. The irony of using it for his headstone would have brought a smile to his face. He'd named it "turtle rock" due to its hump-backed shape. Sometime later, she'll have the stone inscribed.

Silvano brings the backhoe carefully through the gate. She is standing next to the spot where she wants the rock placed, and he maneuvers the stone until she signals to him that she is satisfied.

He idles the backhoe, intending to climb down and join her, wanting to be there to comfort her, but her back is turned, her shoulders stiff and hunched, the canister in her arms, and he is aware that now is not the time.

Should she open the seal on the canister and scatter the ashes? She's really no good at this kind of thing. She wonders what Luke would have wanted and thinks he might have chosen to mix them into the earth he so loved. But she cannot bring herself to do it.

She picks up the spade she'd brought out earlier to mark where the rock would go and begins digging. She kneels down and sets the canister securely in the hole, covering it with dirt and then the pieces of moss she'd disturbed.

Her hands are trembling, and with care, she empties a packet of seeds into her palm, picks up a rock shard, carving small grooves into the soil. *"Primula.* The flower of the Druids, who believed in the immortality of the soul," Luke had once told her.

She rises, feeling the emptiness and perhaps the lightness of nothing left to hold.

A lone goldfinch lights on the top of Luke's rock, fluttering its black and white wings. It tilts its head as if he is curious to know what she's doing there or perhaps why she is leaving. He stays right there on the rock as if to say this is the best place in the world on which to preen.

Silvano sees that she has accomplished what she set out to do. He raises the bucket to back out of the cemetery, but then he stops and calls her name.

"Lucy!"

She turns and looks up at him.

"I'll be seeing you soon," sounding almost as if it is a question.

"Yes," she calls back and waves her hand. "Yes!" And then again, more softly, "Yes."

35

Katherine

She drives into the airport's short-term lot, relieved she can park out in the open. She has to confront her fear of parking garages, and sometime, she will try going into one, but today is not the day. She gets out of the car and walks across to the terminal in plenty of time for Mac's arrival.

She hasn't seen him since he flew across the country at the end of last summer to comfort her. She often thinks about how caring and unselfish an act it was and maybe too much for her to have asked. But there was simply no one else she wanted to see, and those brief hours they spent together had grounded her, spurring her to contact Dr. Rablen. Late last fall, she'd been looking forward to a second visit, this time with the children, but the trip had to be postponed when his daughter fractured her wrist playing soccer.

When he called to tell her they were finally coming, he asked if they could stay at the farmhouse. That startled her. "Won't Veronia be disappointed?"

"Actually, she suggested it. The children are older, and so is Veronia, and her house is too small for all of us. I guess I should have asked you before I told the kids."

"No, Mac. I'd love to have you all. There's plenty of room in the house."

"If you're sure, Katherine."

"Of course, I'm sure."

She is excited to finally meet the children, and she's also worried. The specter of playing the hostess increases her anxiety. She's never spent time with teenagers and has no clue how to keep them entertained.

Again, she'll have to rely on Mac.

She asked him what they liked to eat, and he wasn't much help, saying they weren't fussy. So she googled "foods for teens," made a long list, and yesterday went shopping. She focused on breakfast, snacks, and lunch, so the fridge and the pantry were well-stocked.

She told Mac that she'd treat him to dinners out. "After all, this is a vacation, and there are a lot of new restaurants downtown. It might be fun for them to look around. If you'd like, Veronia can join us."

"Don't worry, Katherine. I've bought open tickets for our return. There's plenty of time to do everything."

She wasn't sure what he meant but thought it had something to do with Veronia. "I imagine she'll want to spend some time with her grandchildren alone?"

"She's looking forward to it."

"Enough said," Katherine thought and let it go.

She'd set up the bedrooms with lighter-weight sheets, new blankets, and towels and put fresh toiletries in the bathrooms. She did all she could think of to make the visit comfortable. So much to think about taking care of others, and she's not used to it.

Holly and her daughter Emma have visited several times since Katherine moved back to the farmhouse. The diaper bag, the portable playpen Holly erects in the sitting room, bottles and jars of food—all of the other paraphernalia even for a brief visit—fascinates and overwhelms Katherine.

"I don't know how you manage all this," she'd said to Holly, who laughed and scooped up her daughter, a beautiful infant with wide blue eyes and a mass of springy curls. She held her out for Katherine to take. "You hold her," she said.

It seemed unnatural, strange, for a woman in her forties not to have ever cradled an infant, and it was tricky shifting the baby, making sure she was holding her properly so that Holly could let go. "What a dear," Katherine said and asked if it would be all right if she could hold Emma for a while.

"Of course, but she'll probably fall asleep."

"I don't mind."

Katherine sat back in a chair that had been her mother's favorite. She could feel Emma's body relaxing and watched as her eyes closed. Katherine put her hand lightly on Emma's chest, and in the next moment, she felt Emma taking hold of her thumb.

She'd felt truly happy with that foray into a world of motherhood she'll almost certainly never experience—having a child of her own.

She goes down the long corridor toward the gate where Mac and his children will arrive, stopping first at a women's room. She dampens a paper towel and presses it against her forehead.

She's too nervous. She's seen lots of photos of the children, and once, a few months ago, Mac had the idea to try a Skype call. It hadn't gone well. The children were silly, laughing when she asked a question and making jokes and faces at each other until Mac had had enough and asked them to leave the room.

But she understood. "They're nervous, too, Mac, about meeting their father's 'long-time friend.'"

"Thank you, Katherine, but they know better."

"Don't be too hard on them."

He laughed. "I think that's the trouble. I never am. They really are good kids."

She wants the children to like her. She looks in the mirror. Her hair is long, loose, and wavy. She's wearing jeans, a denim jacket, and a white t-shirt.

Nothing fussy to draw attention or make her look as if she's dressed up for them.

Months ago, she'd zipped her suits and coordinated blouses inside plastic bags in the spare room closet and only retrieved them for meetings with the investors or with the new clients in Jack's office downtown.

She is continually thankful that Lucy offered her the property. She loves working from home and living in the farmhouse.

She brings her face closer to the mirror and wonders if the harsh overhead lights emphasize the lines that seemed to appear overnight after the attack. To her, they are reminders of what happened, and she thinks they've aged her.

In the last few days, she's ruminated about the time she and Mac had lived together in that small third-floor apartment.

She believes she is more considerate now, not as self-centered or as obsessed with her future. She assumes he may be more assertive. She's aware that he was in love with her, and she probably knew it then, too, but they were so young and inexperienced. At the time, his devotion made her uneasy, a threat to her independence and her career.

She has always loved Mac in her own way but is uncertain about what the future might hold for them.

The Keeper

She reaches the gate, and unaccustomed to close crowds and noise, she puts in earbuds, listening to a Bach concerto, when she feels a hand touching her arm. She turns abruptly, and there is Violet in the midst of all these strangers. She is delighted to see her and removes the earbuds.

"Violet, what in the world are you doing here?"

"I didn't mean to scare you," she says. "I spoke, but you didn't hear me."

"I couldn't hear with the—"

"I know. People wear them everywhere and look silly, like creatures tuned in to signals from outer space."

Katherine laughs. "I used to think the same thing."

"It's dangerous to wear them in the car—I hope you don't."

"No, I never do."

"Good." Violet smiles in a way that Katherine has never seen. Her cheeks are flushed, her eyes sparkling. "I'm meeting Lauren, an old friend of mine. She just graduated college and is now going on to law school." Violet's eyes moisten. "I helped her all the way through."

"That's wonderful, Violet."

"So why are you here?"

"I'm meeting an old friend, too, and his children."

"I miss you at the firm. A lot of people do. Are you working?"

"I'm working with Jack Heft now."

"I've heard of him. Talked to him once or twice."

"I'm sure you have."

"Well, I don't want to be late for Lauren. It was nice seeing you, Katherine. You look rested. Maybe we can get together sometime?"

"I'd like that," Katherine says, and as Violet moves toward a different gate, she is reminded of how kind and supportive she's always been, yet Katherine knows so little about her other than that she lives alone. "Violet, wait!"

She turns. "What is it, Katherine?"

"Would you like to come for dinner some night? I'll ask Lucy to join us."

"Yes, and I'll look forward to it. Any night but the ones I work at the soup kitchen." She waves a cheerful goodbye.

Katherine thinks she'll include Aunt Ellen, too. She and Violet might just hit it off—in some ways; they seem very much alike.

As the growing crowd shifts forward, Katherine moves with them, and then, all at once, Mac is beside her. "We're here," he says.

"Mac," she cries and, without thinking, gives him a warm hug. "You had your ear fixed," she whispers.

"I thought it was time," he says. "Oh, it's so good to see you, Kat. It's been too long," holding on to her for a few seconds longer.

She is so nervous and excited and wonders if the children can tell.

"Katherine, this is my daughter, Caroline."

Caroline is slim, dark-haired with pale skin, very much like Veronia. Katherine holds out her hand, smiling for all she is worth. Caroline takes it and says, "Hello," politely.

A tall boy with dark reddish hair grabs Mac's arm. "Dad, where do we pick up our luggage?"

"Not so fast, Luke. Say hello to Katherine."

Of course, she knew his name was Luke, but to hear Mac say it aloud, she was deeply touched, thinking of her brother and what it would have meant to him to meet this tall, mature-looking boy, his namesake.

For a moment, it's awkward, and then Mac puts an arm around each of his children and, smiling broadly, he says, "Kids, this is my friend Katherine, the woman I've told you so much about. Katherine, this is us."

"It's so nice to finally meet you in person," she says. "Your father has told me so much about you, too."

They look at her as if they are not quite sure of what to say next, and she starts again. "I was thinking about you this morning. Your father told me about your wanting a dog."

Caroline folds her arms and looks at her father. "Yes, Luke and I want a dog. But Dad says no because he travels so much, and it wouldn't be fair to the dog."

"Yes, that's what I heard, Caroline. Well, I've thought that I'd like to have a companion at my farmhouse. I've never had a dog and just don't know where to start."

"After Dad said no, Luke and I went to a few different shelters, thinking we might get an older dog who wouldn't be too scared if it was brought to a kennel when we were away. Dad still said no, but we found out a lot about dogs, so we know what you need to do."

"Really?"

"Yes, we do," Luke says.

"And you'll help me out?"

The children look at each other and then at Katherine. "Sure," Luke says. "We're good with that."

Caroline can't hold back. "We'd love to help, Katherine!"

"That settles it. Tomorrow, first thing after breakfast, we'll all go to the shelter. You'll only be here for a short time, so we have to find the right dog as soon as we can. Is that okay with you, Mac?"

"As long as everyone agrees, the dog stays at the farmhouse with Katherine when we leave," he says.

Caroline gives him a peeved look, and she and Luke walk ahead to find the luggage.

Mac takes her hand. "What a brilliant idea, Katherine." He shakes his head. "And you were worried?"

"Yes, Mac, I was," she says, looking steadily at him. "But not anymore."

36

Rangy Barstow

His new job is in front of him. He was interviewed for the position because he'd lived in the neighborhood and had worked at Moses Rocket. That's what the counselor at the shelter told him. Charter Oak was first hiring anyone who'd been displaced, and a man whose name he can't remember, the one that showed him through the building, had been surprised that he knew right where they were going, along the passageways, through the various basement levels, up back stairs, without any confusion. The man declared Rangy was "meant for the job."

On Monday, he begins work. He feeds Kitty, fills the water bowl Cook has given him, changes the litter box, and locks Kitty inside the room they share. The children living in the shelter are fond of Kitty, and they might try to get in and take Kitty out. He allows them to play with her in the fenced-in yard when he's working there but always heeds Cook's warning to keep her out of the kitchen.

It is a short walk from the shelter to Moses Rocket. Rangy holds the ring of keys he's been given. In the changing room, he goes straight to the locker he's been assigned and opens it with one of the keys. He tried to tell his new boss he had no need for a key and that he could open the locker without one, but before he could manage the words, the man was on to something else.

It seems that here his difficulty with speech, with words, is an asset. Other people do most of the talking and are pleased that he listens so attentively.

Two uniforms are hanging inside the locker, both a bright blue color, the same as those of the other men. They are one-piece outfits with pockets that are deep enough to hold Kitty when he brings her with him on weekends, and the building is almost empty.

He likes his uniform and again feels a sense of pride that he can get up each morning and go to work.

His clean hands smooth the twilled cotton duck cloth. His fingers travel down the lapel, across Charter Oak's logo on the left-side pocket. His trimmed fingernails trace the orange oval, the large red C O, and then go across to the right pocket, over the scripted fine white thread.

R. Barstow
Moses Rocket
Maintenance

About the Author

Joan Vincent is an award-winning poet, corporate designer, and educator. She is the author of the coming-of-age novel *Because Mother Liked to Dance,* a children's picture book, *Molly Marbles,* and a children's chapter book, *The Legend of the Lost Lilies.* She lives with her husband outside of Boston.

For more about Joan, readings, and guest appearances. Please visit her website joanvincent.com; Linkedin; Goodreads.

Facebook: www.facebook.com/mollymarblesthecat/

Member: Women's National Book Association, Boston, MA